Nothing Could Stop Them

"Let's make love," Clarissa said.

Sean turned to face her and sat on the windowsill, his arms folded across his chest. "To punish Susannah?"

"No. Because we want to."

" . . . What about Diana? What about your father's campaign?"

"I'm not proposing that we make love on the street," Clarissa said.

Sean smiled. "What are you proposing?"

"You mean, for the long run?"

Clarissa traced the pattern of the carpet for a while. "I'm proposing that we make a commitment—a commitment to the future."

Suddenly, he was beside her, bending to lift her to her feet, raising her in his strong arms as if she weighed nothing, holding her close to him, bending her back in his arms, kissing her long neck, running his hand down her long back, pressing her hips and thighs against his, finding her lips with his and thrusting his tongue deep inside her mouth. Then his hand was on her breasts, then between her thighs.

Clarissa stepped away from Sean and bent her head like a child so that he could unbutton her dress. He pulled it down over her shoulders and she stepped out of it and with one motion pulled her slip over her head and dropped it alongside the dress, then stepped close to him and pulled at an end of his tie to open it and concentrated on the buttons of his shirt.

FOR LOVE
OF A STRANGER

Lily Devoe

PINNACLE BOOKS NEW YORK

FOR LOVE OF A STRANGER

An original Pinnacle Book edition, published for the first time anywhere.

First printing, October 1983

ISBN: 0-523-42081-1
Canadian ISBN: 0-523-43027-2

Cover illustration by John Solie

Printed in the United States of America

PINNACLE BOOKS, INC.
1430 Broadway
New York, New York 10018

FOR LOVE
OF A STRANGER

Prologue

He would never forget it as long as he lived—the tall blond man and the lean tanned woman hanging out into space four hundred feet above the street, calmly passing the children to safety while flames leaped from the windows around them, the smoke billowing up and up, smudging the bright Acapulco sky.

They looked like ballet dancers, or aerialists, and even wore matching costumes—floppy white muslin pants, loose white shirts with the sleeves rolled up to their elbows. The man's hair was fashionably long and was blown around his face by the warm wind. The woman had her hair tucked up under a white tennis hat; more than half of her face seemed to be obscured by enormous sunglasses, and had it not been for an unmistakable femininity marked by the curve of her hips and the surge of her breasts, she might have been a man herself, so powerfully did she move and with such confident coordination.

1

"Like Superman and Wonder Woman." Jorge Estrada y Valenzuela had gone to hotel management school in the United States and he invoked American comicbook heroes when the newspaper and television reporters sought him out and asked him for his account of what had happened. "They were like Superman and Wonder Woman. They seemed to have no fear—no concern for their own safety. They leaned out into space as though they were standing on solid ground, not at the very top of the tallest hotel in all of Acapulco."

SUPERMAN AND WONDER WOMAN SAVE CHILDREN FROM HOTEL BLAZE. That headline, or variations of it, appeared in newspapers all over Mexico, all over North America, all over the Western Hemisphere, all over the world. And he, Jorge Estrada y Valenzuela, became briefly famous for having given those names to the heroes of the Acapulco Regent fire—the fire in which nobody died. He became something of a hero himself, although after making sure that all the guests were safely out of the hotel he had done little more than watch—watch and create the fantasy that he was watching not human beings but superheroes passing the children to safety. Jorge Estrada y Valenzuela became a hero in the absence of the true heroes, for no one found out who the true heroes were, no one learned the names of the tall blond man and the lean tanned woman who had labored fearlessly and, it seemed, effortlessly amid the flames four hundred feet above the street. There were photographs taken of them, to be sure, but even telephoto lenses had not been able to discern

2

their features. All you could make out of the
woman were the huge sunglasses and the hat.
Some newspapers blew the photographs up in
an effort to identify the heroes, but in the process rendered them even more mysterious—
blobs of gray and white dots without character
or characteristics.

The fire broke out in the kitchen of Buena
Vista, the Acapulco Regent's famous rooftop
restaurant—a restaurant whose spectacular
view of Acapulco Bay, the mountains around it,
the ocean beyond, was the pièce de résistance of
a menu that featured some of the finest food to
be found at any hotel in Mexico—perhaps anywhere in the world. For reasons investigators
were never able to adequately determine, the
fire spread quickly and was soon burning ferociously, devouring draperies and carpets and
tablecloths in great gulps, advancing through
the ornate restaurant with the certainty of an
ocean wave—a wave not of cool water but of
deadly heat.

By the time word reached the front desk,
where Assistant Manager Jorge Estrada y Valenzuela was on duty, the fire was out of control
and there was nothing to do but call the fire
department, dispatch every available bellboy,
porter, maintenance man and maid throughout
the hotel to alert the guests and lead them to
safety down emergency stairways—and, having
done that, simply watch and pray.

The fire started in late afternoon. On any
other day, the restaurant would have been
nearly empty, serving late lunches or early
cocktails to a few tourists who'd had enough of

Acapulco's sand and sun and would be glad to be enjoying a cool salad or a tall drink in air-conditioned comfort while gazing out the huge tinted windows at the glorious setting. But that day was different, for on that day the Acapulco Regent had been the site of an unusual gathering: The city's Chamber of Commerce, in conjunction with the country's Ministry of Tourism, had invited to the hotel a group of schoolchildren, first- and second-graders, from Acapulco's public and parochial schools. Most of the children were from poor families and it was the hope of the gathering's organizers that inviting them to the hotel would be a step toward bridging the chasm of misunderstanding that existed between the row of luxury hotels on one side of the main highway along the beach and the poverty-stricken community on the other. The children were in the restaurant, fifty of them, along with a dozen chaperons and a few other diners, when the fire started.

The Buena Vista restaurant was reached by a pair of escalators running from the Acapulco Regent's fortieth floor, the highest floor serviced by the main bank of elevators. Near the escalators were two emergency stairways leading from the restaurant down to the floor below. About half the people in the dining room, and most of the staff, managed to escape down the escalators and stairs, but the fire spread so rapidly that the other half were trapped. The only way out was along a balcony running around the outside rim of the restaurant. The balcony was only decorative and could not be reached from the main dining room—not with-

4

out breaking one of the huge tinted windows. Some of the children told reporters later that it was the tall blond man who had done just that—swinging at the window again and again with one of the heavy wooden dining room chairs until the window shattered into smithereens.

Like most decorative balconies, this one led nowhere.

"There were twenty or thirty people on the balcony," Jorge Estrada y Valenzuela told reporters. "Most of them were children, but there were a few adults—besides the blond man and the woman." (He had not yet admitted the names he had thought of for them.) "It seemed the end for them—unless the firemen could reach them with ladders from the floors below. Or perhaps helicopters—I don't know."

He was afraid to watch, for he was sure that they were going to begin leaping from the balcony, preferring an irrational leap into the unknown to the certainty of death by fire. In his imagination, he could hear the sound of their bodies striking the tiled walkway that led from the street to the main entrance of the hotel, and he knew that he would be sick, perhaps even faint.

But he watched nonetheless, and saw the tall blond man step up on the rail of the balcony ("Do not stand there," he wanted to shout. "It is for decoration only."), jump upward lightly and gracefully, getting his hands over the cornice of the roof, and pull himself up with one smooth motion. ("Like a gymnast," the assistant manager told reporters.) Lying on his stomach, the tall blond man leaned over the edge of the roof, extending one arm, calling to those on the balcony to follow after him, to use his arm as a lifeline.

"They hesitated. Who would not hesitate? I would not have done what they did. It was so far to fall. . . . Then, the woman stepped forward. At first, I thought she was a man, but . . ." Jorge Estrada y Valenzuela caressed the air with his hands in an international gesture and the reporters laughed and ducked their heads and recorded in their notebooks that the woman had been voluptuous.

The woman lifted a child into the air and the man grasped the child's wrist and lifted it onto the roof. If was a girl. Then a boy. Then another girl. Then two boys, then three girls.

"I counted twenty children lifted up to the roof," Jorge Estrada y Valenzuela said. "Then the firemen arrived and I was busy for several minutes explaining to them the layout of the restaurant. When I could look up again, there were perhaps a dozen people left on the balcony —a few children, and four or five adults, in addition to the woman. The children went up without difficulty, but there were problems with the adults. One of them was a woman— very . . . well, very , . ." The assistant manager made another gesture with his hands and the reporters noted that one of the survivors had been very, very fat.

A man helped the lean tanned woman lift the very, very fat woman. They got her onto their shoulders, but she kicked and squirmed a great deal and would not hold out her hands to the blond man above her. At last, she quieted and held out her hands and the blond man lifted her up onto the roof as easily as he had the children.

"Finally, only the woman was left. There was no one to lift her, so she stepped up on the railing, just as the man had. She waved at him to move aside, and, just as he had done, she leaped up and grabbed the edge of the roof with her hands and pulled herself up—like an acrobat, like the most beautiful, most graceful acrobat that had ever been seen in any circus anywhere —like Wonder Woman. They were like Superman and Wonder Woman."

But who were they really? The reporters wanted to know! Were they guests? Were they among the children's chaperons? Neither, the assistant manager told them. That much was certain: They were neither guests nor were they among the children's chaperons. They were just two people. Tourists who had come to the Buena Vista restaurant to enjoy the view, the air conditioning, a salad, a cocktail.

Were they together? the reporters wanted to know. Were they man and wife? Or lovers? No, the assistant manager said. As far as could be gathered from the maître d'hôtel, who had suffered minor burns and had been taken to the hospital, the tall blond man and the lean tanned woman had not been together. The man had been sitting at a table looking west, toward where the sun would set. The woman had sat on the shady, eastern side of the restaurant. The man had ordered a margarita, smoked a pipe, read a magazine—an American business magazine, the waiter thought. The woman had gazed out at the mountains, only picking at the shrimp salad she had ordered.

But who *were* they? Hadn't the assistant manager tried to find them? With another gesture of his hands, a gesture of helplessness, Jorge Estrada y Valenzuela said that there had been so many things to do, so much confusion, that he had not even thought to look for them until hours afterward, and by then, they had gone.

Where?

"Who knows?" The assistant manager nearly added, Who knows where Superman and Wonder Woman go after they have finished with a mission?

The children said that the man was kind and funny, that the woman was serious and firm. The very, very fat woman said that the man was extraordinarily strong and—she blushed as she said it—"very good-looking." One of the male chaperons said the woman looked "like a movie star."

The fire burned all night before firemen managed to extinguish it. At dawn, a thin plume of smoke rose from the roof of the hotel, just as thin plumes of smoke rose from the shanties in the poor sections of Acapulco only a divided highway away from the row of luxury hotels. Getting out of his car to return to work after a few hours' sleep, Jorge Estrada y Valenzuela stood for a moment looking up at the balcony four hundred feet above the tiled walkway and wondered, as he would wonder many, many more times: Who was that tall blond man? Who was that lean tanned woman? Did they introduce themselves and talk a while? Did they go off somewhere together—to have a drink, to have some dinner? Did they fall in love and go to bed together that very night, notwithstanding how exhausted they must have been? He would have liked to be there—not because he was prurient, but because he was sure that the coming together of Superman and Wonder Woman would have produced an explosion of passion that would have been something to see.

Chapter One

The rainstorm marched across Central Park like an invading army, sending pedestrians on Fifth Avenue and Central Park South fleeing every which way. The wind that was the storm's vanguard plucked rudely at women's skirts, contemptuous of the fact that among them were some of the city's most fashionable denizens. The rain was equally democratic, strafing young and old, rich and poor, strong and weak with equal force. The brutal gusts made short work of umbrellas that were raised in vain hope of fending off the advancing wall of water.

Clarissa Leeds had just stepped out of the Sherry Netherland Hotel when the storm hit the east side of Fifth Avenue. A flash of lightning turned everything a ghastly white, and she flinched from it, thinking for a moment that the photographers had found her once again, and were pelting her with their awful strobe lights. A peal of thunder enlightened her and the wind splashed her face with droplets of water. Clar-

11

issa ducked back in the revolving door and stood by a window in the lobby, watching the deluge, smiling sympathetically at the hapless victims of the storm who hurried back and forth outside.

Had any man among them happened to look at the window, his day would have been made—rain or no rain. And any woman would have had to admit that Clarissa's was no ordinary beauty —that it really did call for adjectives like *incredible* and *stunning*. Clarissa was tall, but a better word to describe her was *long*. She had long, strong legs; a long, narrow torso; a long, delicate neck; a long, oval face. When she walked, her stride was long, and when she gestured with her long arms, her long fingers seemed to reach halfway across the room. But for all her length, there was nothing gawky about her, nothing awkward. She moved like a dancer, with liquid motions that could mesmerize a watcher—and often did. Where she had walked there sometimes stood a row of men, entranced by her loveliness. Clarissa's black hair was long, too, falling to the middle of her back, although on this day she wore her hair up, tucked into a green felt safari hat from Hunting World, a hat whose brim she had pulled down low over her forehead, so as to deflect inquiring glances. She had never worn hats till now—except sometimes in the summer, when she wore a white tennis hat—but she had come to find them a useful defense—especially against the awful strobe lights of the photographers and the probing microphones of the radio and television reporters.

12

Clarissa wore a beige linen suit—a single-breasted, one-button jacket with notched collar and an A-line skirt with a front kick pleat. Beneath the jacket she wore a dark green blouse with its top button open to reveal the lace of a lime green camisole. Her discreet clothes could not disguise the exciting curve of her hips, the glorious thrust of her breasts. Clarissa's brown, low-heeled shoes bore the distinctive red and green bands of Gucci, as did the small suitcase she had set beside her on the floor beneath the window.

"Taxi, Miss Tyler?"

It was a moment before Clarissa realized that the doorman was talking to her, for he had called her by her maiden name. She had registered under her maiden name and had been struck that it had been so long since she had used it that she had formed the letter *T* differently from the way she had in the past. Rather than giving it a distinctive filigree, she had made it of two stark, straight lines—a stick figure that reminded her of a scarecrow, or a cross on a grave.

Clarissa swung her Burberry raincoat over her shoulders and turned up its broad collar. "I need a taxi, yes. I have to be at Grand Central by six-forty. But with this rain, do you think there's any hope?"

The doorman thought to himself, but could not say out loud, that if she cared to venture out in the street she could have a dozen taxis, a score of taxis. A woman as beautiful as she could get a taxi in the Sahara Desert, or the Amazon Jungle, or at the South Pole. But he just touched the brim of his hat, for it was his job to get her a taxi—he would have slain a dragon for her if she had asked—and although he wasn't sure he could summon one in this rain, he would die trying if it would mean getting her radiant smile of thanks, if it would mean hearing the music of her soft southern accent. "At your service," he said, and went out the door, holding his umbrella before him like a bayonet, ready to do battle with the elements.

Miss Tyler, Clarissa thought. When had anyone last called her Miss Tyler? In college, at Mary Washington, in graduate school at Juilliard, teachers had called her Miss Tyler. Occasionally, when she was at her parents' home outside Louisville, Kentucky, one of the servants would call her that, out of habit. But for five years now she had been Mrs. Leeds, Mrs. Peter Leeds. Representative Leeds and Mrs. Leeds. Mrs. Leeds. It had been something of a surprise to her to discover that she was still Mrs. Leeds, and could remain Mrs. Leeds as long as she cared to, even though Peter was dead.

The rain, though it did not seem possible, was coming down harder. It filled the gutters with rushing water and turned the pavement into a shallow river along which the cars and taxis aquaplaned, sending up plumes in their wake, splashing pedestrians who ventured too near the curb. A bus went by, for some reason nearly empty, though it was the height of the rush hour; its bright interior looked cozy and its passengers seemed to be enjoying their dry passage down the avenue, looking out at their less fortunate, damp compatriots. A young couple sat by a window, the woman with her head on the man's shoulder; she sat up straight and looked out the window at something he pointed to, then laughed and put her head back down on his shoulder. Clarissa would have liked to be on that bus, sitting next to a window, looking out at the tumult that the rain had caused, feeling safe and dry and in good hands. She wondered how far downtown the bus went. Perhaps it went all the way to the Battery. She could get the ferry there, and ride across the gray, rain-swept harbor to Staten Island. Perhaps by then the rain would have stopped and she could walk through quiet residential neighborhoods, looking in windows at families sitting down to dinner—mothers and fathers and children together, warm and dry and safe and in love with one another.

Clarissa had not ridden on the ferry since her days at Juilliard. Sometimes, when the pressure just got to be too much, when she had practiced until her fingers ached and her arms and back screamed in protest and her eyes could not make out notes on the staffs but only a jumble of black dots that danced mockingly before her, when she would rather have died than play the violin again—at those times, she and Sarah Stevenson would take a taxi down to the South Ferry and ride across the harbor to Staten Island. Sometimes they would have a hamburger at a quaint, old-fashioned diner near the ferry terminal in St. George, but more often they would turn right around and come back, feeling refreshed and renewed by the salt air and the wind, ready—anxious, even—to pick up their instruments again—those instruments, Clarissa's violin, Sarah's cello, that a few hours before they would have renounced forever.

No. She had ridden on the ferry more recently —with Peter. He'd come to New York for a fund-raising breakfast and she had come along to visit Sarah and Sarah's husband Abraham, at their apartment in the Hôtel des Artistes. Before going back to Washington, Peter and Clarissa had had a late lunch at the Windows on the World, the restaurant at the top of the World Trade Center, then had walked down through Battery Park to the ferry terminal and had taken a boat across to Staten Island and back.

In his light gray suit, his soft blue shirt, his bright yellow tie, Peter had looked like a fashion model posing for a magazine spread, like a movie star. She had stood with her feet apart, not holding on to the railing, imagining that she was the captain of this ship, and that it was not a shabby ferryboat, going from here to there and back again, endlessly, but a sleek liner, crossing the high seas to high adventure.

On the way back, they had shared the fantasy that they were immigrants, arriving in the New World. Peter had talked of his dreams of making that New World an even better place in which to live; he had made a promise never to let that dream dissipate. It was, he had said, a promise to his constituents, to himself, to her father, Senator Dwight Tyler, his mentor—and above all to her.

But to Clarissa's dismay and eventual horror,

it quickly turned out that Peter wore his vaunted political ideals with the same smug satisfaction as he did his Dunhill suits and André Oliver ties. Life in the fast track didn't enhance Peter's spirit—it made him smaller and meaner, arrogant, full of himself, and convinced that he was above the petty rules that constrained lesser men.

As his hunger for power-for-the-sake-of-power intensified, so too did his increasingly indiscreet womanizing. To what extent Clarissa was aware of all this no one could have said, for she kept her misgivings and her disillusion locked in her heart. That Peter was no longer the earnest and crusading boy she had married was undeniable, but her own pride forbade overt recriminations or retaliation.

All too soon, however, it began to be clear that Peter was playing out of his league. For all his outward worldliness and drive, he was the kind of guy senior senators and representatives ate for breakfast. He began searching for influence outside the accepted corridors of power —a little mixing in with organized crime here, a little bribe-taking from foreign industrialists there. Unfortunately, one of his sub-rosa contacts turned out to be an undercover agent for the FBI. Caught red-handed, there was nothing to do but face the music, or end it.

He had chosen the latter. On the evening of the day the House Ethics Committee voted unanimously to recommend an investigation of the charges against him, Peter had locked himself in the study of their Georgetown townhouse, consumed a quart of Kentucky bourbon, and shot himself in the right temple with a .45 caliber pistol left over from his days in Vietnam.

Clarissa shook her head to clear away the memory. For three months she had been a widow. Yet she was still Mrs. Peter Leeds, and could be for as long as she wanted.

"Miss Tyler?" It was the doorman, looking downtrodden.

Clarissa smiled. "No luck?"

"Not yet, I'm afraid. It's Friday night, and, well, everyone's trying to get away for the weekend."

Clarissa stooped to pick up her suitcase, pulled her Burberry close about her, and gave a tug to the brim of her hat. "I'll just have to take my chances out on the street, then. Maybe I'll have better luck over on Madison."

"I'm awfully sorry, Miss Tyler."

She touched his arm gently. "Don't be. I should have known to call a radio cab. It's really the only foolproof way on a rainy Friday evening. Now it's too late, and I'll just have to pay the piper."

The doorman looked at the place she had touched and thought that if he were a younger man, if he didn't have a wife and children, he might have done something as romantic as to never get his coat cleaned again. "The storm just came up. Just a few minutes ago, it was a beautiful day."

Life was like that, Clarissa thought, and went out the revolving door into the rain.

But there was some luck in life, as well, for just as Clarissa turned the corner onto Fifty-ninth Street, a taxi pulled up to the curb in front of the Playboy Club and a couple of portly men tumbled out and trotted into the club. Thank God, Clarissa thought, for Hugh Hefner. She curled her upper lip over her lower and brought forth a most unladylike but highly effective whistle—her brother, Dwight Tyler, Jr., known to everyone as Frére, had taught her how to do it when they were kids—and ran for the taxi, her long legs flashing, bringing a little joy into the lives of the rain-sodden males who trudged along on either side of the street.

The taxi driver, looking in his rearview mirror, thought he must have died and gone to heaven. He thought for a moment that the woman running toward his cab had come out of the Playboy Club, then realized that she had come from down the block. Nevertheless, she was as beautiful as any woman he had ever seen in *Playboy*—much more beautiful, in fact, and, notwithstanding the fact that she was fully clothed—a thousand times more erotic. Imagine his consternation, then, when the right rear door of his cab opened just then and a man got in, a man who, unnoticed, had dodged between cars from the other side of the street.

"Grand Central," the man said.

"No!" the taxi driver said.

The man laughed. "You're on duty, aren't you?"

"Yeah, but . . ."

"You know where Grand Central is, don't you?"

"Yeah, but . . ."

"Then take me to Grand Central."

"But . . ."

Just then, the left rear door of the cab opened and Clarissa got in. She had run the last few yards with her head down, holding on to her hat, and hadn't seen the man getting in the taxi. "Am I glad to see you. Grand Cen—oh . . . oh, no."

The man smiled. He was tall and fair and had blond hair combed straight back. His hair was wet from the rain, but would when dry, Clarissa knew, have a soft wave in it. He wore a tan doublebreasted suit, a dark blue Ralph Lauren shirt, a dark blue knit tie and dark brown hand-made loafers with tassles. On the seat beside him was a leather attaché case with a copy of the *Wall Street Journal* tucked into its side pocket. "Grand Central, you were about to say? I'm going there, too. I'll be glad to share the cab, but I'm afraid I'm not going to give it up. I'm late as it is."

Clarissa ducked her head so that the brim of her hat hid her face. She held the collar of her Burberry up to cover her right cheek.

The taxi driver looked in the rearview mirror. Half a loaf—or, in this case, two loaves —was better than none. "Grand Central, ma'am?"

Clarissa's heart pounded and her face was flushed. Her stomach was a knot. She wanted to look at the man again, to be absolutely sure. But she was absolutely sure. And yet, it couldn't be. It wasn't possible. It was something she had never thought would happen, and yet it was something that some part of her had always known would happen, had always hoped would happen. But not now. It couldn't happen now. It wasn't the time or the place. It wasn't right. She shook her head. "No."

There was a loud silence. The taxi driver looked at Clarissa in the rearview mirror. The man looked at her from where he sat. She was sure his gaze was burning through the fabric of her Burberry, through the brim of her Hunting World hat.

"No," she said again, and got out of the cab and walked swiftly back toward Fifth Avenue.

The taxi driver watched her in the rearview mirror, then turned to the man. "Not our lucky day, I guess."

The man murmured, "I guess not."

Chapter Two

Sean Howard offered a silent prayer of thanks when he spotted the empty cab outside the Playboy Club. He'd just emerged from the General Motors Building, where he had his office. He ran for it, tucking his attaché case under his arm, imagining that he was in college again, playing rugby for Yale, having just taken a lateral from the scrum half, shooting past the opposing fullback before he even registered that Sean had the ball. He offered a hip to a panel truck and took it away, swiveled past a long gray limousine, and dived into the taxi as he would have dived over the goal line.

It was typical of Sean's life, actually, to have no trouble whatever finding a cab during a rainy Friday rush hour in New York. He was used to finding the things he wanted at hand. Not that he had been spoiled as a child and a young man. Not that he was particularly lucky —although he did feel that he was in the right place at the right time more often than not. But it was not simply a matter of being in the right place at the right time; it was a matter of knowing that it *was* the right place, that it *was* the right time. It was a matter, too, of knowing exactly what he wanted and being ready to do what was necessary to have it at the moment it presented itself. When he talked about it, trying to explain it to others, he used a metaphor from racquet sports, which he played nearly every day—tennis in the summer, squash and racquet ball in the winter. In racquet sports, there was a decided advantage to hitting the ball on the rise, hitting it when it was still ascending from the court. By hitting the ball on the rise, one got the benefit of its maximum momentum and threw one's opponent's timing off, making him feel continually rushed. "It isn't that I hit the ball that much harder than others," Sean would say, "but I hit it sooner."

Sean had played squash at noon that day, soundly drubbing George Sherston in three fast games at the Manhattan Racquet Club. Then, as if to illustrate that the battles of business were won with the same techniques used on the playing field, he had accepted Sherston's offer to do the decorative work on La Tour almost before Sherston finished making it.

"Don't you want to think about it?" Sherston said. He was still wet from his shower.

"I have thought about it," Sean said. "I was only waiting for you to make an offer."

Sherston's voice got a little high-pitched. "Don't you want to talk it over with your people?"

Sean smiled. "George, I have no people. I

24

didn't get to where I am by having people to go to."

Later that afternoon, standing at the window of his office high in the General Motors Building, watching the rain clouds forming over the New Jersey Palisades, Sean imagined, as he imagined often, how the skyline to the southwest would look when La Tour had asserted itself into the air over Manhattan.

La Tour was Sean Howard's pride and joy, his impossible dream. It was to rise fifty stories, tapering slightly from its base to its peak in a manner that suggested rather than imitated the Eiffel Tower in Paris. Although trained as an architect, Sean had never actually practiced. As long ago as his undergraduate days at Yale, he'd come to the conclusion that the true master builders were not the designers but the men who acquired the space and put up the money. But he had had an active role in the design of La Tour, a design whose plans and scale models had already won high praise from the city's architectural community.

La Tour was to be many things in one. Its ground floor atrium would house a shopping mall whose shops would be annexes, so to speak, of the city's most elegant commercial establishments—Gucci, Cartier, Madler, James Robinson, Kron, Martha, Tourneau, Countess Mara, Dunhill. At one end of the atrium would be a legitimate theater whose interior was modeled after the finest of the classic old Broadway theaters; at the other would be a small, intimate movie house that would feature the cream of the current crop of films. The first twenty floors of the tower would be rented to commercial clients; the remaining thirty floors would be for condominium apartments. The commercial space had been two-thirds rented within three months of the initial offering; the apartments were spoken for within a week.

All that luxury was to be set against a most unlikely backdrop, for La Tour was to rise on the block of Broadway between Forty-eighth and Forty-ninth streets, just to the north of that combination Casbah, black hole, skid row and red-light district known as Times Square. The block had been occupied by a discount phonograph record store, a fast-food emporium, a pornographic movie theater, a video games arcade, a shop selling everything from posters of the latest flash-in-the-pan blonde in a soaking wet shirt to silly hats to cocaine spoons, a topless dance hall, another fast-food outlet and another video games arcade that was, as well, the headquarters for a local drug kingpin and his minions. In short, it had been an average block in a subhuman neighborhood until Sean Howard's bulldozers had come along and leveled it mercilessly and without a trace of nostalgia.

When the rain came it gave Sean great pleasure. It was so . . . extravagant. There was so much of it. When the phone rang and his secretary buzzed him on the intercom and said that his lawyer, Daniel Freedman, was calling, he was reluctant to turn away from the window and deal with business.

"See your picture in the paper?" Freedman said.

"Did you see yours?" Sean said and laughed, for in the photograph that had appeared in that day's newspapers—Sean, Freedman, some construction workers, some city officials, all gathered at the La Tour construction site for a ceremony honoring Sean for his contribution to the renaissance of Times Square—Freedman had had his hardhat pulled low over his eyes. "I barely recognized you."

"That was intentional," Freedman said. "I have a reputation to protect—a reputation for advising rational men."

Sean laughed again. Visionary. Crackpot. Humanist. Egotist. Realist. Dreamer. Pioneer. Madman. Those were just some of the sobriquets he had earned as a result of his plan to build La Tour on the nether reaches of Times Square. Even Freedman, who had watched him gamble and win in the past, was among those who pelted him with some of the less complimentary names. "Your name's in the caption. People will think you're just shy—or got a hat that was too big."

"Just calling to say that it's still not too late to reconsider," Freedman said. "The place'd make a dandy parking lot. It'd take a couple of days to pave it over and put up a fence. You could be in business by the middle of next week."

Sean laughed again. "Dan, this island's going to tip over if there's any more building on the East Side. The future lies to the west, the way it always has in America. We'll raise a score of beautiful buildings on the West Side—just you wait and see."

"You're the only person I've ever known,"

Freedman said, "who uses 'score' that way."

"Lincoln did," Sean said.

"I didn't know Lincoln."

"Dan, that neighborhood isn't terminally ill. This'll be a piece of cake compared with what we did on the waterfront."

"One minute you're saying how hard it's going to be," Freedman said, "the next minute you're saying it's going to be a piece of cake. I don't like these telltale mood swings."

"I said a piece of cake compared with the waterfront. Of course this'll be hard, Dan. I wouldn't do it if it weren't."

"Per arduous ad astris, or whatever it is."

"Per arduua ad astra," Sean said. "Through adversity to the stars."

It was Sean's motto. Only difficult prizes were worth going for. It was the motto, too, of the British Royal Air Force, in which Sean's grandfather, Thomas Howard, had flown in two wars. On graduating from Yale's School of Architecture, Sean had enlisted in the United States Air Force, following in the footsteps of his father, Lieutenant Colonel Thomas Howard, Jr., who had followed, at least symbolically, in his father's, and who had been killed on a bombing raid during the Korean War. It was 1964 when Sean enlisted, and the war in Vietnam was becoming a reality.

Sean had his doubts about America's involvement in the war but none about his duty to his country. In early 1965 he found himself stationed at the U.S. air base in Da Nang, South Vietnam, one of the pilots sent there to fly bombing raids against North Vietnam in the operation

code-named Rolling Thunder. But he never got
to fly those raids, never got to fly in war at all,
for shortly after arriving in Da Nang he was
wounded in the chest and stomach by the ma-
chine-gun fire of a party of Communist suicide
raiders who burst through the perimeter one
night, spreading mayhem as they went, wound-
ing a dozen Americans and damaging several
planes before they were cut down. Sean was invalided out to Honolulu for a month of inten-
sive care, followed by six months of convales-
cence in a San Diego military hospital.

The rain made Sean's chest ache. It would
also make his trek to Grand Central to catch a
train for Connecticut even more hassle-ridden
than usual. "Anything else, Dan?"

"Just remember. It's still not too late to reconsider. Like I said, the place'll make a dandy
parking lot."

Sean laughed. "Good night, Dan. Have a good
weekend."

"Umm," Freedman said.

Sean usually walked to the station, but forget
that in this weather! It was too late to call for a
cab—he'd take his chances on the street. He
knew where to look, out on Fifty-ninth Street,
near the Playboy Club.

But before he could get his things together
and leave, the phone rang again and his secretary buzzed him and said that a reporter from
the *Post* was on the phone, a woman named
Penelope Hammill.

"What does she want?"

"Something about an interview. I tried to get
her to tell me more, but she wouldn't. Sorry."

"That's okay. Why don't you go home? I'll see you Monday."

"Thanks. Have a good weekend."

Sean sat on the edge of his rolltop desk and punched the flickering button. He enjoyed pretty good relations with the press, for which his calculated accessibility was in large part responsible.

"Penny Hammill, from the *Post*. We're doing a series of important young New Yorkers. We're calling it 'Movers and Shakers.' You interested?"

"I'm sure it'll be an interesting series," Sean said.

Penelope Hammill laughed. "Nice. I like a nice wit in a man. I want to interview you. When can we get together? I'll need an hour. Maybe two."

"I'm pretty busy these days," Sean said.

"Good. That'll make it more interesting. I'll spend a day with you, then. I'll tag along with you, sit in on your meetings, do the interview in bits and pieces—in taxis and whatnot. Maybe I'll even buy you a drink. How about Tuesday?"

Sean had to smile at her directness. "I'm afraid next week's impossible. The meetings I have are with people who wouldn't want to be eavesdropped on—"

"Who?" Penelope Hammill said.

He could see her with a pencil poised, ready to write. "Why don't you give me a call in the middle of the week? In the meantime, could you put something in writing? I'd like to have your proposal on a piece of letterhead."

"Nice. A careful man. I like a careful man. . . ."

You want it in writing, you'll get it in writing. . . .
I'll be talking to you."

Sean hung up but didn't make a move to
leave. He had been the subject of such interviews before, had no problem giving them. For
without being immodest, he knew that he was a
mover and shaker and that his was a story that
would make good reading. On returning to New
York after recovering from his wounds, he had
politely rejected an offer from his mother to become a consultant to the real estate firm she
had inherited from her father; instead, Sean
had borrowed $100,000 from his mother and
started his own real estate operation. Within six
months, he had negotiated the financing of a
luxury apartment house in Brooklyn Heights, a
building that had once been a fashionable hotel
but that had fallen on hard times and had become a single-room-occupancy dwelling for
welfare recipients. The apartment house, River-
edge, blazed a trail that was followed by devel-
opers all over New York, who seized on the in-
spiration of buying up inexpensive existing
property—old hotels, former warehouses and
factory buildings—and converting them into
condominiums and cooperatives.

As befits a trailblazer, Sean became a million-
aire and moved on to new challenges. He repaid
his mother's loan, got himself an office in the
General Motors Building and built office buildings, apartment houses, a downtown branch of
the Museum of Modern Art, a private athletic
club, even a discotheque. His most ambitious
project was North River Plaza, a mix of residential and commercial buildings, including a

restaurant and a movie theater, built on the banks of the Hudson River in an area of abandoned piers and decaying warehouses. North River Plaza was credited with beginning the renaissance of New York's waterfront, just as it was hoped that La Tour would begin the renaissance of Times Square.

But Sean was reluctant to grant an interview at the moment. For even though he knew it would help La Tour, he also knew that any interview would inevitably turn to the subject of his marriage, and it wasn't a subject he cared to discuss. Sean had married Susannah Evans on the day he had arrived in New York from San Diego. They had met during his senior year at Yale, where Susannah was a student in the School of Dramatic Arts. They had been a beautiful couple—tall, strong blonds who were enough alike in physique and temperament that many people assumed they were brother and sister. They lived at first in a tiny penthouse apartment on Riverside Drive. With Sean's first successes, they moved to a three-bedroom apartment in River House, that elegant alp that rises above the East River just south of Sutton Place. Susannah pursued an acting career, and got some good parts in off-Broadway plays. But real stardom eluded her, for she was much too beautiful to play anything but merely beautiful women. And the marriage began to go bad; or rather, they began to recognize that youthful enthusiasm was not enough to sustain a marriage; they began to recognize that they did not love each other very much. Susannah tried a traditional remedy for loveless marriages—

she got pregnant; she didn't tell Sean that she had stopped using her diaphragm and told him that she had gotten pregnant in spite of it, which sometimes happened, didn't it? Susannah loved being pregnant, loved herself for being pregnant, and Sean found himself loving her more—and liking himself more—as a result. They moved to Connecticut, to the estate Sean had inherited when his mother had died the year before. Beautiful, damned Zoe was born on Labor Day, which they were never able to make a joke of, suffering from leukemia, and died a year later.

Sean sought surcease from sadness in his work. North River Plaza was just taking shape and there was a myriad of details to attend to. He worked until late at night and took the last train to Connecticut, arriving home with just enough time to wash up, catch a few hours' sleep and get back to the city for another long, driven day. More and more, he began spending nights in town, staying at the River House apartment, which they had kept even after moving to the country. Sometimes he spent weekends there.

Then Susannah decided that she wanted to move back into the city. She wanted to look for acting work again, to resume her career. But she had been away too long; her old contacts were no longer useful to her and even her loveliness had been faded by sadness and discontent.

Sean saw her plight and used his influence: An old friend of his mother's was a member of the board of the Guild Hall in East Hampton. Could she help Susannah get work with the

Hall's summer repertory company? Without an audition Susannah was offered the part of the schoolteacher in *Picnic*. She didn't want to take it; she wanted to make it on her own, not with Sean's help. He persuaded her, arguing that everyone needs a break in life. She accused him of simply wanting her out of his hair for the summer; he replied that he planned to take at least a month off, and would work as much as possible, when he had to work, at home—home being a summer house on Gin Lane in Southampton that he had rented for that purpose.

Driving out to the East End of Long Island the week before rehearsals were to begin, their Mercedes was hit broadside by a Trans Am that ran a red light on a street crossing the Old Montauk Highway in Quogue. The driver, a teenage boy with a long list of traffic violations, had three cans of beer on the bucket seat beside him and three empties on the floor of the backseat. Susannah was left paralyzed from the waist down and would spend the rest of her life in a wheelchair. The driver of the Trans Am was killed. Sean walked away virtually unscathed.

Sean devoted himself to Susannah's care. He had specialists flown in from all over the country to attend to her. He hired a full-time nurse and a full-time cook and housekeeper at the house in Connecticut, where they had always gotten by with day help, liking, when they had liked each other, to spend their evenings altogether alone. Susannah reminded him that their marriage had been plummeting downhill out of control well before the accident. He reminded her that they were still married nonetheless—in sickness and in health, just like the man had said when they'd taken their vows.

Susannah adjusted quickly to her plight, learning to use the wheelchair without assistance and insisting that she enjoyed having so much time to read and think. She even started to write, for she had an idea for a play and wanted to try her hand at it.

The phone intruded itself into Sean's reverie. He answered it automatically, then glanced at his watch and kicked himself for not just letting the service pick it up. It was Carolyn Evans, Susannah's mother, calling from Palm Beach, where she had lived year-round ever since her husband's death two years ago. Sean wondered if she had tuned into his thought, for she had a psychic streak in her.

"I've been thinking about coming north sometime soon," Carolyn Evans said. "I just wanted to make sure the coast was clear."

Sean laughed. "The coast is clear but the weather's not. It's pouring rain. Did you talk to Susannah?"

"I called, but she had that infernal answering machine on. She must be taking a nap."

"She's probably writing," Sean said. "She puts the machine on when she's working."

"Sean?"

"Yes?"

"How is Susannah? How is she really? Don't tell me what you think I'd like to hear."

Sean shut his eyes for a moment and breathed in and out deeply through his nose. "I'm worried about her."

"I could sense it," Carolyn Evans said. "That's why I called. Worried, how?"

"It's complicated," Sean said. "On the one

hand, she's found a way to keep mentally alert and active; the writing really takes her mind off the fact that she's . . . crippled. On the other hand, the writing is a constant reminder that she's crippled. By doing something she never did before, she makes herself always aware that she's not the way she was. She was a very physical woman, Susannah. She was . . . into her body, as the expression goes. Being deprived of that is a terrible emotional strain. She copes, but she's always aware that she's coping."

"Is she still taking those drugs?"

"She has a prescription for Valium, but she doesn't take it that often."

"Are you sure?"

"No . . . but it's not because I don't care, it's that . . . well, I try not to be looking over her shoulder all the time."

"I know you care, Sean," Carolyn Evans said. "You don't have to tell me that. Look, I don't want to keep you, Sean. I know you must be trying to get started on your weekend. I just had this . . . feeling, so I thought I'd call."

"You will come up and see us, won't you?" Sean said.

"Oh, that was just a pretext. I don't want Susannah thinking that I'm looking over her shoulder, either."

"Carolyn?"

"Yes?"

"Come and see us."

Carolyn Evans laughed. "Perhaps I will. I'll call you next week, after I've had a look at my schedule . . . Be well, Sean."

"Thank. You, too."

Sean's Rolex watch told him that now he'd really have to hussle for that train. He took a deep breath, and braced himself for the Herculean task of navigating the sodden streets of Manhattan. He'd get a cab, though. He just wasn't the type who got stuck in the rain.

Chapter Three

"Where're your bags?" Sarah Stevenson Newman asked. She was sitting on the hood of a
Jeep Cherokee, her feet on the bumper, reading
a book. She marked her place with a finger as
Clarissa approached, but didn't get down to
greet her, withholding her affection by way of
saying that she didn't like the look of things.
The train clanked into motion and moved north-
ward along the track. It had rained in Connecticut, too, and the parking lot was bright with
small mirrorlike pools, some of them golden
from the setting sun.

Clarissa held up her Gucci case, striking a
pose like a model in a fashion show.

"That's *a* bag," Sarah said. "I distinctly said
bags. I distinctly said you were not just staying
for the weekend. I distinctly said—"

"Don't be a yenta, Stevenson," Clarissa said.

Sarah stared, then roared with laughter, tipping backward until she was nearly lying on the
hood. "Yenta,"—she mimicked Clarissa's soft

southern accent—"Yea-en-tah. God, that's priceless." She sat up suddenly and admonished Clarissa with a wag of her finger. "Yiddish, my dear Wasp, is not for every tongue. You should only use Yiddish if you can make it sound as though there're several thousand years of experience behind what you're saying. Try it again. Yenta."

"Yenta."

"*Yen*ta!"

"*Yen*ta!"

"Better. Not great, but better." Sarah hopped down from the hood of the Cherokee, stuck her book in the hip pocket of the seersucker overalls she wore over a dark blue T-shirt, put her hands on Clarissa's shoulders and looked her up and down. "Where're your *bags?*"

Clarissa laughed and put her arms around Sarah and squeezed her as hard as she could. "Oh, Stevenson, it's so good to see you. How I've missed you."

Sarah stayed stiff, keeping her arms folded against her stomach. "Your *bags?*"

Clarissa laughed again. It had been a long time since she had felt like laughing. "My bags are at the hotel. I haven't checked out yet because—"

"Clarissa. You promised."

"—because I have to go back to the city on Monday," Clarissa put up a finger that warned Sarah not to interrupt, "to go back just for the day. I'll bring the rest of my things out then. And I'll stay all summer, as I promised."

Sarah frowned dubiously. "Go back to the city for what?"

"It's a secret." Clarissa put a finger to her lips.

"Clarissa!"

"Okay, it's not a secret, but it's a surprise. I want to tell Abraham, too, so you'll just have to wait till we get to your house."

"Till we get *home*," Sarah corrected. "I want you to call it home."

" . . . Till we get home, then."

Sarah scuffed at the sidewalk with an L. L. Bean boot. "I don't know. It sounds to me like you want to have a way out if you decide not to stay."

"That's because you're a yenta."

Sarah shrugged. "When you marry a Roman, do as the Roman does . . . Oh, Tyler, it's so good to see you."

And they dropped their game-playing and got into each other's arms and held on for a long time, not moving, not speaking, just feeling their friendship being rekindled, remembering.

They had met on their first day at Juilliard. They had sat on opposite sides of an aisle at an orientation lecture and had at one point exchanged amused looks at a particularly fatuous remark made by the dean of students. Afterward, they had introduced themselves and shaken hands and gone off to have coffee together. Sarah played the cello, Clarissa the violin, and that very evening they had played the first of countless duets together—a piece by Vivaldi.

Clarissa was a natural musician, but Sarah, though she had to work harder at it, was the more accomplished player, for she was driven by her love of music to an extent that Clarissa, who could do many things well—ski, ride horseback, play tennis, swim, sail, paint—was not. When Sarah fell in love, it was, predictably, with a musician, Abraham Newman, a man ten years her senior, one of the country's most accomplished violinists. Their marriage was a milestone on Sarah's road to a full-time career in music, for she and Abraham joined together not only in matrimony but as one-half of a string quartet, the Antonio Quartet, that was slowly gaining a world-class reputation.

"So," Sarah said when she had gotten the Cherokee started—it had taken a while, for there was something wrong with the solenoid ("Whatever *that* is," Sarah said)—and had turned onto a road leading west away from the station, "how are you? How are you really? Don't say what you think I want to hear. Give it to me straight."

"I'm managing," Clarissa said. "That's about the best I can say for myself. The worst thing—I suppose I should've expected it, this being the Age of Gossip—the worst thing is the publicity. The reporters won't let up, even now. They hang around constantly—Washington, at my parents' —wanting to know where I'm going, where I've been, what I've been doing. Freedom of the press, I've learned, means freedom to harass the hell out of whomever they want."

"That's why I wanted you up here," Sarah said. "It'll make a big difference—having a secret hideout."

Clarissa looked out the front window at the trees rushing by overhead. It already felt like a hideout, or at least the path to one—like the places she had retreated to in childhood, when being a senator's dutiful daughter just got to be too much. "I hope it'll stay a secret. If it can't, I won't stay, of course—but I have to go to Washington at least two or three times in the next couple of months. I'm afraid if I'm seen coming and going reporters'll start getting interested and follow me up here."

"Then why go? I mean, what's in Washington?"

"That's where the custody hearing will be."

"So you're going ahead with that?" Sarah glanced at Clarissa and saw her nod determinedly. "Won't that just make more publicity?"

"I have to do it," Clarissa said. "I have to." For getting custody of Diana was the only way, she thought, to keep herself whole, to keep herself sane, to salvage something from her miserable marriage, and something of her self-respect. Diana Leeds was Peter's twelve-year-old daughter by his first marriage to Rachel Abern. Rachel's father was a noted horse trainer, Peter's father a noted breeder of horses, and Rachel and Peter had been childhood sweethearts. But not adult sweethearts.

After the divorce, Rachel married Edward Owen, a San Francisco lawyer and yachtsman. She had dropped Diana entirely and devoted herself to following her husband around the world from one boat race to another. Diana had lived with Peter and Clarissa and had been the light of Clarissa's life. When Peter killed himself, Rachel had an attack of something she called responsibility, but that others called guilt or just contrariness, and went to court to try to gain custody of her daughter. Clarissa would have none of it, for as far as she was concerned, Diana was neither Peter's daughter nor Rachel's, but her own, for there was an empathy between them that surpassed the ties of blood.

Rounding a curve, Sarah slowed down and pointed out her window toward the stone gates of a huge estate whose grounds rose up from the road like a small mountain, on whose summit stood a beautiful modern house of bleached white wood and glass—the only modern house Clarissa had ever liked at first glance. "Nice, hey?" Sarah said, looking at Clarissa with a wry smile.

"That's it?" Clarissa said. "That's your house?" She slapped her cheek lightly in mock astonishment. "That's home?"

Sarah laughed. "Are you kidding? Our place is no dump, mind you, but it can't compare to that showplace. Oh, look—" Sarah pointed at a figure coming around the corner of the house— a woman in a wheelchair, pushing herself along with smooth, easy motions of her long arms. "The lady of the house—the mysterious Susannah Howard."

"Mysterious how?" Clarissa strained to see the woman better, but she could not make her out over the huge distance.

Sarah waved at the woman and got a wave in return, then accelerated along the road. "Oh, I guess she really isn't so mysterious, really. Just . . . tragic. She was in an auto accident. She and her husband, Sean Howard—the real estate big-gie—were hit by a drunk kid. She was paralyz-ed. Sean barely got a scratch. The kid died. Things hadn't been going so well for Sean and Susannah at the time. After the accident, he did everything he could to make her comfortable, insisted that they live together as best they could even though they might never love each other again. It was rather noble of him, I thought, although Abraham thinks he's martyr-ing himself unnecessarily. After all, he was totally blameless, and there's really nothing in the life he's living now for *him*. You'll meet them on Sunday. We're having a little garden party, with some music, to raise money for a local chamber music group, and they'll be there."

"Sarah, I don't think I can. Meet people, I mean. It's just too soon. Would you mind if I just holed up in the attic or something?"

"Don't give it another thought. I figured you'd probably feel that way. But it won't be the attic you'll hole up in. You're going to have the guest house all to yourself." And with that, as if she had timed it, Sarah swung the Cherokee into the drive of an estate that made Clarissa's heart soar. It reminded her of her native Kentucky, with its rolling hills and loblolly pine trees. In the distance was a pond that was nearly a lake, and at the top of the hill was a charming stone house with a round tower rising above it. "Castle Perilous," Sarah said. "The guest house is in the trees by the pond—I call it the swamp. I'll take you there later."

"What a beautiful house," Clarissa said.

"Don't let appearances fool you. Inside, it's a mess. God saves me from the joys of do-it-your-self renovation! When Abraham suggested we take four months off from touring to work on the house, it sounded like the best thing in the world to me. I didn't realize that he was just angling for cheap coolie labor."

"I love it," Clarissa said. "I love my home." Getting out of the Cherokee, she looked across the grounds toward the neighboring estate. She saw a momentary flash of metal as a car went along the drive toward the house, which was hidden from view by a grove of trees. Mr. Howard had come home, she guessed, home to the tragic Susannah. When the scandal surrounding Peter had broken, Clarissa had thought often about what it was going to be like to be married to him. It would, she imagined, be rather like being married to an invalid. She had been sure she would be able to manage it, but she hadn't been sure how—or why. She wondered how Sean Howard managed it. Before she could wonder further, she was enveloped in a welcoming embrace by Abraham Newman, who looked very like a bear in a down vest over a ragg wool sweater, baggy corduroys and high gum boots.

"Welcome," Abraham said. "Welcome, welcome, welcome."

Going into the house with Clarissa's bag, Sarah called, "Tyler thinks I'm a yea-en-tah."

"A what?"

"A *yen*ta," Clarissa said.

Abraham laughed a great bear laugh, tugging

at his red-brown beard with pleasure. "Tyler's right. She's absolutely right."

"Aren't you cold?" Sean said, bending to kiss Susannah as he got out of his Mercedes.

"I'm burning up," Susannah said. "I'm on fire."

Sean laughed. "Oh?"

"I did it, Sean. I did it." Susannah tipped her chair back and spun in tight circles, finally stopping and looking up at him, her face flushed with pleasure. "I finished my play. All it needs is to be retyped, then I can send it around."

"Terrific. I'm amazed. Not that you finished it, but that you did it so quickly."

"Eleven weeks," Susannah said, fighting off a smile of pride, then giving in to it. She was dressed in a deep maroon silk blouse that brought out the touches of red in her blond hair, dark gray slacks and black, low-heeled Ferragamo shoes—the sort of outfit she had taken to wearing since the accident, an outfit that made her look very much the career woman. Before the accident, she had dressed with the studied casualness of an aspiring actress. She looked very elegant in her new outfits, but they did something else to her, too; they gave her a kind of reserve, shrouded her in a coolness that Sean often found difficult to penetrate. They were emblematic of their relationship since the accident, for although they were perfectly polite to each other, there was an enormous distance between them.

Sean bent to kiss Susannah again, trying to bridge that distance to express his genuine pleasure at her accomplishment. "Congratulations. I'm delighted—and very proud. I hope you asked Delilah to make something special for dinner. We'll have to unearth one of our better wines, and maybe have some champagne. I also hope . . ." But he did not go on.

"You hope I'll let you read the play," Susannah said, for she had read the significance of his hesitation.

" . . . Well, yes. I'd hate to have to wait till opening night."

Susannah turned her chair to face the setting sun, which had sunk beneath the treetops and was perched on the rim of the earth, taking a last look around before disappearing for another night. "The main reason I haven't let you read it yet is simple—unadulterated fear. I don't know if it's any good. I can't bear to find out that it isn't. You understand that. You're the same way. You cover up your drawings when I come into the study if you're not ready to show me what you've done."

"I'm the same way," admitted Sean.

"The other reason I haven't let you read it," Susannah said, "is that . . . Well, as someone said, you can only write about what you know."

"Umm," Sean said.

"It's not *about* us," Susannah said. "Or rather, it's not about *us*. The protagonist isn't an actress . . . a cripple. Her husband isn't an architect, a builder. They don't live in the East.

48

They live in New Mexico. But, well, there are resemblances."

Sean put a hand on Susannah's shoulder and watched with her as the last segment of the sun slipped beneath the rim of the earth beyond the trees. "Susannah, if and when you'd like to show me the play, I would truly like to read it. For now, let's just be very happy for you, and not worry about anything else."

Susannah put her hand on his for a moment, then returned it to her lap and clasped it with her other hand, as if making sure it didn't get away again. "I'm not allowing myself to think too far ahead. Too many things can happen before the curtain goes up on any play. I've been around the theater long enough to know that. But . . . well, if I'm any good at this, I could be on my own. You wouldn't have to take care of me anymore."

"Is that what you want?" Sean asked.

"I don't know. I guess I think it must be what you want. You're a young man, Sean. You could have another child—many children. I often ask myself why you want an invalid on your hands."

"I don't think of you as an invalid, and I don't feel as if I have you on my hands."

Susannah looked up at Sean, his face golden in the last deflected rays of the sun. "I guess what I mean is, I hope you don't have me on your conscience."

Sean thought a moment before answering. He felt responsible for the failure of their marriage, and he *had* been driving when the accident occurred. To say nothing of the fact that going to East Hampton in the first place had been his idea. He tried—not for the first time—to brush these thoughts aside. "No. Not on my conscience. But I do think I owe you a comfortable life. If you ever feel that you want to be on your own again, just say so. You can always depend on me. All you have to do is ask."

Susannah examined the palms of her hands for some hint of the future. "Don't you ever think you might fall in love, Sean? With someone who can share your bed as well as your board?"

"I'm not looking to fall in love, Susannah, and I think love only comes to those who're looking. I have a wife and a home and I'm happy—so I'm not looking."

But after taking Susannah inside and going upstairs to change for dinner, Sean faced up to the fact that the bedroom he was in was his bedroom—Susannah's was across the hall—and that what he really had was not a wife but a housemate—a housemate who had written something she wouldn't let him read, who rarely talked to him about anything but quotidian things, who when she looked at him for longer than a glance seemed to be seeing him through a veil, seemed to be seeing not him at all but someone she imagined him to be.

Sean wondered about the drugs Susannah took, wondered if she took far more than he knew. He considered going into Susannah's bathroom—a bathroom that had been renovated for use by someone in a wheelchair—and looking in the medicine cabinet to see just what was in there. But he only considered it, for it was not his way to creep about peeking at her

things. He had never, for example, considered sneaking a look at Susannah's play, even
though she kept it out in a manila folder on top
of the desk in the study where she worked. But
he decided that he would bring the subject out
into the open.

"I take a Stelazine now and then," Susannah
said. "At night. They help me sleep."

Sean nodded.

"What're you getting at?"

Sean shook his head. "I only wanted to
know."

"Well, I've told you."

And Sean let it go at that, although he knew
that she was lying.

That night, lying in his bed, trying to sleep,
Sean heard himself saying: *I'm not looking to
fall in love, Susannah. I think love only comes to
those who're looking. I have a wife and a home
and I'm happy—so I'm not looking.* Not a wife—
a housemate. Not a home—just a place to live. It
was true that he wasn't looking, but he was not
surprised when he shut his eyes to see the
image of the woman who had gotten into the
taxi during the rainstorm. He had seen her
image earlier, when he had shut his eyes for a
moment in the smoking car of the train from
Grand Central.

What with her Hunting World hat pulled
down over her eyes and the collar of her Burberry turned up, he had not seen her well, and
couldn't picture her clearly now. But he had
seen enough to be interested—in who she was,
in why she would not accept his offer of a ride
to Grand Central, in why she had fled so deter-

minedly. He had a feeling that she had fled from *him*, not simply from the fact that he had been a strange man come upon unexpectedly in a taxi she had set her sights on. But if that were so, then mustn't it be that they knew each other somehow? He tried again to see her more clearly, for he wanted to understand why there was a feeling inside him almost of nostalgia, or pleasant longing for some time and some place in the past, a feeling of having loved and having been loved. That couldn't be, of course. You didn't love someone, then forget them. You weren't loved by someone, then forgotten by them. Maybe it hadn't really been love. Maybe it had been just a connection—something more than a glance exchanged across a crowded room, but not much, not necessarily.

Whatever the feeling was, he wanted to understand it. He wanted to feel it again.

Chapter Four

"A horse?" Clarissa asked. "You two have a horse?"

"Rather," Abraham said, trying to sound aristocratic, but sounding, as always, pure Brooklyn.

"Tally-ho," Sarah said.

It was Saturday morning and they were eating breakfast at the huge round oak table in the center of the Newmans' enormous kitchen. The sun poured in through the kitchen window, gleaming on ceramic tile and copper cookware, and turning the polished floor the color of the honey they ladled on their muffins.

"Kentucky isn't the only state where it's legal to ride horses, you know," Sarah said.

Clarissa laughed. She had been there only a little more than twelve hours and she had already laughed more than she had laughed in a year. "Oh, I know. It's just . . . well, you two just aren't the horsey type."

Sarah whinnied. "How's that?"

With a wink, Abraham said, "You should see me in jodhpurs. They bring out the red in my beard."

Clarissa looked at him through narrowed eyes. "Do you know what jodhpurs *are*, Abraham?"

Abraham feigned indignation. "They're those ridiculous red coats you wear in that ridiculous effort to catch a poor, innocent fox."

"I think they're pants, Abe," Sarah said out of the corner of her mouth.

Clarissa laughed.

Abraham shrugged. "In any case, yes, we have a horse. Or rather, we borrowed one from a neighbor."

"The Howards," Sarah interjected. "We drove by their house last night."

Clarissa nodded.

Abraham went on to say that they had been sure Clarissa would want to ride and when they had mentioned to the Howards that they were expecting a guest who was an expert horsewoman, they had immediately offered the loan of one of the four horses in their stable. "Her name's Maggie, I believe. I suppose that means it's a she—"

"A mare," Sarah muttered.

Clarissa reached out and took Abraham's hand in her right and Sarah's in her left. "Thank you. What a wonderful thing to do. I haven't been riding in months. I've missed it terribly. It's terrific to know that I can. Maybe I'll go out this afternoon."

"If I were you," Sarah said, "I'd go out this instant. Abraham here is getting that glint in his eye that means he's thought of some other room we can tear apart so we can rebuild it exactly the way it was. If you hang around here, you're liable to get drafted."

"You're certain to get drafted," Abraham said, rolling his napkin up tightly and flicking it like a whip.

Clarissa thought for a moment. She had thought she would spend the morning listening to some music on the stereo in the guest house, and might even dare to practice for a while, using a violin from among the Newmans' collection of instruments. But something told her to wait until she had her own violin. That had been the secret that Clarissa had wanted to wait to tell to Sarah and Abraham together: She had found a man, an elderly musician, retired from the New York Philharmonic, who was considering selling his Stradivarius. He had severe arthritis and could no longer play, and although it would pain him to part with the glorious instrument, he felt it deserved to be played, rather than to sit silently in his apartment. But he was concerned that he sell it to a serious musician, not merely to a collector, who wound hang it on a wall.

When Clarissa told him that she was going to be staying for a time with Abraham and Sarah Newman, and would be taking lessons from Sarah, he was very impressed. He had one other potential buyer with whom he had to meet, and he wanted to hear each of them play before he made his decision. It was to meet with him for a second time that Clarissa was going to go into New York on Monday. And though she felt she should practice, for she had not played the violin seriously for a long time, she also felt that she should not take up any other instrument beforehand, that the Stradivarius and she should come together as strangers, and make music together in a way that strangers often can—and intimates cannot. "Well, if I'm going riding, I'll need some boots. Mine are at the hotel."

Sarah made a casual gesture that said that they had anything she could possibly need. "The boots are in the back hall, along with a pair of jodhpurs"—she looked at Abraham significantly—"and a hacking jacket and one of those funny hard velvet hats you horsey folks wear. The saddle and bridle're there, too."

"But . . . where did you get everything?" Clarissa said.

"They're Susannah's," Sarah said. "You're the same size."

Clarissa ducked her head. "I don't know if I should."

"Because she's crippled? Nonsense. She offered the boots and clothes without my even asking. She doesn't need them, Clarissa. There's no need to get maudlin about it."

Dressing in Susannah Howard's clothes—they fit to a T, even the boots—Clarissa didn't feel maudlin. She felt eerie, for to fit so well into another woman's clothes made her feel she and that woman must have something in common. She wondered what.

The mare was brindled and gentle. She came to Clarissa at the edge of the paddock Abraham had fashioned in a grove of trees behind the house—there were bales of hay in it and an old bathtub that served as a watering trough—and nuzzled at Clarissa, searching out and finding the carrot she had brought down from the house.

"Hello, Maggie," Clarissa said. "You thought for a moment there that I was your mistress, didn't you? Well, I'm afraid I'm not. But I can assure you, I know what I'm doing, so don't give me a hard time."

The mare sensed her expertise immediately and stood quietly as Clarissa put on the saddle and bridle and mounted up. Clarissa kept her at a walk for a while, moving out of the paddock and around the bottom of the hill, past the guest house and pond, heading toward a line of trees where, Sarah had told her, there was a path that many of the horseback riders in the neighborhood used. But the mare wanted to run, responding to the hint of summer in the air, and finally so did Clarissa. She moved the mare to a canter, loosening the silk scarf around her neck so that the wind would cool her, for the morning was getting warm. The scarf streamed behind her as she rode.

Sean rode angrily, not staying to the path but taking a difficult course through the trees, reining the big gray gelding left and right, right and left, literally risking his neck among the low branches.

He replayed the conversation he had had that morning with William Middlebrooks, whom he had run into at the general store where he had gone to buy a newspaper. Middlebrooks was an old friend. Well, perhaps *friend* wasn't the right word, although he had been at Yale with Sean, had lived in River House for a time when Sean and Susannah lived there full-time, and was now a neighbor, having an estate about a mile from the Howards', Middlebrooks wasn't someone with whom Sean had ever talked about much more than the weather. He was more than an acquaintance, and he was proximate, but he wasn't a "friend."

Middlebrooks was the Manhattan district attorney, and his conversation that morning had been about more than the weather. It had been about an investigation his office was conducting into corruption in the construction industry —an investigation that was leading, tangentially perhaps, but leading nonetheless toward La Tour. There was nothing definite, nothing provable, nothing even litigable, but there was a hint, a suggestion, a suspicion that one or more of the contractors involved in the project had been paying bribes to city building inspectors to overlook certain irregularities and violations of building codes. Furthermore, there was a hint, a suggestion, a suspicion that the same contractors, in turn, were being paid off by subcontractors to accept deliveries of inadequate building materials or to hire those subcontractors to do work on the tower even though they had not submitted low bids.

"It's the kind of thing that may turn out to be nothing, Sean," Middlebrooks had said. He was on his way to play tennis at the Wendover Club, and wore flannel shorts, a Fred Perry shirt, Fred Perry sneakers, a cable-knit sweater with blue and red trim around his neck. He had an oversized Prince racquet with which he stroked imaginary backhands as he talked. "Sometimes people tell me stories to get me off their backs and on someone else's. But I want you to know that I'm going to look into it and that I may want to ask you a few questions."

"Isn't it a little irregular, Bill?" Sean had said. "Talking about a case to someone who's potentially involved?"

Middlebrooks stopped swinging as an attractive teenaged girl rode up to the store on a moped, dismounted and went inside. A bachelor, one of the city's most eligible, according to publications that keep track of things like that, Middlebrooks watched her until she was out of view. "It would be irregular if you were involved, Sean, but there's no suggestion of that. I'm telling you because sometimes things like this go on in a way that's slightly illegal but not illegal enough for me to build a case. By telling you . . . well, maybe you can have a look around and, well, get your own house in order. I'm not interested in sending people to jail—just in making sure that things are on the up and up, that this building ends up being safe and sound. I'd say you have the same interests. If you can get done what I'm not able to, because I have to toe the line a little more than you do, well, I'd say we'd both be very happy."

The teenaged girl came out of the store with a paper bag and a newspaper. Middlebrooks watched her load her purchases in a wire basket on the rear of her moped, mount up and ride off. He looked at Sean and rolled his eyes, as if he had fallen in love.

Sean remembered something about Middlebrooks at Yale. He was always falling in love with things that could not be his—a woman who was committed to someone else, a book that belonged to someone else, a jacket or a tie that someone else wore regularly and fondly. Sean had thought at the time that Middlebrooks was feigning a desire for the unattainable because he didn't really know what he wanted; he thought the same, now. He also thought that Middlebrooks didn't want to ever truly commit himself to anyone or anything. "I appreciate your telling me this, Bill."

"I thought you would." He paused and then asked rather hurriedly, "Oh, and how's Susannah?"

"She's fine."

"Give her my best, Sean."

"I will."

And Middlebrooks had trotted to his car, swinging his Prince overhead to limber his service motion.

Bastard, Sean thought as he rode. If he had a case, he wouldn't tell me. He only told me to let me know that he'd like to have a case, a case involving one of the city's most important real estate entrepreneurs, instead of the nickle-and-dime cases that so far had been the only cases he'd been able to build. There was nothing illegal going on at La Tour. Sean was sure of that. He was sure of it because he oversaw every single detail of the project—down to the doorknobs and the restroom faucets. He had a hand in drafting every contract and he spot-checked materials practically daily to make sure he was getting what he'd paid for. More often than not, he gave work to the highest bidder, pretty much believing that you almost always got what you paid for. He knew personally every contractor and subcontractor on the job, and he knew their foremen and assistant foremen, as well. No. Middlebrooks didn't have a case—not even a hint, a suggestion, a suspicion. He would only *like* to have a case, just as he would like to have the teenage girl. But he just didn't have the balls to really go after either.

Sean urged the big gray gelding down a ravine and up the other side, riding parallel to the path through the trees. As he reached the other side, he glimpsed a figure riding just ahead of him, keeping to the path. It was Susannah.

He reined in the gelding and shook his head in disbelief. It wasn't possible, or course. Susannah could ride no more. But who had it been? For just an instant, the thought passed through his mind that he had seen a ghost. For just an instant, he got cold all over.

Sean hauled the gelding's head over and went through the trees to the path pursuing the mysterious rider, who was already out of sight. He kicked the gelding just once with his heels and rode full tilt.

Rounding a bend in the path, he glimpsed his quarry just turning another bend farther along the path, and realized that the brindled horse she rode was Maggie, and remembered about Sarah and Abraham Newman's guest. They had said she was an expert horsewoman—what an understatement! Sean was an expert horseman himself, but he had doubts about his ability to overtake her, even though he rode the swifter mount. He hit the gelding lightly with his quirt and the horse surged forward even faster. The trees were a blur around him and the ground sped by beneath like a quick-running stream.

Suddenly, he stopped, hauling the reins so violently that the gelding nearly skidded on its hind legs. Its forelegs pawed fruitlessly for the ground that had been beneath them just moments ago. Fluttering to the trail up ahead of Sean was a blue and gold silk scarf.

Sean dismounted and let the reins drop to the ground, holding the gelding in place as effectively as if he had tied it up, and trotted along the path and bent to pick up the scarf. He hesitated for a moment before lifting it from the ground, for something told him that it was a talisman of particular power.

Hermes, the label said. The name of an exclusive shop Sean knew, but also the name of a Greek divinity, the messenger of the gods. He smiled at the idea that he was getting messages from such high places as Olympus, folded the scarf carefully and put it in the pocket of his hacking jacket. It left a scent on his fingers that he had never smelled before but that he knew he would never forget.

Sunday was warm, almost hot, and the guests at the Newmans' garden party wore summer clothes and thought summer thoughts and talked of summer things to do. Susannah wore a royal blue caftan with gold thread around the yoke and a gold pair of sandals on her useless feet. Sean wore white duck slacks and a Navy blazer over a striped Lacoste shirt. He had on fashionably battered Sperry Topsiders with no socks. After just a little while in the sun he felt that he was getting the beginnings of a tan. He was glad that summer was really on the way.

The local chamber music group played first, and played very well, for they were avid amateurs—a dentist, a lawyer, a housewife and a schoolteacher. After a short intermission, Sarah and Abraham played—Bach and Vivaldi and Pachelbel and Mozart—played so beautifully that the birds got quiet. Afterward, there was a feast that did as much for the guests' bodies as the music had done for their souls.

Sean excused himself from a group of people and went after Sarah, who was on her way inside the house to give some instructions to the maids. He caught up to her in the rose bower. "It was just beautiful, Sarah. What a treat to hear you play."

"I'm so glad you could come," Sarah said. She shaded her eyes from the sun and thought what an extraordinarily handsome man he was, despite the reservoir of sadness in his eyes. "We really don't see enough of each other, neighbors or not. It's not all that different from living in the city, is it? We don't get together much more often, really, than people there do who live in the next apartment. And they take the rap for being 'unneighborly.' "

"You *are* on the road a lot," Sean said.

"Don't remind me." Sarah pulled her hair back from her temple. "See these gray hairs? One for every airplane I've been on in the last year! But we're going to be here all summer. I can't tell you how delighted I am—even if Abra-

63

ham's idea of a vacation is to saw wood and hammer nails from dawn to dark."

"That can't be very restful for your guest," Sean said.

Sarah cocked her head and looked at him with mock suspicion. "How did you know we have a—Oh! Of course! We borrowed your horse. She had a wonderful ride this morning. She's very grateful for your generosity."

"Does she have a name?"

Sarah frowned. "I thought her name was Maggie."

Sean laughed. "The horse's name is Maggie, yes. I was referring to your guest."

Sarah ducked her head and scuffed at the bricks of the bower with a sandal. "I don't mean to be secretive, but . . ."

"But it's a secret?" Sean said.

"Not exactly. It's just . . . well, she's going through a difficult time in her life. She came up here to get away from things, people, that were making it more difficult. I hope, in time, she'll come out of herself a little bit. I know she will. But for a while, anyway, I think she'll be keeping pretty much to herself. She didn't care to come up here today, for example. She's down at the guest house."

"Which still doesn't explain why you won't tell me her name," Sean said. "I'm not prying, I just . . . well, I just like to know who's riding my horse."

Sarah nodded, but didn't lift her head. "You see, the thing is . . ."

"She's famous," Sean said. "You have Greta Garbo here visiting you. Or Elizabeth Taylor. Or Barbra Streisand."

Sarah laughed. "I wouldn't let Barbra Streisand set foot inside the gate. I abhor Barbra Streisand. Anybody who spells Barbara that way—Bar Bra. Every time I see it I think of metallic lingerie."

Sean laughed and touched Sarah's shoulders momentarily. "Okay. I won't ask any more questions. If you want to have a mystery guest, that's up to you. But if I should happen to see her, should I just avert my eyes, or can I say hello?"

"Say hello," Sarah said. "It'll do her good. Now, if you'll excuse me . . ." And Sarah went inside the house.

Susannah waved to Sean, and when he went to her she said she was getting tired and wanted to go home and take a nap. "But you stay—please. It's such a nice party."

"I'll take you home, at least."

"I can call Martha and have her come get me."

"I'll take you," Sean said. "I'll walk back. I want to walk off some of this food."

After he had driven Susannah home, Sean returned to the party on foot by way of the grounds, walking around the pond and past the guest house. The guest house windows were open and the flowered curtains fluttered in the warm breeze. Music played on a stereo inside—Bach, guessed Sean to himself, although he wasn't sure.

He went up on the porch and knocked on the door.

"It's open," a woman called in a voice as soft and warm as a breeze.

Sean put his hand on the doorknob, breathed

65

in and out deeply through his nose, and opened the door, keeping his feet on the doorsill, for he knew that he was not who she expected. "Hello."

"... Oh ... Hello." She had been sitting in an easy chair in a corner of the living room, one leg draped over the arm, a book in her lap, a pair of half horned-rim glasses perched on her nose. When she saw who it was, she got up in one quick, fluid motion and stood with her back to a window, her hands out behind her, as if ready to bolt from this intruder.

"I'm sorry to disturb you," Sean said. "I hope I didn't frighten you. My name's Sean Howard. I live next door. I ...." He fumbled in the pocket of his blazer and took out the scarf and shook out the folds. The breeze, sneaking through the door, filled it like a spinnaker. "I found this. I believe it's yours."

Clarissa put a hand to her throat, as though she had lost the scarf only moments ago. She wore a light blue silk blouse, white cotton pants with a drawstring waist and white ballet shoes. She wore no bra beneath her blouse and as she moved the fine silk lightly caressed her nipples. "It is, yes. It blew off while I was out riding. I looked for it along the trail, but I couldn't find it. I thought it must have blown into the underbrush."

Sean heard himself saying something about how he had picked it up lest it be accidently trampled by other riders, lest it startle another horse, about how he had recognized Maggie and had surmised that her rider was the Newmans' guest, about how he would have brought it by yesterday but had gotten tied up with errands and then had had to go out to dinner at friends'. But he wasn't concentrating on what he was saying. The words just formed themselves, assembled themselves into sentences that might or might not have made sense—he couldn't say. For he was stricken by her beauty. It wasn't the kind of beauty that takes your breath away, but rather that gives you breath, that makes you feel alive and glad to be alive. It wasn't a heavenly, untouchable beauty; it was earthly and even a little earthy, for her body had a sensuality that only comes from use—use on horseback, use in sports, use in making love. And he was stricken by the realization that—there could be no doubt about it, even though she wore no hat and did not have her hair tucked up into it, even though she wore no trench coat with its collar turned up against inquiring glances—that this was the woman who had gotten into the taxi the other rainy afternoon. "I'm . . . Excuse me for staring, but, well, we've met, haven't we . . . in a way?"

Clarissa could only nod. She could not form words at all, for in order to form words there must be more organization of thoughts, and her thoughts were all a-jumble. She thought: *This is the man from the taxi. This is the man from . . . from the past. Impossible. He doesn't know me. Not surprising. My hair is down. I'm not wearing a hat. I'm not wearing sunglasses. I had a tan. It was two years ago. I was different. He was different, too—but not that much. His hair was a little longer. He had a tan—not as dark as mine —a golden tan. He was wearing casual clothes.*

He's here. He was in the taxi. He was there. Here. There. Impossible.

Sean smiled warmly. "You see? You should've accepted my offer to share the cab. We could've ridden up together on the train. How is it I didn't see you on the train? Because I rode in the smoker, I suppose. And then, when I got to the station, I went across the road to get some tobacco at the little store there, and I didn't see you get off."

Clarissa nodded again, not because she really heard but simply to acknowledge that she knew he was speaking. She was stricken, too—by the impossibility of it, and by his beauty, by a handsomeness of a kind she had never encountered in any man—a handsomeness that seemed to be a manifestation of some interior order, some harmony of his mind and heart and soul. And yet she could see in his eyes that some effort was being applied in order to achieve this harmony, that he had to work to keep the order from turning into disorder.

Sean put out a hand, as if to modify what he had just said. "But I also understand that you wouldn't want to share a taxi with a stranger . . ." He paused, wishing they had something else to talk about other than the taxi ride they hadn't shared. He could think of nothing. He couldn't think at all. "Well . . . I won't disturb you any longer. Here's your scarf"—he took a step toward her—"it's a very beautiful scarf. I'm glad I found it before it got ruined."

Clarissa nearly took a step away as he stepped toward her, then told herself to get a grip on things, and went to meet him in the center of the room. Their fingers touched as the scarf was passed from hand to hand. "Thank you. And thank you for the loan of your horse. She's magnificent."

"I'm glad to . . . I'm . . . I'm glad. Yes, she is magnificent, Miss . . .?"

"Tyler. Clarissa Tyler."

They shook hands. Her hand was long and cool, his strong and warm.

"I'm glad to meet you," Sean said. "If there's anything—anything at all—I can do to make your stay here more enjoyable, you must let me know."

Clarissa nodded. "Thank you. I will."

"If you need a car, I have two. I also have three other horses." Sean wanted to name everything he owned, but he checked himself. "Anything at all."

"Thank you," Clarissa said, "for everything."

After mumbling an incoherent good-bye, Sean forced himself to turn and go out the door and down the steps and walk across the lawn. He didn't head for the garden. He didn't head back to his house. He walked toward the woods, wanting to be in a place where he would be enclosed, protected, yet free to wander. He felt in the pocket of his blazer for his pipe and tobacco, but he hadn't brought them with him. When he took his hand from his pocket, he raised it to his face and smelled her smell.

Standing by the window, watching him walk across the lawn, Clarissa thought how in her memory he had always been connected with the smell of smoke—great billowing clouds of smoke, and with the sounds of roaring flames and the cries of children.

69

Chapter Five

The violin fit in Clarissa's hands like a child in its mother's arms. The ancient wood was polished by 250 years of handling. The instrument's smell triggered memories of Europe—of museums filled with unknowable treasures, of narrow streets redolent of history, of monuments that had outlasted by far the events and the individuals they had been erected to commemorate.

And when Clarissa touched the bow to the strings, the violin emitted a sound so beautiful that she nearly stopped playing in order to hear it better, nearly forgetting that it was she who was responsible for it. Responsible in part, for the instrument seemed almost capable of playing itself, seemed to have a life of its own that was not dependent on the fickle, unpredictable lives of humans.

David Stein, the violin's owner, settled back in the worn plush easy chair of his studio in a building across the street from Carnegie Hall, placed his fingertips, gnarled by arthritis, together beneath his chin, and with a nod told Clarissa to play on. Behind him, in the shadows of a corner of the room, stood James Morgan, the young man who was contending with Clarissa for the right to buy the violin. David Stein had met with each of them separately on Monday and had talked with them for a long time about their backgrounds and about their aspirations for the future. He had let each of them hold the violin, but had not let them play it. On Wednesday, he had telephoned each of them and summoned them to his studio on Friday for the crucial performance.

"Maybe you think I'm putting you under a little too much pressure," Stein said when he greeted them that morning. "And there's no question that it does. But my decision will be a matter of opinion—a matter, if you will, of taste. If each of you hears the other play, you'll at least know something of the nature of my taste. You may not share my taste, for taste is, after all, a personal thing. But taste is also something, as the saying goes, that there is no disputing. It'll be less arbitrary, I think, if you each hear the other play than if you were to play for me privately, then were to be informed, by phone, or by letter, of my decision."

Clarissa played a Bach sonata she had played as a student at Juilliard. Her black hair fell about her face as she tucked the violin under her chin and swayed to and fro as she bowed. The acoustics of the room were exceptional, the studio having been built expressly for the purpose of playing music, and the notes danced lightly about the room, each a link in a fine chain of golden sound that grew longer and longer, gradually making contented captives of its listeners.

There were flaws in the chain, for Clarissa had not played in a long time and her fretting fingers had no calluses and her bowing arm soon grew tired from tension. Once, she lost her place on the page, being unaccustomed to reading the notes and having to read them one by one, rather than, as she had when she was more fluent, as she would again, phrase by phrase. But at least, she thought with the part of her mind that was free to observe what was going on, at least she had not stopped. Nor did the imperfections distract from the emotion that suffused her playing. For her heart was not out of practice, and it gave to the music an ardor that could not be marred by a few false notes, by a slight inconsistency in the rhythm.

David Stein heard the emotion in Clarissa's playing and smiled behind his twisted fingers. James Morgan heard it, too, and he shifted from one foot to the other in the shadows, at once swept along by the power of the music and at the same time trying to fight it. He had played first—a piece by Schumann—and had played with a technical brilliance that had left Clarissa cold with anxiety. But it had been playing that impressed itself only on the mind—cerebral music-making that had not one whit of passion in it. Listening to Clarissa play, James Morgan knew that he had lost, knew that the note-perfect performance he had given was being ousted from the memory of the one-man judge and jury by Clarissa's rapturous display—just as it was being ousted from his own memory. And when Clarissa finished, when the last links of the chain were in place and the whole still hung in the air like an evanescent web, not collapsing but only slowly fading, like a light that has gone out but whose ghost still lingers, James Morgan stepped out of the shadows, applauding lightly, and walked across the room and extended his hand to Clarissa.

"Brava. Brava. The violin is yours—unquestionably"—he turned to look at David Stein, but turned back before Stein could even nod his head.

"I'm not used to being bested, but in this case . . . Well, I'm honored." And he bowed and turned-ed away and with a nod to David Stein left the studio, slipping quickly out the door as if to keep even a note of the music from escaping, shutting the door gently behind him as if not to disturb the delicate framework that still stood resonating in the air.

Clarissa raised her eyebrows at David Stein. "I hope that's your opinion, as well. I hope the poor man didn't jump to the wrong conclusion."

"Then you haven't been listening to what you've been playing." David Stein got up slowly from his chair and walked to the window looking out over Fifty-seventh Street, holding out his hands to the sunlight that streamed in the window, as if the healing light and warmth might straighten his twisted fingers. "One day, I think, you will be making music there, across the street, at Carnegie Hall."

Clarissa smiled. "I'm not as young as I look. I'm thirty years old. I've wasted a lot of time. I don't know if I can make it up."

"Your hands may have been idle," David Stein said, "but your heart has been making music all the while. That, finally, is all that matters. Even I—" he held up his hands and turned them this way and that, "even I, with these hands of mine that can no longer hold a bow, that can no longer form themselves around the neck, even I, when I am asked by a stranger what my profession is, say, 'I am a musician—a violinist.' If I am asked to play, of course, I must say, 'I cannot.' But that isn't quite accurate. My hands cannot play, but my heart can play at will. My heart is tireless and nimble—as is yours. Whatever it is you have been doing these past few years, years when you have not been playing, does not mean, had anyone asked you what your profession was, that you could not have said, 'I am a musician—a violinist.' "

Clarissa held the violin close to her breast, feeling, almost, that the instrument had a heart and that she could feel it beating in time with her own. "Then the violin is mine?"

"Indeed."

Clarissa laughed. "For the price you mentioned, of course. I have the check right here. It's all made out." She put the violin down gently in its case and rummaged in her bag.

"Then you must have known, in advance, that you would be the better player," David Stein said. "That kind of confidence comes only from the heart, as well. The fingers, the hands, the body—they really exude that kind of confidence."

Clarissa looked toward the door. "He was very gracious to say what he said. I'm not sure I'd have been such a good loser."

David Stein rubbed his white beard thoughtfully. "I thought I detected a slight subterfuge in his action. Nothing dishonest—he meant what he said. But . . . well, I imagine that you will be hearing from that young man again. He was smitten by more than your music."

Clarissa had known that, and she liked it. It had felt good to know that an attractive man was interested in her. And James Morgan was very attractive. Thin but strong, with long brown hair that he was forever raking his slender fingers through to pull it away from his face. He had been dressed in the urban-cowboy fashion that was lately a la mode—a blue-and-white-checked shirt with pearl-snap buttons, a suede sport jacket, worn blue jeans, a tooled leather belt with a silver Lone Star Beer buckle, ornate Tony Lama boots with sharply pointed toes. He worked as a copywriter at an advertising agency, he had said, but his first love was music. And women, she could almost hear him add, though of course he said nothing of the kind.

When Peter killed himself, Clarissa had been sure that she would never get involved with a man again. Men were weak, inconsistent, unreliable. They hurt women—and worse, they didn't know they did. Better to be alone—with herself, with her music, with Diana, if it turned out that that was in the cards. But lately she had begun to feel differently. Not that she would put herself once again in the position of being hurt. But if the right man came along—and she didn't know yet what would constitute rightness—Clarissa would be willing to consider the possibility of a relationship with him. For one thing, Diana needed a father—not a father like her sailor stepfather (was stepfather even the right word for what Rachel's husband was?), but a father who could love her as he loved Clarissa. For another, Clarissa wanted to have a child of her own. She didn't know where that wish fit in with her wish to resume playing music, to try to have a career as a musician, but she knew that it was so.

Clarissa knew that James Morgan was not the right man. There was an inconsistency in his eyes that warned her not to get too interested in him. But at least she knew that she was beginning to feel again, to unbutton, at least, if not cast off entirely the protective shroud she had had tightly pulled about her for all these months.

Clarissa glanced at her watch and made a startled sound with her tongue against her teeth. "Oh, dear. I must be going. I have a train to catch." She closed the violin case carefully and gathered up her things. "Thank you so much."

David Stein took the certified check Clarissa held out to him, folded it and put it in the pocket of his sweater. "I'm not going to cash this right away. I'm going to wait until I hear from you that you are giving a performance to which you would like to invite me. Then I will cash the check and use some of the money to buy flowers for your dressing room and a bottle of champagne with which to toast your success."

Clarissa frowned and bit her lower lip. "Oh, dear. I'm afraid . . . I would hate . . ."

David Stein laughed and gently touched Clarissa's hand. "If you're thinking you're afraid I might die before you give such a performance, don't worry. I'm not that old . . . I'm merely expressing my confidence in you, my dear young woman. It's not the worst thing in the world to have someone who believes in you."

"No," Clarissa said softly. "No, it isn't. But a concert—there are so many fine young musicians—"

"Of whom you are one," David Stein said. "Nor need it be a public concert, like one at Carnegie Hall—though that will come to you in time—I'm sure of it. Merely a performance—a performance to which you would like to invite me. I'm sure the time will come when you feel you are ready for such a performance." And with that he bent and kissed her cheek. "My blessings, my dear."

Clarissa bit back a few tears, picked up the violin case and held it close. "I'm grateful for it, and for this beautiful instrument . . . and your confidence . . . your belief in me." She turned and went out the door.

"T G I F," Sean's secretary said as she looked into his office on the way to the elevator.

And though Sean disliked the expression, he, too, was thankful it was Friday. It had been a hell of a week. On Monday, the crane that lifted building materials to the upper stories of La Tour had developed a crack in its boom and had to be dismantled and the weakened strut replaced. On Tuesday, Sean had learned that one of the investors in the project had been putting up money that was not altogether his, having embezzled it from his partners in an independent motion picture production company; the lawyers and bankers were trying to figure out what belonged to whom. On Wednesday, William Middlebrooks had phoned to say that he had a witness who was prepared to say that the chief foreman on the La Tour project was aware of, if not directly involved in the alleged briberies and kickbacks. (He had also extended his regards to Susannah.) On Thursday, some reinforced concrete slabs delivered from a supplier in Pittsburgh turned out to be the wrong size and had to be sent back. On that Friday morning, Sean had had a particularly unsettling conversation with Ken Forrest, his oldest and closest friend.

They had had breakfast together at the Algonquin, where Forrest, who illogically spent winters in a cold climate and summers in a hot one, was stopping over enroute from Livingston, Montana, to Key West, Florida. A novelist who had enough loyal readers to constitute a following, though they did not make his books bestsellers, Forrest had known Sean since their days at Yale, where they had been members of the same fraternity and had played rugby together. They had followed separate but parallel paths after graduation, Forrest enlisting in the army when Sean joined the air force. Forrest had been in Vietnam when Sean was wounded, but he hadn't learned of it until a year later, when he looked Sean up after finishing his tour of duty. Forrest lived in New York for a while, writing his first book, supporting himself by betting on whatever sport was in season, and on the horses, which raced all year round. After his first book was published and was sold to the movies—the movie never got made—Forrest moved to Montana, where, he said, "there was room to think." His second book was made into a movie, which deviated so greatly from the novel that he demanded that his name be removed from the credits; the movie was a hit, however, and the money enabled Forrest to get a place in Key West in which to summer. ("Damn right it's hot," he said by way of explaining his curious choice of lodgings. "And it's colder than hell in Montana in the winter. But that's the goddamn point. It's either too hot or too cold to go outside, so I just work all the time. Why the fuck would a writer want to live where it's *nice?*") Notwithstanding the distances between them, Sean and Ken had stayed in close contact, having long telephone conversations every couple of weeks, exchanging brief but pointed letters on almost a monthly basis, making sure to visit whenever business took one of them even vaguely close to where the other was.

The argument started obliquely when Forrest said he was thinking about writing a nonfiction book about Vietnam veterans, about the bum rap they had taken from start to finish. "Too many of them have gone down the tubes. Drugs, breakdowns, suicides, a lot of one-man car wrecks nobody can prove were suicides but sure as hell look like they were. A Seventh Cav buddy of mine put a bullet through his head a while back. Maybe you read about it—Peter Leeds, the congressman."

Sean had read about it, and he nodded. "It's hard to blame that on Nam. He got caught taking a bribe."

Forrest waved away the suggestion. "Yeah, but who's to say he didn't learn all there is to know about corruption in Vietnam?"

Sean stopped a forkful of roast beef hash halfway to his mouth and looked up at the ceiling. "Clarissa Leeds."

Forrest leaned down and followed Sean's gaze. "Where?"

"His wife's name was Clarissa, wasn't it?"

"That it was. Hell of a looker. So fine, in fact, that I had to decline an invitation to be an usher at the wedding. I was afraid I'd commit some kind of mayhem, or just lie down and cry—anything but watch her tie the knot with another man—even a buddy." Forrest cocked his head and tried to make something out of Sean's expression. "Seen a ghost?"

Sean shook his head and went on eating for a while, although he couldn't have said what he ate or how it tasted.

"Come on, old-timer," Forrest said. "Don't just leave me hanging here. What about Clarissa Leeds?"

"She's a guest of my next-door neighbor, in Connecticut," Sean said. "She's using her maiden name, Tyler, to avoid publicity, I guess, so I didn't make the connection . . . that's all."

Forrest laughed. "If that's all, then I'm a brain surgeon." He waited a moment, then made a motion with his fingers of wanting Sean to fork over whatever he was withholding."

"Really," Sean said. "That's all."

Forrest pushed his plate away and spread his elbows on the table and spoke conspiratorially. "Sean, old buddy, this thing you got with Susannah—"

Sean laughed. "It's called a marriage."

Forrest raised his eyebrows doubtfully. "Oh, come one, Mr. Integrity. It's no marriage and you know it. It's your way of doing time for a crime you never even committed."

Sean bristled inwardly, but as always, he let Forrest go farther than anyone else would even have dared. "It's not like that," he said evenly. "We need each other."

"Susannah needs you, you mean."

"Yes."

"Well, what about you?"

"Ken, I can't just leave her."

"You practically left her, once—burying yourself in your work the way you did."

"That was after the baby died—and before the accident."

"Which was just that," Forrest said.

"I know that," Sean said. "Forget the psycho-analysis, okay?"

"Sometimes I wonder what you know and don't know. Sometimes I think maybe you think it was your fault."

Sean crumpled his napkin in anger. "Lay off it, Forrest. No matter whose fault it was, it happened. And Susannnah was hurt. And I won't abandon her as long as she needs me."

"So, it's just a—what would you call it—a marriage of convenience? Or, should I say, Susannah's convenience." Forrest held his hands up defensively. "I've known you for a long time. I've got a right to say what I think."

"What you think is wrong," Sean said.

Forrest shrugged. "You're the one mentioned Clarissa, not me."

Sean had to laugh. "You mentioned her husband. I mentioned that I met her. That's all. It's a way people have of talking. It's called chitchat."

"She is a looker, isn't she?"

" . . . Yes, she's a looker."

There was a long pause, during which they fiddled with silverware and folded and unfolded their napkins and looked around the dining room, not seeing what was right in front of their eyes. Finally, Forrest leaned across the table and grasped Sean's hand in his. "I love you, you old fuck, you know that, don't you?"

Sean nodded.

"And I'm only saying what I'm saying because it matters to me what your life is like. I know you think your life is fine. But I've known you too long, Sean, not to see that there's something in your eyes that's never been there before, something that doesn't belong. If I had to give a name to it—that's my business, after all, giving names to the looks in people's eyes—I'd call it resignation. It feels to me like you've given up. And that's not something I've ever known you to do."

The arrival in the dining room of an author

better known than Forrest caused the subject to be changed to that author's work, and it didn't get changed back. But now, in late afternoon, settling into a seat in the smoking car of the train to Connecticut, filling his favorite Wilke pipe with imported Rhodesian tobacco from his fine leather Dunhill pouch, Sean replayed the conversation and knew that Forrest was right; he had resigned himself to a life whose only emotions were cool and controlled. And he had resigned himself to celibacy, to a life without sparks, without heat. That it was his duty to care for Susannah made it understandable, he supposed, even acceptable. But the evil thing about duty, he knew from his time in the air force, was that it involved more than devotion to a task, to a cause, to an individual or to a nation; it required closing one's eyes, shutting off part of one's brain, ceasing to ask questions, to inquire, to learn, to grow. It required, as Forrest had said, giving up.

Chapter Six

"Son of a bitch!" Sarah growled, as the motor of the Jeep sputtered and died for the umpteenth time. "It's the goddamn solenoid. Now what do we do? Abraham is out with the Toyota, and there are no taxis in this goddamn town. Care to spend the night here at the train station while your million-dollar violin is slowly destroyed by overexposure to the elements?"

Clarissa grinned weakly, and tried to hide the alarm she felt at having the Stradivarius—even in its virtually impregnable case—subjected to the sudden summer squall that rained down on the train station. "Don't you have a neighbor you could call?" she asked, trying to keep her voice even.

"Let me give it a try," Sarah groused, and went stomping off to the pay phone by the station. In what seemed like an eternity of minutes she was back, unmollified, to tell her friend, "Well, so much for the neighborliness of suburbia. I couldn't rouse a single person. But I called a mechanic about twenty miles from here, and after I promised him fealty forever after, he agreed to come over and give us a hand. It could be an hour or so before he gets here, though."

Clarissa groaned inwardly, and tried with little success to shield herself from the rain that was blowing furiously in from the side of the Jeep.

The sound of a man's voice made the women turn to see Sean Howard leaning across the front seat of a dark green Mercedes to call to them out the window. "Anything wrong? Or are you just basking in the sunshower?"

Sarah laughed giddily. "Why, hello, Sean. Yes. Yes, something's wrong." She gestured at the empty parking lot. "We're stranded here and the goddamn Jeep has just dropped dead."

Laughing, Sean got out of his car and walked over to them, looking leaner than ever in his doublebreasted blue suit. Typically, he had a tidy little umbrella that he kept in the car for such emergencies. His blond hair ruffled in the wind. He tried not to smile at Sarah's recitation of her woes, nodded seriously as though her plight were the worst ever experienced by a human being, and held out a sympathetic hand when she had finished. "Why don't I give you a lift?"

Clarissa, with her back to them, wrapping her jacket around the violin case, took note of the fact that her heart was beating abnormally fast.

"But the goddamn Jeep," Sarah said. "I don't like to leave it here, and besides, I have a mechanic coming."

Sarah thought for a moment, then threw up

her hands in a gesture of discovery. "But I'll tell you what! It would be more of a help than I can say if you'd take my friend back to the house. She's carrying the kind of merchandise that would simply adore the dry comfort of your Mercedes."

Sean looked at them both in bewilderment, but asked no questions. He'd have given Clarissa a lift if she had been carrying a fortune in contraband drugs. "I don't like to abandon you here, Sarah, but I'll do anything you say that would lighten your load."

Clarissa felt like a schoolgirl. She couldn't admit even to herself how much she suddenly welcomed the prospect of being alone with the magnetic Sean Howard. Too, and this was even more serious, she was desperate to get her violin to safety. A part of her knew that she was worrying unnecessarily, but it was not the part that held sway at the moment.

"What do you think?" she said to Sarah awkwardly. "How long do you think this mechanic will be?"

"Sweetie, he'll get here when he gets here. I'm not going to melt. Now say thank you to the nice man, and let him get you out of here. By the way," she added breathlessly, "I guess this is the kind of occasion that calls for introductions."

"We've met," Sean and Clarissa said together.

Bread and butter, Clarissa thought, remembering a ritual from childhood of saying that phrase to exorcise whatever spirits were responsible for two people's saying the same thing at the same time.

"Bread and butter," Sean said out loud.

Clarissa smiled, then dropped her eyes.

Sarah put her hands on her hips. "You've *met?* Why, I had no idea. But then, I've always been the last to know everything."

Clarissa felt Sarah's eyes on her, but didn't look at her. That she and Sean had met was doubly surprising to Sarah, given that only the night before Clarissa and Sarah and Abraham had had a long talk about him, and about Susannah. Clarissa had heard the whole sad story of the separation, the accident, the tragic aftermath. . . . She had said nothing about his coming to the guest house to return her scarf.

"Miss Tyler?" Sean said. He was standing by the Mercedes, holding the passenger door open, umbrella aloft.

Clarissa touched Sarah's arm. "Will you be all right?"

Sarah waved her hand nonchalantly. "Of course. There's still plenty of light. If the worst comes to the worst, I can swim home. I'm mostly concerned about you—and your cargo. But . . . well, speaking of knights in shining armor . . ."

Clarissa took note of the fact that she was blushing. Feeling simultaneously guilty, elated, and relieved, she rushed to Sean's car, cradling the violin against her chest.

Sean got in the car, started the engine and drove out of the parking lot. With a wave to the hapless Sarah, Sean accelerated and turned onto the road leading toward their estates.

"What is it exactly that you have there? Is it an instrument?"

"It's a violin," Clarissa said. "A very old one."

Maybe it was the unnerving exhilaration of having won the instrument in the first place, or her near-panic at being stuck in the rain with it, or the shock and surprise of being with him so unexpectedly. Whatever, Clarissa found herself opening to this man in precisely the way she had resisted so strenuously before. Prattling happily, she told him something about David Stein and his curious competition for the violin. Something, but not everything. She didn't tell him that David Stein had said he would not cash the check until she gave a performance he was invited to. She didn't tell him that because she knew that he would say he hoped that he would one day be invited to a performance. And she didn't tell him that James Morgan had been smitten by more than her music. Not that it was the sort of thing she would have told a stranger in any case, but she was aware that she was not telling him, though she didn't know why she wasn't.

"You must play very well," Sean said, and thought—*How could she not play well? How could she not do well anything she put her hand to?*

Clarissa told him a little about her days at Juilliard and that she had eventually stopped playing for a time—she didn't say why—and that she hoped to begin again, under Sarah's tutelage.

"I hope that one day I can hear you play," Sean said.

You see? Clarissa thought.

The rain stopped as suddenly as it had begun, and all at once the world was bathed in golden evening light. Nearing an intersection Sean slowed suddenly. "Have you seen the Dells?"

"The Dells? Are they neighbors?"

Sean smiled and turned off onto the other road. "No. They aren't people. They're . . . a place. I'll show you. It's not far. It won't take long. You might like to ride Maggie there one day. It's a beautiful place to ride."

The Dells was the local name for a huge meadow filled with flowers and wild grasses, not very far from the road but hidden from the eyes of those driving past by a dense growth of trees. The meadow was reached by means of a narrow path that led through the trees from the roadside. It was a magical place, particularly enchanting in the light of the sudden clearing.

Sean stood back and watched Clarissa drink it in. The material of her dress was thin, silky, and as she stood between him and the setting sun he could see her long legs distinctly silhouetted. He felt that he should move to another vantage point, for it was a violation of her privacy, yet he wanted to look at her, to admire her fine figure.

Clarissa turned and saw his eyes on her and blushed again, but did not drop her eyes. "It's beautiful. You say you can ride up here?"

"I could show you—tomorrow, perhaps, or Sunday. If you'd like."

"We'll have to see," Clarissa said. She had not been noticing the scenery all that much. She had been remembering the conversation she and Sarah and Abraham had had the night before about Sean and Susannah Howard. Sarah had repeated her contention that Sean

90

had done the noble thing in caring for Susannah after the accident. Abraham had countered that the noble thing would have been to recognize that the marriage wasn't working, that his wife had needs he could not fulfill, and vice versa. Reconciling with his wife had not been noble, but feeble.

"What do you think, Tyler?" Sarah had said.

Clarissa had said that she didn't have an opinion, that she didn't know enough to which to base one. But she had said this: "The danger in caring for someone is that you're a constant reminder of their need."

"Exactly," Abraham had said. "That's why I say he's a chump."

Not a chump, Clarissa thought now, looking into Sean's eyes and seeing the sadness and the pain. Just a man who's trying to do right in a situation where there is no right or wrong, where the best is none too good. "We should be going," Clarissa said, pointing at the setting sun. "I want to be there to wait for Sarah."

Sean started along the path, then turned to face Clarissa. "I feel a little awkward . . ."

"Oh?"

He looked at a point somewhere above her head and tried to think of how to put it. "It turns out that we have a mutual friend. Ken Forrest."

Clarissa nodded. "He was a friend of my husband's, really, but I know Ken, yes."

"We went to college together," Sean said. "We've kept in touch over the years. He was passing through town and we had breakfast this morning, in fact. Your husband's . . . death came up. He and Ken were in the same outfit in Vietnam and, well, I made the connection. I just . . . I just didn't think it was right to pretend I didn't know. I thought it was fairer to tell you that I did."

"I appreciate that," Clarissa said.

"I'm sorry about your husband's death," Sean said.

"It was a suicide, you know," Clarissa said. "I've done a lot of thinking about it, and I've decided that the survivors of suicide victims should not be felt sorry for. A suicide is a liberation, after all, isn't it? It's an escape. I don't think the survivors should be denied the right to have escaped, as well—to have been liberated— Does that sound cold and unfeeling?"

"I can understand that you'd want to get on with your life," Sean said.

"Exactly. Therefore, don't feel sorry for me. Feel—as much as you can, given that you hardly know me—glad." Clarissa took the top button of her dress between thumb and forefinger and rubbed it, like a worry bead. "I guess it's only fair that I tell you that I know something about you and your wife."

Sean smiled. "There are no secrets around here."

"It wasn't gossip. Please don't think that."

Sean nodded. "I appreciate your telling me, too." He looked into her eyes with gratitude, but then the look slowly changed to one of perplexity, for he wondered once again about this feeling of nostalgia that this woman induced and he wondered how such a thing could be.

Clarissa saw the look in his eyes and thought

she understood it, but she didn't say anything—although it would have been so easy to say, *Yes, we've met before—before the guest house, before the taxi, long before. Not met, exactly, but . . . crossed paths. Remember . . . ?* She didn't say anything because to do so would be to invite him into her fantasy world, with all its comfortable and comforting furnishings and accoutrements, so unlike reality with all its odd shapes and sizes. For the moment, perhaps forever, the fantasy had to be protected against reality.

Later in the car, driving back to the main road, Sean struggled to think of something to say other than what he wanted to say, which was *When can I see you again? Can we go riding, or for a walk, or a drive, or, or . . . ?* At last, he said, "Do you go into the city often?"

"Twice this week, but I hope not again for a while," Clarissa said.

"I ask only because should you ever need a place to stay overnight, I have an apartment that's yours to use for the asking. I only stay there once every few months or so. Otherwise, it's empty. You need only call me"—he reached into his pocket and handed her a business card —"and I'll tell the doorman to let you in."

Clarissa thanked him and said she would keep the offer in mind and put the card in her bag. They drove the rest of the way in silence.

Chapter Seven

Two weeks later, Clarissa went to Washington for an appearance before the judge hearing the case of the custody of Diana Leeds. Summer had come prematurely but fully fledged to the capital, and the streets were sticky and the air suffocating. Clarissa's lawyer, Lester Roth, told her she needn't have come, for all that happened was that Rachel Owen's lawyer appeared to ask for an extension in filing certain documents on behalf of his client. But Clarissa wanted to be there, for she hoped that the judge would be impressed that, unlike Rachel, she was not leaving everything in the hands of her counselor, that she was making a personal commitment.

After the court session, Clarissa and Lester Roth had lunch at the Washington Hilton. He reminded her, as he had reminded her numerous times, that it was important that she live an exemplary life for the duration of the custody case. "Any hint of scandal, and yours is a lost cause. And it doesn't even have to be truly scandalous—just something mildly unorthodox."

"You mean like swimming nude in the Reflecting Pool?" Clarissa said.

"I mean like going out on a date with the wrong kind of guy," Roth said between forkfuls of shrimp cocktail.

"I've explained to you, Lester," Clarissa said, "that I lead the life of a nun. I exercise, practice, read—a hot night is watching TV with the Newmans and going to bed at ten. The only men I see are Abraham and maybe some of the handymen he has working on the house, or the gardener."

"That's exactly what I'm talking about," Roth leaped in as if he were attacking some weak testimony. "Don't go having an affair with the gardener. The newspapers'll make it sound like Lady Chatterley and then some."

"The gardener's seventy-five if he's a day," Clarissa said with a smile.

"That'd make it even worse," Roth said.

Clarissa put a hand over his. "Lester, I assure you I'm not available."

Congress was still in session and Clarissa went to McLean, Virginia, to spend some time with her parents. She went riding with her father and played tennis with her mother on the court behind the comfortable colonial farmhouse. Her mother had developed a devastating two-handed backhand and won in straight sets with the loss of only two games.

"You've obviously been playing the violin too much," Abigail Tyler said. "You're dreadfully out of shape."

"That's not so. I go riding every day—sometimes twice a day. If I played tennis six hours a day, the way you do, we'd see who was out of shape."

"Riding," Abigail Tyler said. "Yes, well—riding is good for one thing, I suppose."

"Don't get Freudian with me, Mother. I ride for the exercise, not because my libido's out of whack."

"Isn't it?"

"Mother, for God's sake."

Abigail Tyler held her glass of iced tea to her forehead, cooling it. "I've known of women your age who've lost their husbands and just ... dried up."

"I didn't lose my husband," Clarissa said. "He killed himself. And I'm not drying up. This is a time for me to grow, Mother. When the time comes, I'll be ready for a kind of relationship I couldn't have had with Peter in a million years."

"I just worry that you're by yourself so much," Abigail Tyler said, "isolated up there in Connecticut."

Clarissa laughed, for part of her mother was still fighting the Civil War, and that part thought of Connecticut as enemy territory.

"Do think about coming back here in the fall," her mother went on. "The fall social season in Washington is really quite wonderful."

"You seem to forget I met Peter during the fall social season in Washington."

"Peter was a rotten apple, Clarissa. Don't chop down the whole tree."

And out riding with her father, Clarissa got some more advice.

"I know Mother didn't tell you," Dwight Tyler said. "She knew I wanted to tell you myself. There's to be a formal announcement at a press conference on Thursday. Clayton wants me to be his running mate."

"Oh, Daddy. Vice-president? Congratulations."

"I'll be sorry to leave the Senate," Dwight Tyler said. "I've been there a long time. I've felt it was the place I could do the best job. But this country's in a bad way. Everywhere you hear people saying it has no great leaders any longer. I'm one of those heard saying it, in fact. But, recently, I heard myself saying it and I said to myself, 'Dwight, old sport, *you'd* make a great leader.'"

"You will, Daddy," Clarissa said. "No conditional tenses about it. You *will*."

They rode in silence for a while. Then her father said, "It puts an additional burden on all of us, Clarissa, to live exemplary lives."

"I just heard this speech from my lawyer, Daddy," Clarissa said. "I don't intend to be the merry widow."

"You must understand my position, Clarissa. I don't hold you at all responsible, but the simple fact is that Peter's transgressions were very damaging to me. Being asked to run for vice-president is a gesture of the party's confidence in me, but it's a gesture that can be withdrawn as easily as it was made."

Clarissa reined in her horse, and when her

father had turned and come back to her, she spoke evenly: "You must understand *my* position. My goal in life, at the moment, is to get custody of Diana. A secondary goal is to begin playing music again. Both honorable goals. Neither will be an embarrassment to you. I will not discuss it further." And she turned her horse and rode off alone, too fast for her father to follow over such difficult terrain.

Clarissa flew back to New York the next evening. Instead of taking the Connecticut limousine, she got a taxi to Manhattan, for she wanted to go to Schirmer's and pick up a piece of sheet music—Bach's Chaconne for solo violin. A sales man at Schirmer's told her on the phone that they had the piece and would hold it for her. She would take a train from Grand Central to Connecticut. She wondered if Sean Howard would be on it. She had not seen him since the afternoon he had driven her home from the station. Though he had said he might call to invite her to go riding, he had not, and a few days later Abraham had pointed out to Clarissa a newspaper article saying that a building Sean was erecting near Times Square was the subject of an investigation by the New York County District Attorney into corruption in the construction industry. Obviously, he had things on his mind other than riding.

New York was, if anything, hotter than Washington. As the taxi crossed the Queensborough Bridge, Clarisa thrilled at the sight of the twilight skyline, the lights in the windows of offices just going on and making the buildings look as though they were set with jewels. A moment later, all the lights went out, as if a giant hand had thrown a giant switch.

"Not again," the taxi driver said.

"What is it?" Clarissa said.

The taxi driver looked at her in the rearview mirror. He could think of no one he would rather be stuck in traffic with on the Queensborough Bridge. "Looks like another blackout. That's just the way it happened in sixty-five and in . . . what was it—seventy-six? Seventy-seven? I forget."

Clarissa had only read about New York City's two famous electrical power failures. In 1965, she had been just twelve years old—Diana's age —living in Louisville and Washington, innocent and carefree. In 1977—she knew that the second blackout had been in 1977—she had been twenty-four, traveling in Europe with Sarah after their graduation from Juilliard, a little less innocent, but still carefree. "Do you think we can get off the bridge?"

"Doubt it, ma'am, if it's like the other blackouts. The traffic lights're out, too. Everything's out. Subways, elevators, phones. Your best bet's to go back to the airport, get on a plane back to wherever you came from. Get on a plane going anywhere. Anywhere but this dump. The Big Apple. Hah."

Clarissa thought about going back to the airport for a moment, if only to get the Connecticut limousine, which went by way of the Whitestone Bridge. However long it would take, it would surely take less time than trying to make her way through Manhattan. But there was something intriguing about the city's having suddenly gone black. She remembered the newspaper accounts she had read of the other blackouts—tales of heroism and generosity, of people trapped in elevators and falling in love, of New Yorkers dropping their traditional reserve and banding together to help one another through a time of adversity. And she remembered the phenomenon that had been noted nine months after the 1965 blackout—a sharp increase in the number of babies born—an increase finally attributed to the fact that on that November night many couples—either because it solaced them during the hours of uncertainty or because they had nothing better to do, there being no television, no movies, no theater, no clubs or bars or restaurants—had made love.

Romance. Intrigue. Manhattan seemed to be offering Clarissa something. She took a bill from her bag and put it in the slot in the taxi's protective window and opened the door and got out. "I think I'll walk. I'm sorry to leave you stranded here, but . . . I gave you a fifty. That should cover the trip and the time you'll have to wait here."

"Hey, lady," the driver said, "you can't walk on the . . ." But she was gone, walking between the rows of cars, carrying her small suitcase in one hand, her pocketbook in the other, swinging them rhythmically for balance, her long legs flashing. Heads emerged from windows of cars all along the way as she passed as men tried to get a longer look at this unexpected apparition, this moment of beauty in what was shaping up to be a grim evening.

At Second Avenue, traffic was at a standstill in every direction, for the driver had been right —there were no traffic lights working. Clarissa gave up the small hope she had had of getting another taxi or a bus and set out to walk over to Fifth Avenue and down to Schirmer's. As she walked, she bucked a tide that had already begun to form and was moving in the opposite direction—veterans of previous blackouts who knew that one way out of Manhattan to the east was over the bridge she had just walked off. There was resignation in the faces of some of those she passed, bitterness in the faces of others, in the faces of some fear and uncertainty. There was also in the faces of some a look of excitement, of taking part in a great adventure. With so many people on the sidewalks, overflowing into the streets, there was in the air an atmosphere of carnival.

Many shops and stores along Clarissa's route had closed or were closing. Others stayed open, lighted by candles or flashlights. Schirmer's was about to close when Clarissa arrived, but the salesman at the door took one look at her beautiful face and heard her plight in her soft, charming accent, and led her inside the store and guided her by the light of his flashlight to the back of the store and found for her the Bach Chaconne that had been put aside for her. He would have tried to find Bach himself, if she had asked.

Having accomplished her mission, Clarissa

decided that there was no point in trying to make it to Connecticut that night. She would go to the Sherry Netherland and get a room and make the trip in the morning, when things certainly would have been sorted out. But it took nearly half an hour to walk to the hotel, and the hotel was booked solid.

"I'm terribly sorry, Miss Tyler," the desk clerk said, flipping needlessly through the registry by the light of a candle. "If only I'd known . . ."

"There was no way you could have. I'll try the Pierre and the Plaza."

With a long face, the clerk said that it would be no use, that he knew that the other nearby hotels were booked as well. If she wanted to wait in the lobby or the bar, however, he was going to begin calling other hotels as soon as phone service was restored. He had a list of other Sherry Netherland regular patrons who were seeking accommodations and could put hers on it, although there were quite a few people ahead of her.

"Do that," Clarissa said. "I'll leave my bag with the captain. I don't think I'll just sit here, though. I want to see what's going on outside. I'll come back in an hour or so. If you get to my name before I get back, just make a reservation and say I'll be there shortly. Anyplace will do."

Clarissa crossed Fifth Avenue and made her way to the fountain across from the Plaza Hotel. It was a good vantage point for watching the stream of pedestrians going past. The sky was nearly dark now, and the buildings all around were black silhouettes against the sky.

Suddenly, magically, the lights in the General Motors Building across Fifth Avenue came on. People cringed from the light at first, fearing some new catastrophe. Then, realizing what had happened, they let out a cheer. The blackout was over.

But in a few moments, it was clear that it was not over, for no other buildings lighted up. Clarissa heard people saying that the building must have an emergency generator. Then she remembered that Sean Howard had his office in the General Motors Building. She crossed her legs and wondered if she should go up and see if he were there.

Almost against her will, all of her initial reluctance to have anything to do with him was melting into thin air. Though she tried to deny it to herself, the enchantment of their few meetings lingered in her mind, and it struck her that there was an element almost of destiny in their sharing the adventure of the blackout together. Besides, hadn't he told her he had a place in town she could use whenever she liked?

You're a little fool, she chided herself as she determined to force herself to wait a little while longer to see if the lights would go back on. But a half hour went by and nothing happened. When she checked back in with the desk clerk at the Sherry Netherland, he told her in tones wringing with regret that since the phones were still out he'd been unable to do anything for her yet. Squaring her shoulders and telling herself she had no choice, she strode to the General Motors Building, found Sean Howard Enterprises on the directory and took the elevator to the forty-fifth floor.

The glass doors to the office were open, and a cleaning woman ran a vacuum cleaner around the reception area, but there was no one at the receptionist's desk and a feeling that there was no one around anywhere.

"Excuse me," Clarissa called over the noise of the vacuum cleaner. "Excuse me."

The cleaning woman turned and saw Clarissa and switched off the machine.

"Is Mr. Howard still here?" Clarissa said. "Do you know if Mr. Howard's still here?"

The cleaning woman shrugged in a way that said she didn't speak English.

"I'll look around myself," Clarissa said, and she opened a door off the reception area and looked inside. It was a supply closet, filled with stationery and jugs of bottled water for the water cooler. In the corner were a squash racquet and a tennis racquet. "Oops," Clarissa said and shut the door.

"Hello," Sean Howard said. He was standing in the doorway of another office on the other side of the reception area, leaning against the post, his hands in the pockets of a pair of beige pleated slacks. He wore a white shirt and a blue and red tie. He had a pencil parked above his ear.

"I'm not snooping," Clarissa said. "I just guessed wrong."

"You guessed right that I'd be here," Sean said. "I'm glad of that."

"There's been a blackout," Clarissa said, then

laughed. "You know that, of course. I'm . . . I'm in town and . . . and I thought—" All of a sudden she felt like a schoolgirl. How ridiculous!

"You'd like to use my apartment. I'm delighted."

Clarissa poked at the thick carpet with the toe of her Gucci shoe. "You don't seem surprised to see me."

"I've been waiting for you," Sean said.

"Waiting?"

Sean stood away from the door and held out a hand that invited her to come into his office. She hesitated, then went through the door, not looking at him as she passed.

To the cleaning woman, Sean said, *"Nada mas. Gracias,"* and the cleaning woman unplugged the vacuum cleaner and wrapped up the cord.

The office was bright and spare. There were colorful Mexican scatter rugs on the floor, an architect's drawing board against one wall, a wooden rolltop desk against the other, a comfortable couch in the center of the room facing the big windows that looked out over Fifth Avenue. On the walls were some framed architect's drawings of buildings and some prints. There was a large framed photograph of some rugby players leaping for a ball, their hands high over their heads, their fingers straining to make contact. Clarissa recognized one of the players as Sean Howard, perhaps fifteen years younger.

Sean stood by the window and motioned for Clarissa to join him. Way below, she could see the fountain where she had been sitting for so long. "I've been waiting for you," Sean said again. "I saw you sitting down there."

"You saw me? But it's so far . . . and it's . . . it's dark."

Sean smiled. "It wasn't quite so dark when you first sat at the fountain. And, at any rate, you stand out in a crowd." He hurried on before she had time to react. "I wasn't sure that you'd remember my offer to use my apartment whenever you needed. I tried telepathy. I flatter myself that it worked."

"My name's on a list at the Sherry Netherland," Clarissa said. "The clerk's going to call other hotels when the phones come back on. Perhaps there'll be a room for me somewhere. Perhaps there's one already."

Sean touched her arm lightly just above the elbow. "I'm afraid I insist. It's a very big apartment. It has three bedrooms. There's no way you're going to get a room in a decent hotel tonight. Do you fancy spending the night in some shelter at Grand Central?"

Clarissa laughed. "I flew in from Washington this afternoon. I was on the Queensborough Bridge when the blackout happened. I could've turned around and gone back to the airport, gotten a limousine to Connecticut. But I came ahead. I thought it would be an adventure."

"And it is," Sean said. "The next exciting installment will be to try to find a place to have dinner. I'm sure some place'll be open. Are you game?"

Clarissa let herself look in his eyes for the first time since she had entered his office. They were warm and kind. The pain that she had seen

107

in them seemed somehow assuaged. In its place was a brightness—almost a playfulness—the same look that was in the eyes of the young rugby player in the photograph. "I'm not only game," she said, "I'm starved."

Chapter Eight

Sean had hired a limousine for the night, for he had been planning to stay in town anyway, for a dinner meeting with his lawyer, Daniel Freedman. Just after the blackout happened, Freedman had managed to get through on a phone that was still working and had said he would have to cancel, for he lived in Brooklyn Heights and was going to have a long trip home. As Sean and Clarissa left the General Motors Building, he found the driver, Eddie, waiting at the curb.

"I thought we'd try the Sign of the Dove," Sean said to Clarissa. "We can ride if you like, but the traffic's still a mess and it'll be quicker to walk. And it's a nice night, otherwise."

"I'd love to walk," Clarissa said.

Sean told the driver to go to the Sherry Netherland and get Clarissa's bag and when traffic thinned out to take it to his apartment at River House, then pick them up later at the restaurant.

They walked up Fifth Avenue to Sixty-fifth

Street, then turned east toward Third Avenue. Streams of pedestrians headed north on Fifth, Madison, Park and Lexington, but there were only a few other walkers sharing their route.

"How did it happen, anyway?" Clarissa said. "The blackout, I mean?"

"If it's like the others, some kind of overload on the system. It was a hot day and a lot of people had air conditioning on for the first time since last summer. I guess the system wasn't ready for the drain. Are you a veteran of the other blackouts?"

Clarissa told him that she had been a schoolgirl in Louisville during the first blackout and that during the second she had been traveling in Europe. "And you?"

"In sixty-five I was in San Diego. In seventyseven I was in Europe, too, on business. In Paris."

"I was in Vienna," Clarissa said.

"Almost a coincidence," Sean said.

Almost was close enough, thought Clarissa. And given the other great coincidence in their lives, it seemed they weren't coincidences at all, but were intended. Once again, she did not feel that she could tell Sean about that other coincidence. Once again, she felt that she had to protect fantasy from reality. "So we're both blackout virgins. Were you in San Diego on business, too? You would've been a very young businessman in 1965. A baby tycoon."

Sean laughed. This was more like it—to be talking about unimportant moments in their lives as strangers do when getting to know each other instead of talking about the tragedies that become part of the public record and thereby serve as obstacles to getting to know each other. Of course, San Diego had not been such an un-important moment. "I was in a V.A. hospital there. I'd been wounded in Vietnam."

"You were there, too?" Clarissa said. "Another coincidence."

Sean heard in her tone of voice a warning that she didn't want to talk about her husband.

They walked in silence for a while, their pace checked by the seriousness of all the subjects they were skirting. Finally, Sean said, "You don't have to worry that I'm going to lead you down any memory lanes you don't want to travel. I promise."

She smiled at him gratefully, and didn't have to say a word.

At Lexington Avenue, a young man stood in the middle of the street, directing traffic. He was dressed in a black formal suit with tails, a top hat and big clown shoes. His face was paint-ed white and he was performing his voluntary chores in pantomime. Signaling to a bus to move south along the avenue, he pretended to hitch a rope to its front bumper and to pull it with a mighty effort until it got rolling. After some traffic had passed, he stopped it so pedes-trians could cross by putting up both hands and leaning alarmingly far forward, as if pressing on the cars with a great invisible barrier. As Sean and Clarissa began to cross, he convert-ed himself into a headwaiter, draping an imaginary napkin across his arm, holding up two imperious fingers and directing them to an imaginary table, one of whose imaginary chairs he pulled out and held for Clarissa.

Clarissa nodded a thank-you and pretended to sit on the imaginary chair, leaning an elbow prettily on the imaginary table.

Some passersby laughed and applauded her performance. Sean laughed and applauded, too, and when Clarissa got up from her imaginary chair, folded her imaginary napkin and placed it on the imaginary table, he took her arm above the elbow and held it with a strong tenderness that told her what she already knew, from the laughter and the applause and the joy in his eyes—that he had fallen in love.

The restaurant was crowded, for it seemed that on such a night lots of people were in the mood for festivity. Sean was a regular customer, however, and the maître d' gave them a table almost immediately. Clarissa excused herself to go to the ladies' room and on the way back ran smack into James Morgan, her adversary for the violin. He was with a redhead who had her hands around his neck and was nibbling on his ear.

"Well, hello there, Miss Tyler," James Morgan said.

The redhead let go and looked Clarissa up and down, then glanced at James Morgan sharply. She hadn't missed the warmth in his voice.

"Penny, this is . . . it's Clarissa, isn't it? This is Clarissa Tyler. Miss Tyler, this is my friend, Penelope Hammill."

Penelope Hammill offered Clarissa her hand, then took it back almost immediately, and

112

turned to latch onto the arm of a tall, dark man who was passing by. "Warren! Where have you been hiding?"

"Nice to see you," Clarissa said, and began to move away.

James Morgan moved with her. "I've been trying to get in touch with you."

"Oh?"

"I wondered if you'd like to have dinner some night. I called David Stein, but he insisted he doesn't know your number."

"He doesn't. And I'm afraid I can't have dinner. I don't get into town much."

"I have a car. I'll come to where you live. Wherever it is."

"Really, I can't. Thank you, but no thank you."

He leaned close to her. "I think we could, uh, make some nice music together."

Clarissa craned her neck like an angry cat. "Your friend is listening."

James Morgan laughed. "Penny? That's all she is—a friend. Penny's with the *Post*. You've probably read her column. Look, who're you here with? Penny'd like to know. She'll put an item in the paper. A photographer'll be here in a while. He'll take your picture. You'll be famous."

"Good-bye," Clarissa said, appalled at his suggestion, so glibly tendered. She turned quickly and went to the table where Sean stood waiting, having watched the exchange from a distance.

"Anything wrong?" Sean said, holding a chair for her to sit.

"No," she said, but as she glanced back toward the bar she saw James Morgan and Penelope Hammill with their heads close together and saw Penelope Hammill form the words *Clarissa Leeds*. "Can we go somewhere else? Anywhere else?"

"Of course. But tell me why."

"I'll tell you when we get outside," Clarissa said.

But getting outside was no easy matter, for the crowd had grown. Worse yet, the photographers had arrived, and Penelope Hammill was prodding him into position to take a picture of Clarissa Leeds and her escort. The strobe exploded in Clarissa's face and the light tore at her eyelids.

"Sean?"

Sean turned at the sound of a woman's voice and saw the redheaded woman waving at him.

"Sean Howard, right?"

He turned away without answering and hurried after Clarissa, who was already out the door and walking up Third Avenue. He ran and caught up to her and took her arm. "Don't worry."

"I'm not worried. I'm infuriated."

"Has it happened often?"

"For a time, it happened every day. I thought it was over, but their appetite is unquenchable. Damn them. Damn them all."

They walked in silence for a while, heading north on Third Avenue, going nowhere, getting caught up in the stream of people still making their way home through the blacked-out streets.

At Seventy-first Street, Sean took Clarissa's

arm gently and checked her stride and faced her. "I don't like the way I feel. I feel trapped—or rather, I feel as though I just escaped from a trap. But I was there of my own volition. I'm with you of my own volition. I wasn't caught doing something illegal, immoral, clandestine. I was simply trying to have dinner with a friend. The immoral thing is to think that something else was going on. I'll leave that to the lady journalist. For myself, I only want to feel what I was feeling just a little while ago—happy to be with you, happy to be getting to know you, happy to have some time to do it in. I don't want to feel like a victim."

Clarissa looked into his intelligent eyes for a long time, then nodded, once, sharply. "You're right. I was feeling like a victim. That's the way I've felt when it's happened before, even though I knew everything you just said. I guess . . ."

"You guess what?"

"I guess . . . I guess maybe I felt it was just a little bit immoral to be having a good time."

Sean smiled and gestured at those slogging homeward. "You mean, when everyone else is being . . . inconvenienced?"

Clarissa smiled. "That and . . . well, men haven't been my favorite gender for quite a while now. Do you want to go back to the restaurant?"

"It would show them a thing or two," Sean said.

"Then let's show them," Clarissa said, and put her arm through his and turned him around and started to cross the street. "Let's show them three or four things. The bastards."

When they got back to the Sign of the Dove, the crowd had thinned somewhat, and there wasn't a vulture in sight. Without so much as a raised eyebrow, the maitre d' reseated them, and they were soon launched on a happy stream of good wine, good food and good talk. It was one of those rare moments in the beginning of a relationship where the sheer joy two people are beginning to take in one another covers the whole world with a magic glow.

During a lull in the conversation, her last drop of reserve melted away, Clarissa looked him squarely in the eye and said, "You were magnificent, you know." Reality was a threat to fantasy no longer.

He stared back and, after only a split second, said simply, "Of course. Acapulco. I can't believe it's taken me this long to figure it out."

They reached across the table for each other's hands, and held each other in a long look that Penny Hammill would have kicked herself for missing, had she only known.

Chapter Nine

"Peter had an affair with a woman who produces current events programs for the public television station in Washington. He was one of her favorite guests—and I guess you'd have to say that she was one of his. It turned out that it wasn't the first affair he'd had, but it was the first I found out about. I was angry. I was hurt. I wanted to be by myself. So I went to Acapulco, to stay at a friend's.

"It was lovely there. Just me and the maid. The house had a private beach and a pool and I never had to leave. I didn't want to leave. All I wanted was to be by myself.

"But one afternoon I got restless. Nothing irresistible. I didn't want to go disco dancing or riding on one of those parachute water-ski things they have or diving off the cliffs. Nothing strenuous. I just wanted to get out of the house for a while. I put on something of a disguise— just put my hair up under a tennis hat and wore my less than best clothes and a pair of dark glasses and that pretty much took care of it. I actually ran into an old friend of Daddy's who didn't give me a nod, so I guess the disguise worked.

"I drove downtown, went to a few shops, then went to the hotel to have something to eat. Shrimp cocktail. I seem to remember that I ordered shrimp cocktail. I didn't have any appetite for it when it came. Seeing all those kids in the restaurant depressed me. They reminded me of Diana. Diana's Peter's daughter by his first marriage. Diana's wonderful. I'll tell you all about Diana some other time. . . .

"Anyway, there I was—picking at my shrimp cocktail, drinking my margarita, when all of a sudden people started yelling fire. *Fuego!* And sure enough, there was a fire. And there you were, breaking the window with a chair. I had a crazy memory association: There's a movie of *Madame Bovary*—it's wonderful. They're at a ball, her first big society do, and they're dancing, dancing a mad waltz that takes them round and round the room—a big room with windows all along one wall. They go faster and faster. Suddenly, she feels faint, and sort of slumps in his arms. He turns to the footmen standing all around the room and says, 'Madame is fainting. Break the windows.' All around the room you hear the command repeated. 'Break the windows.' 'Break the windows.' And all the footmen pick up chairs and . . . break the windows. Crash, crash, crash—all down the length of the room, with the camera following along. Crash, crash, crash. When I was a child I thought that was the most wonderfully, extravagantly ro-

mantic thing a man could do for a woman—
break all his windows because she needed some
air. I still do, I guess. . . . Anyway, there you
were, breaking the windows. And, well, you
know the rest. . . . Somehow when we found
each other again, it didn't seem right at first to
bring the whole thing up again, to break the
magic. But now . . ."

"But now," Sean said, "here we both are."

"Yes," she breathed. "And the magic's
intact."

It was four o'clock in the morning and they
were sitting on the carpet in the living room of
Sean's River House apartment, their backs
against the silk-covered banquettes, sipping
brandy from huge snifters. The lights had come
back on at two o'clock. They had noticed a
brightening of the sky and had gone to the
window to see the lights coming on in Queens,
on the other side of the river, and in Brooklyn,
to the south, and on Roosevelt Island, in the
middle of the river, and then on the FDR Drive,
right below them.

Then it had been Sean's turn to tell her a little
of how he had happened to be in Acapulco. He
had been in Mexico City on business, and had
wound up his affairs sooner than expected, and
decided to spend a few days by himself—
Susannah was visiting her mother in Florida.
He had stayed at Las Brisas and had spent most
of his time beside his suite's private swimming
pool. Restless, he'd decided that afternoon to
take a drive, and for want of anything better to
do, had just wound up at the Acapulco Regent,

in whose famous rooftop restaurant with its
famous view he had sat down to have a drink
and a pipe while he looked through the latest
issue of *Fortune*. Of course, she knew the rest.

Clarissa swung her snifter in a slow circle,
watching the brandy slide to and fro up and
down the sides of the crystal. "Since you left
right away, you probably didn't see the newspapers. They called us Superman and Wonder
Woman. The hotel manager, I think it was, told
reporters that's who we'd reminded him of."

Sean smiled ruefully. "What sobriquets! Can
you stand it?"

"Don't you like Superman?" Clarissa asked.
"You'd rather have been called . . . the Lone
Ranger?"

Sean laughed.

What a wonderful laugh, Clarissa thought.
And what a beautiful man. Sean had changed
into a pale blue Lacoste shirt, a pair of tan
cotton slacks with a drawstring waist and big
patch pockets. On his feet were navy espadrilles. The light from the single lamp made his
blond hair shine brightly and modeled his
strong arms.

Sean felt happily full of laughter and smiles
and he realized just how little he had laughed
and smiled of late. *How wonderful to laugh*, he
thought. *And what a beautiful woman*. Clarissa
had dressed after her shower in a mauve, silk
short-sleeved blouse and silk pants. (How happy
that driver had been to lug her suitcase all over
New York!) Her feet were bare—she had beautifully high arches—and she had her hair held up
in back with a silver comb. A strand of hair fell

alongside her cheek, and he wanted to move it away from her face with his fingers and to touch her cheek.

"So, here we are," Clarissa said.

"Yes."

"Impossible. It's impossible that we're here together and that we're here together is impossible."

"Impossible as in . . . not advisable?"

"Yes," Clarissa said.

Sean shrugged. "You needed a place to stay. . . . You *need* a place to stay. Which reminds me—you should've called Sarah and Abraham when the power came back on."

"They're not expecting me. I didn't know how long I'd stay in Washington. . . . You didn't call your wife."

Sean studied her face to see if there was cattiness behind the remark, but he could discern none. "I was planning to stay in town anyway. I had a dinner meeting scheduled with my lawyer."

"I've read about your . . . your problem with the district attorney," Clarissa said. "Are things all right?"

"So-so."

Clarissa took a sip of brandy and held it in her mouth for a moment before swallowing. "You don't want to talk about it?"

"Do you?" Sean said.

Clarissa laughed. "Not especially. Not now. Eventually, I'd like to know all about it."

Softly, Sean said, "Eventually . . ."

Clarissa cocked her head. "Eventually, what?"

"Exactly," Sean said.

Clarissa shook her head in bewilderment. "You've lost me."

Sean smiled. "Eventually, what? That seems to be a good description of—" he held his hands up, searching for a word, "of our . . . relationship. It's clear we can't have a relationship—now. So—eventually, what?"

Clarissa took a deep breath and let it out slowly. "I'm glad you said that—said that we couldn't have a relationship. It's true—we can't. I'd've said it if you hadn't. But I'm glad you did . . . I didn't want to have to reject you."

"I hope you don't feel I was rejecting you by saying it," Sean said.

She shook her head. "No."

They sat in silence for a long time, looking into their brandy glasses, looking into each other's eyes, stealing glances, when the other was looking away, at the other's face and body —but not looking too long, for looking too long made each of them ache.

"I hope," they began together, and they laughed.

" . . . You hope what?" Sean asked.

"No. You go first."

"I hope . . . we aren't going to start feeling sorry for ourselves."

"That's what I was going to say."

"I'm not surprised."

Clarissa tipped her head back against the banquette and studied the ceiling for a while. It told her nothing. She tipped her head forward. "I hope we can be friends. I'd like to be able to tell people about us—about how we crossed paths in Acapulco and then met again, years later, in a taxi on a rainy afternoon in New York. It's a nice story."

"Do you think people will believe it?"

"Sure. Why not?"

"I want to make love with you," Sean said.

"Oh, I know. I want to make love with you."

"But we can't."

"I know."

More silence. More looks into glasses, into each other's eyes, more stolen glances. Sighs—together.

Sean smiled. "I think it's time you got some sleep."

"What about you?"

"I can't sleep."

"Me neither."

They laughed.

"Breakfast, then?" Sean said.

"Breakfast. I could eat breakfast, yes. I could eat three."

"Waffles?"

"Oh, God," Clarissa said. "Would you really make waffles?"

Sean made waffles and bacon and coffee and they ate breakfast at the campaign table by the window, watching the sky grow pink over Queens. They pointed together as the sun peeked above the horizon.

The phone rang.

"Reality," Clarissa said.

"It's awfully early for reality to be calling," Sean said, getting up to answer the phone.

"Reality gets the worm," Clarissa said.

It was Daniel Freedman. "See your picture in the paper?"

"We had this discussion already—remember?"

"Sure I remember. I'm a lawyer. Lawyer's never forget. I'm talking about a different picture. You and your good-looking friend."

"Oh, Christ. The *Post?*"

"Oh, damn," Clarissa said softly, for she understood the significance of the word. More than understood—she had been expecting it.

Freedman read from Penelope Hammill's column—with feeling: " 'Wasn't the blackout romantic, dear readers? You don't think so? You were stuck in a subway train under the East River? You were trapped in an elevator halfway up the World Trade—' "

"Could you skip to the bad news, Dan?" Sean said.

"I thought you'd like to hear it in context. I mean, it has a context."

"Skip the context," Sean said.

"You're the client," Freedman said.

"You're not billing me for this time, are you?"

"Depends on whether you want me to do something about it."

Sean sighed. "Read me the bad news."

" . . . 'Well, you would have thought it was plenty romantic if you had dropped in to the Sign of the Dove last night. Just about anybody who is anybody was there, including a new duo—Sean Howard, the divinely handsome real estate entrepreneur, and Clarissa Tyler Leeds, the stunningly beautiful widow of Representative Peter Leeds, whose suicide in the wake of a bribery scandal is still the talk of our nation's capital—' She also mentions that you are very much married to the invalided Susannah Howard."

"Damn her," Sean hissed.

"You want to do something about it?"

"For example?"

"Deny it."

"You said there was a photograph."

"Yeah. Nice picture . . . especially of her. You look a little peaked."

"In that case, I think I'll just brood about it for a while," Sean said.

"You want me to brood, too?"

"Not if you're going to bill me for it."

"Like I said, you're the client . . . I know this has nothing to do with Middlebrooks's thing, but, well, it's not going to help."

"I know."

"Not that it's any of my business."

"Thanks for calling, Dan. I'll talk to you later."

"Umm," Freedman said.

Sean hung up the phone, stuck his hands in his pockets, poked at the terracotta floor with an espadrille, then finally looked at Clarissa. "It wasn't reality calling. It was notoriety."

She nodded.

"I'm sorry," Sean said.

"For yourself?"

He shook his head.

"For me?"

"I suppose I'm sorry for Susannah," Sean said. "She's the real victim, more than either of us."

"And Diana," Clarissa said, and she told Sean about the custody case and about her lawyer's warning. "My father's not going to be happy about it, either. My father's going to run for vice-president. It'll be announced in a few days. You're sworn to secrecy. He asked me to . . . have a care about my social life, and then *this* has to happen."

Sean poured another cup of coffee and leaned against the sideboard as he sipped from it. "When you're ready to go up to Connecticut, let me call my limousine service and have somebody drive you up. I don't want you riding the train, sitting next to somebody reading the *Post*."

Clarissa smiled gratefully. "I accept." Then she got up with one smooth motion and came to him and took the cup from his hand and put it on the sideboard and got into his arms and kissed him on the mouth. They were rigid at first, but slowly they relaxed and melded together. They moaned softly at the sweet sensations that coursed through them, and flowed even more closely together.

Trembling, they broke apart, then breath coming in ragged gulps, only their eyes still linked.

"My God, Clarisssa, what are we going to do?" Sean said finally.

"Even if we can't be together," she said brokenly, "we will always have each other. As for all the rest, I just don't know."

You could almost see the fragments of their shattered hopes littering the room around them.

Chapter Ten

"Oh, God. How awful. How miserable. How . . . heartbreaking." Sarah punctuated her estimate by tossing a pebble into the pond, beside which she and Clarissa sat, startling a duck. "I was sure the story was going to have a happy ending. If you're going to get your picture in the paper, with intimations of scandal, you should at least have gotten something nice out of it."

"I did. I got a kiss. I've never felt so much love in a kiss."

Sarah threw another pebble, behind the duck, to see if it would turn around. It didn't. "I've never liked Susannah . . ."

"Don't," Clarissa said. "That's not fair."

"All's fair in love and war."

"It's not love and I don't want it to become war."

"You said it was a loving kiss."

"Loving," Clarissa said. "There's a difference."

And another pebble. "Susannah's on drugs.

She's an addict, practically. Stelazine. She's—"
   "Sarah!"
   Sarah shrugged. "I can't help it if people talk." She threw another pebble. This time the duck swam toward it, thinking it might be food. "I wonder where that duck's mate is. I thought ducks mated for life."
   "I thought it was pigeons," Clarissa said.
   "It certainly isn't people."
   "Sometimes it is."
   "I think Susannah's dragging Sean down."
   "Sarah. Please stop. Besides, the other day you said you thought he was noble to stay with her."
   "That was before you fell in love with him."
   "Sarah!"
   Sarah threw up her hands. "I can't help it. I'm heartbroken. How're you going to deal with the fact that you and Sean are in such close proximity? Isn't that going to make things difficult? I mean, the temptation of knowing he's just over on the other side of that hill!"
   "If it were question of temptation," Clarissa said, "then it wouldn't matter if he were just over the hill or in another country. Either way, we'd find a way to be together. But it's not a question of temptation. We understand the impossibility of it. One isn't tempted by the impossible."
   Sarah threw another pebble. "How heartbreaking," she said again.
   Clarissa got up and folded her chair. "I'm going for a ride."
   "I thought we were going to play some music."

"Just a short ride. I need to be bounced around a little."

"I think . . ." Sarah began.

"You think what?"

"Oh, nothing. It was an obscene thought."

"You're impossible. I'll meet you for music in half an hour."

Clarissa rode Maggie at a trot. She and the mare were getting to know each other well, were getting to know each other's quirks and the limits of each other's patience. Neither had given in much to the other. They had reached a détente rather than a true compromise, which meant that each respected the validity of the other's demands, even though they couldn't always accede to them.

And they rode. First at a trot, then a canter, then a gallop, jolting out of Clarissa the lethargy she had felt coming over her when telling the tale to Sarah, a lethargy born, she knew, of heartbreak.

After her ride, Clarissa played the Bach Chaconne—badly.

"Don't be discouraged," Sarah said, sitting beside her, astride a wooden chair in the kitchen, looking over her shoulder at the music. "Segovia said—he was talking about the guitar transcription, but I think it applies to the original—that it was a piece to be studied all your life, but not to be played until you were sixty."

"Then I haven't started too late, after all," Clarissa said.

"You played it wonderfully for someone who's rusty," Sarah said. "You play it wonderfully for someone who's *not* rusty, but it didn't soar. Why don't you try again?"

Clarissa tried it again, and played it better, with greater fluidity and grace.

"Play it the way you would play it for someone you were in love with," Sarah said.

Clarissa gave her a look. "I don't want to have this conversation again."

Sarah tried to pinch a smile from her face. "It's just an analogy. When I'm playing badly, I try and pretend I'm playing only for Abraham. It always works. It's like making love; you know all the moves, but it really only works when you're making them on someone you really love, someone you're trying to communicate with, instead of just trying to get a rise out of, so to speak."

Clarissa played the Chaconne again, and the music became incarnate and filled the room with its beauty. She made mistakes, to be sure. She hesitated, was uncertain, phrased incorrectly or unimaginatively, but she played with animation and intelligence, played a singing line, with nuance and sharp accents.

When she was done, Sarah said, "Wow."

"I can see what Segovia meant," Clarissa said. "I think sixty might be too young to play it. Seventy-five might be about right."

Sarah leaned over and kissed Clarissa on the cheek. "Dinner's at seven. We're having scallops. There's a good movie on the tube tonight. *Madame Bovary*. Ever seen it?"

"Yes," Clarissa said and laughed in spite of herself.

Walking back to the guest house, Clarissa felt like skipping. She was in love with Sean

Howard. She couldn't deny it to herself no matter how strenuously she denied it to Sarah. She couldn't help it. She didn't want to help it. She liked it—liked being in love with him. Look at how well it had made her play, for she played for him. Look at how happy it made her—made her want to skip.

And made her want to dig a hole in the ground and crawl into it. For she *had* to deny it to herself—even more strenuously than she denied it to Sarah. She *had* to help it. She had to want to help it. She mustn't like it—mustn't like being in love with him—no matter how well it made her play, no matter that it made her want to skip. For it couldn't be. It was impossible.

As she stepped up on the porch of the guest house, something made Clarissa turn and look across the grounds in the direction of Sean's estate. Since arriving home that morning she had not looked in that direction once. She had told herself that she would have to train herself not to look in that direction ever again. It wouldn't be a terrible hardship. There were other directions in which to look, other vistas. Turning now, she told herself that she would see nothing anyway, for trees fully screened the grounds of Sean's estate. But she was wrong, for the trees were not leaved all the way down to the ground, and through their trunks she could see a flash of metal as Sean's Mercedes went up the drive toward his house. He had come home—home to his wife.

"Well," Susannah said icily as Sean walked into the living room. "I'm glad you didn't have

133

to endure the blackout all by your lonesome self last night." A copy of the *Post* lay cast aside on a nearby table.

"Susannah, don't." Sean spoke calmly. "Clarissa Leeds is the woman who's staying at the Newmans. I'd mentioned to her at their party the other day that if she ever needed a place to stay in town, the River House apartment was available. When she got stuck in the blackout, she looked me up. That's all there is to it."

"How perfectly obvious," she said bitterly. "And do you treat every stray who wanders in out of the night to dinner at the Sign of the Dove?"

"Susannah, I'm sorry, but I'm not going to have this nasty little scene with you. We had a friendly dinner, nothing else. Do you think I'd have an assignation at one of the most public places in New York?"

"Oh, go fuck yourself," she said dispiritedly. Her eyes were dull, her face flaccid. This was not a woman he knew. He watched with fear in his heart as she reached into a pocket for a vial of pills and downed two of them without benefit of water.

"For God's sake, Susannah, don't you think you should lay off those things?" he said involuntarily, unable to check himself.

"Why the hell should I?" she snapped, her voice suddenly rising. "Do you think it's the tranquilizers that are paralyzing my legs? Do you think if I stopped taking them I could waltz into the Sign of the Dove with you and get *my* picture in the paper?"

Sean broke. "My God, your self-pity disgusts me," he breathed in a low voice. "Do you think you're the only person in the world whose life isn't perfect?"

A look—stricken, astonished, wounded—flashed across her face, and he was instantly appalled at himself for having lashed out at her. He went to her immediately, awkwardly embracing her. "We mustn't let this happen to us, Susannah," he said urgently. "Not ever."

Through her tears, she said, "What a mess I'm making of things." Gently, she pushed him away. "I have really good news, and all I've managed to do is create an ugly little incident that will spoil my surprise."

Her face had brightened, though, and eager to escape the morass into which they'd fallen, he asked her quickly, "What's up?"

Susannah turned her chair to look out the window. "I've sold my play." Her eyes were better now, he noticed, her face less slack. Was it the play, or merely the drugs going to work? "Stephanie Chonin wants to produce it. She produced *Red Christman*, that mystery that's been running forever."

Sean knew who Stephanie Chonin was. She was an officer of the League of Broadway Theaters and had met with Sean several times about his plan to build a theater in the ground floor of La Tour. "Congratulations. I'm stunned. Not because she wants to produce it, but because it's all happened so fast."

"Beginner's luck," Susannah said. "It almost makes me feel guilty. People spend years writing plays and more years trying to get them mounted. I hope it doesn't mean I'm going to fall on my face quickly, too."

"There's no reason to think that," Sean said. He leaned over and kissed her cheek. "Congratulations. I'm very proud of you."

Susannah lightly touched the place he'd kissed with a fingertip. "I'll have to do a rewrite—probably lots of rewrites. Stephanie has a lot of ideas on how to improve the play. They're good ideas, but they'll take a lot of work. She wants to work together. I told her about the house in Bermuda. I thought it might be very quiet there."

Sean nodded. The house in Bermuda had been built by his grandfather in the twenties. It had been willed to Sean's mother and then to him. Though he didn't get there often, it was one of his favorite places in the world. "I think that's a terrific idea."

"It'll be terribly expensive to staff it," Susannah said.

"Not so terribly."

"I hate to ask it of you."

"I'm glad to give it."

"I should've said something to you before I mentioned it to her."

"Nonsense. It's your house as well as mine."

Susannah took his hand in both of hers. "I have something else to ask."

"Ask."

"Could you come with me? I'm going to need a lot of support to do this. It would mean a lot to have you there."

"All right. I will."

Susannah laughed a small, nervous laugh. "Just like that?"

"Just like that."

"You're not going to say you might have to come back now and then because of work?"

"I might—particularly because of this grand jury of Bill Middlebrooks's. My work I can take care of from a distance, but I have to be at his beck and call. But I can't anticipate what he's going to want from me, so I won't try."

Susannah looked away. "Is Bill out to . . . get you, Sean?" She said haltingly. "Is that what you think?"

Sean had to laugh. "Bill's ambitious, I suppose, but I don't think of him as out to get *me*. There is corruption in the building industry. I only know that I'm no part of it."

Susannah looked at Sean directly. "I'm not asking you to come to Bermuda to get away from that woman."

"Please don't call her 'that woman.' There's no need to. Nor is there any need to get me away from her."

"People will think that's why we've gone away."

"What people think is usually pretty much out of the control of the people they're thinking about."

Susannah lifted Sean's hand to her mouth and pressed her lips against it. "It'll be nice to be in Bermuda, won't it?"

"Yes," Sean said, but he felt burdened by a terrible weight. The weight was his heart, which felt like a rock in his chest. Not like a rock, actually, for it was soft, almost tender. It felt big and empty. It felt incompetent to its task of pumping blood through his body. It felt used up and useless. For he was in love with Clarissa, and he knew that he had been since their paths had first crossed, and that he always would be, although their paths might never cross again.

Looking out the window, looking across the ground of the estate toward the trees that screened his property from the Newmans', he thought how ironic it was to be so near and yet so far.

Sean turned toward a sound from the upstairs. "Do we have a burglar?"

Susannah laughed, somewhat sardonically. "I nearly forgot. My mother's here. I'm afraid I was horrid to her. She's been in the guest room for hours. She said she would've left, only she wanted to see you."

After dinner, Sean and Carolyn Evans sat alone in the living room and shared their mutual concern.

"Hysterical doesn't begin to describe her behavior," Carolyn Evans said. "She was completely out of control. She said it was because of the newspaper item, but that didn't seem possible. It wasn't a jealous rage. It seemed a rage, almost, against herself, against the fact that she's crippled. She seemed to be raging against her impotence."

"I hope working on the play will help her," Sean said. "She was fine—or at least better—during the time she was writing it. Since she finished it she's been in a kind of limbo. I know how I feel between projects. It is a kind of impotence."

"This woman, Sean," Carolyn Evans said. "Is she . . . ? Are you . . . ?"

"No."

Carolyn Evans sighed. "In a way, I'm disappointed. God knows I appreciate what you've done for Susannah—what you're doing for Susannah. But, well, I love you, and I want you to be happy."

"Happiness is relative, isn't it? I'm as happy as I can be, all things considered," Sean said.

Later that evening, alone in his bedroom, Sean allowed himself to acknowledge just how worried he was about Susannah. Hearing the unmistakable click of the safety top of a bottle of pills, Sean wondered if she was already on some irreversible downhill slide and contemplating hastening the process. He nearly ran to her bathroom and opened the door without knocking.

"Why, Sean," Susannah said with great composure, "what brings you in here?"

"I'll never leave you, Susannah," Sean said. "I don't want you to think that. I don't want you to give up."

Susannah looked at him for a long moment, then said, "Thank you for saying that. Sometimes I think about it. It would be so easy."

"Don't give up. You're at the very beginning of what could be a wonderful new career. You must let yourself have that experience."

Susannah smiled. "I think I will."

Chapter Eleven

Diana Leeds called Clarissa by her maiden
name, Tyler, the way Sarah Newman did. And
Clarissa called Diana Pat, after the character
played by Katherine Hepburn in the movie *Pat
and Mike*, which was Diana's favorite movie.
And Diana was a lot like the character Pat: She
was an expert tennis player, swimmer and
horsewoman. She was fluent in French, Italian
and American expletives. She was adept at writing poems and essays, and she made a sensa-
tional Western omelet.

On a beautiful summer morning two weeks
after the blackout, Diana was making a Western
omelet for herself and Clarissa in the kitchen of
Abraham and Sarah's house. After her father's
suicide, with Rachel Owen's consent, Clarissa
had arranged for Diana to finish out her term at
a boarding school abroad. They both dreaded
the separation, but it was the only thing Clarissa could think of to protect the child from the
incessant harassment of the media. When the

school year had ended, protesting all the while, Diana flew to San Francisco to spend some time with her mother and Edward Owen. Now she was with Clarissa, her favorite place in the world. They had a little precious time together before she took off for a month in Italy as part of a student exchange program sponsored by her school.

"Do you know what they call Western omelets in California?" Diana asked. She leaned against the sideboard, a spatula in one hand, the other on her blue-jeaned hip, her long, long legs crossed at the ankle. She had her long blond hair pinned up in back and wore a blue and gold headband around her forehead.

"Easterns?" Clarissa said.

"Denvers. Isn't that weird?"

"Not any weirder than calling them Westerns, I suppose."

"I think it's weirder. California's weird. In California, they put mayonnaise on hamburgers."

"Yuck," Clarissa said.

"You can say that again. California's grotesque. Do you know what Gertrude Stein said about California? She said it about Oakland, actually, but it applies to the whole state."

Clarissa knew, but she also knew that Diana liked to impart information and didn't enjoy discovering that she was not among the first to know something. "What?"

"She said, 'There is no there there.' Get it? There is no *there* there." Diana put a little hip into the phrase the second time.

"I get it," Clarissa said. "So you've started reading Gertrude Stein."

"Nah. Christopher told me about it."

"Christopher?"

"He lives next door to Rachel and Edward. He has a Kawasaki. I have a crush on him."

"A Kawaski? He's a little older than you, then?"

Diana ducked her head and poked at the omelet with the spatula. "A little."

"How little?" Clarissa asked.

"Christopher's eighteen." Quickly she added. "That's not such a big difference. I mean, when I'm twenty, he'll be twenty-six. And when *I'm* twenty-six, he'll only be thirty-two."

Clarissa listened as Diana prattled happily on, and marveled at the child's resiliency. Her life had been scarred by terrible tragedy, and yet she seemed brighter, more ebullient, more in love with life than most kids her age. Clarissa felt a wave of relief as she remembered that Rachel Owen had agreed—albeit begrudgingly —to keep the Penny Hammill column from Diana. It was a concession that Lester Roth had wormed out of Rachel and her lawyer when the latter had called him to register Rachel's protest against Clarissa's "carryings-on."

"I'm warning you, Clarissa, this is exactly the sort of notoriety you have to avoid," Lester had chided her. Brushing aside all her protestations of innocence, he continued, "I'm not talking reality. I'm talking appearances. This is great grist for Rachel's mill. You have to be above even the slightest hint of impropriety."

Miserably, she had agreed to try to do better, worried sick that Rachel would never keep her word, would use the business of her dinner with Sean as a weapon against her with Diana. But Diana in fact seemed completely oblivious to the whole issue. Clarissa could only hope that things would stay that way, until the time was right for Clarissa herself to tell Diana the truth.

Diana dashed out the omelet and buttered toast and sat at the table. They ate in silence for a while, savoring the delicious concoction. Then Clarissa said, "Other than Christopher, was there anything you liked about California?"

"Nope."

"Just like that?"

Diana shrugged. "What more can I say? A dump is a dump."

Clarissa laughed. "You know there's a chance you might have to live there."

"No way!" Diana expostulated.

Clarissa said, "I think you should be realistic, Pat. There's no guarantee that I'm going to get custody of you."

"Christopher's pre-law at Stanford," Diana said. "I had a long talk with him about the case."

"And?"

Diana took a bite of omelet, then said, "He wanted to know why Rachel didn't want custody at the time of her divorce from Daddy. I told him it was simple. She knew Daddy would fight her to the death, and she didn't want to be bothered. The only reason she's pursuing it now is that she'd do anything to screw you. I mean, Mom has her qualities, but maternal devotion isn't one of them. I know she doesn't *really* want to be saddled with me—she just wants to make sure *you* don't get me."

"I see," Clarissa said, hating the world that was driving Diana to this forced insouciance.

"A big problem," Diana went on, "is that since Rachel's remarried, she's become a ready-made nuclear family. That doesn't help our case."

"What do you suggest?" Clarissa asked mildly.

Diana blotted her lips with her napkin and said, "Get married. But not just because it would be good for your case. I want you to be happy."

Clarissa reached out and took Diana's hands in hers. "You make me happy, Pat. Knowing you're alive makes me happy."

Later, they walked by the pond. They wore shorts and the tops to bikini bathing suits and some workmen putting shingles on the roof nearly fell off trying to get a better look, not believing that a prepubescent girl could be so sensual, not believing that any woman could be so beautiful.

"I think there's something you should know, Pat," Clarissa said.

"Shoot."

Clarissa took a deep breath. "A few weeks ago there was a picture of me in a newspaper— along with a man I was having dinner with. The reporter who saw us didn't know that we were just friends and wrote a story implying that we were having a romance. The man is married, you see. The story was in a gossip column that's syndicated all over the country and Rachel's lawyer got hold of it. My lawyer thinks it might not be the greatest thing that ever happened."

Diana stopped and stood in front of Clarissa and looked into her eyes for a long moment. "You sound unhappy. Were you in love with him?"

Clarissa couldn't look into Diana's eyes. "It's a long story."

Diana, in one smooth motion, sat cross-legged on the grass. "I've got all day."

Clarissa laughed.

"Come on, Tyler. I told you about Christopher. Now you tell me about this man." Diana wriggled her bottom, "Come *on*! What's his name?"

"Sean," Clarissa said, and she sat down on the grass and told Diana the whole story.

"God," Diana said when she had finished. "What a great story! He lives right *there*? When do I get to meet him?"

"You don't. He's gone away," Clarissa said, and her mind wandered back to the day Sean had come to say good-bye.

He had knocked on the door at breakfast time on the Saturday after the blackout. Sarah and Abraham were out and Clarissa had been in the kitchen baking bread. Her hands had been covered with flour, and the workshirt she wore knotted at the waist had been unbuttoned down to her navel to let some air in, but she didn't think she would have buttoned it even if her hands had been clean. Sean had said that he was going to Bermuda for as much of the rest of the summer as he could manage and that he had wanted to let Clarissa know that his stable of horses was hers to use if she wished. All that she had to do was phone the groom to let him know she would be coming by.

Sean had said that he supposed Clarissa would be gone when he got back. She had said that she would, either to Washington or New York, depending on how things worked out with Diana.

"Good luck," Sean had said.

"And good luck to you."

"I suppose people will think I'm leaving because of us," Sean said.

"People think too much," Clarissa said. "If only they'd ask, instead of going off half-cocked. But, of course, that would spoil all the fun."

" . . . Well." Sean half turned and opened the screen door.

"Wait," Clarissa said, and went to him with her right hand out, then remembered that it was covered with flour. She ducked her head and put her hands behind her embarrassedly.

Sean smiled. "In that case . . ." And he took her in his arms and kissed her on the mouth.

Clarissa bent her head back and looked into his eyes and saw the pain in them give way to pleasure, to a kind of contentment she never expected to see there.

They sighed a long sigh in unison.

"Good-bye," they said together.

And he had gone.

Rousing herself from her reverie, Clarissa put her arm around Diana's shoulder and pulled her close. "How about a horseback ride?" she said.

147

"Terrific!" said Diana. "Race you back to the house." And she was off like a young gazelle.

Maggie, the brindle mare, fell forever, as if in slow motion. Diana flew through the air like an aerialist, her hands stretched out before her to grasp a trapeze that wasn't there. She didn't cry out. She simply soared, then descended slowly, her hands striking the ground first, breaking her fall. She rolled over and over, dissipating the force of her impact and ended up standing on her feet, her hands on her hips, an expression of annoyance on her face. Then she ran to the mare, who was trying to regain her feet, and grabbed the reins and tried to keep her on her side.

"Diana!" Clarissa reined in the gray gelding, dismounted and ran toward the girl and the horse.

"I'm okay," Diana said. "There's something wrong with her legs. I thought she tripped or something, but the trail's clear. There's something wrong with her legs."

"Come away from her and sit down for a minute."

"I'm okay."

"You're also in shock. It happens when you fall. Come over here and sit down."

Clarissa led Diana to the side of the trail and sat her against a tree. Gently, she wiped the perspiration from the girl's face with her silk scarf.

"I feel funny," Diana said.

"Sure you do. Your body gets pumped full of adrenaline when something like that happens.

It takes a while for things to get back to normal. Let met see that wrist—"

"Ow! Ow, ow, ow!" Diana cringed away from Clarissa's touch.

"I think it's broken. I'll make a sling with this scarf. Hold your arm against your chest."

"Shit. It's my right hand. My tennis hand. My golfing hand. My writing hand. My omelet hand. Shit, shit, shit!"

"Easy, Pat. You'll recover. There's no such thing as a terminal broken wrist."

Clarissa knotted the scarf behind Diana's neck and made her lie back on a hummock of grass in the shade of the tree, then went to look at the mare, who had gotten to her feet and stood quivering in the center of the trail, her ears laid back, her neck arched with pain, her nostrils flaring, her breath coming in anguished pants. Clarissa picked up her reins and tied them to the big exposed root of a tree and got the gray and mounted up. "I'm going to the house to call a doctor and a vet. Maggie won't try to move and don't you, either. I'll be right back."

"Tyler?"

"What, babe?"

"I'm sorry."

"You didn't do anything. I'll be right back."

The doctor was young and handsome. The vet was old and gnarled. The doctor said it was a hairline fracture and would heal without a cast.

"No cast?" Diana said mournfully. "I thought I'd at least get a cast."

The doctor laughed and ruffled her hair.

Diana felt with her good hand the place he had touched.

"She foundered," the vet said, picking a weed from the side of the trail and sticking it in the corner of his mouth. "Laminitis. It's an allergic reaction to protein. She probably ate too much new grass. The blood vessels swell up. Wouldn't be a problem if horses were like humans, but they ain't. Their feet are rigid, not soft like ours, so when the tissues swell it creates pressure, terrific pressure. It's like jamming your feet into a shoe that's a couple of sizes too small."

"I've been around horses all my life," Clarissa said. "I know what laminitis is."

"Yes, ma'am."

"She's from Kentucky," Diana said.

"Yes, miss."

"I didn't mean to sound rude," Clarissa said. "It's just that she's not my horse, and I want to get in touch with the owner as quickly as possible. If she has to be . . . well, what's your prognosis?"

"Yes."

The vet thrust his hands in his back pockets, then shrugged. "Most folks put a foundered horse down."

Diana cried out "Oh, no!"

Clarissa held her close. "The doctor can do things for the pain, Pat, but foundering causes permanent damage. She'd be unsound. She couldn't be ridden anymore. She might stumble again. And she's prone to more foundering unless she has a very special diet."

"Surely her owner would take care of her," Diana said. "She's worth it."

Sean's groom arrived with a van and he and

the vet carefully loaded the mare into it. The vet had given her a shot and the pain had subsided enough that she could walk tentatively. Diana couldn't watch and let herself be led away by Sarah, who had come down from the house.

"I'd like to call Mr. Howard myself," Clarissa said to the groom, "if you don't mind."

The groom touched his cap.

"You should talk to him, too, of course, but I'd like to break the news myself."

"There's a phone in the stable, ma'am. You can call from there. I have Mr. Howard's number in my office."

Clarissa had expected to hear the sound of great distance on the line, but the line sounded as it would for a local call. She guessed that Bermuda was closer than she thought.

A woman answered—a maid, Clarissa hoped, though she sounded more waited upon than waiting.

"My name is Clarissa Tyler. I'm calling for Mr. Howard. I'm a guest at his neighbors', Mr. and Mrs.—"

"Hello, Mrs. Leeds. This is Mrs. Howard."

Clarissa noted the use of her married name, and of Susannah's. "May I speak to your husband, please? One of his horses had an accident. Maggie, the brindle mare."

"What sort of accident?"

"She . . . she foundered. She has laminitis. It's a swelling of—"

"I know what laminitis is," Susannah said shortly. "I suggest you have the groom call our vet. He'll put her down."

"I don't want her put down," Clarissa said.

151

"I appreciate your concern, Mrs. Leeds," Susannah said, "but a foundered horse is of no use to us. Besides, it's a very painful affliction. Surely you don't want the horse to suffer merely for the sake of sentimentality."

"Can I speak to your husband? I think the horse can be saved. I know she can. I've seen it done. I'd like to talk to your husband about it."

"Mrs. Leeds, I'm sure you can understand that I'm not inclined to have you talk to my husband about anything."

" . . . I can understand . . . Well, then, please ask him if he wants the horse put down."

"I'm perfectly capable of making that decision myself, Mrs. Leeds. Because I'm a cripple doesn't mean I have no knowledge of horses. If you would please get off this line I'll call the groom myself."

"Save your dime," Clarissa said. "He's right here." And she handed the groom the phone.

Chapter Twelve

"He's here," Diana said.

Clarissa stood by the kitchen window, her forehead against the glass. "Who?"

"Sean Howard."

It was a moment before Clarissa registered what Diana had said. She turned and saw that Diana was sitting at the kitchen table, reading a newspaper. "What're you talking about?"

Diana held up the first section of the newspaper with her good hand and pointed with her chin at a photograph on the front page. "Here's his picture. He's cute."

Clarissa went to her and took the newspaper and read the picture's caption. Sean Howard and his lawyer, Daniel Freedman, were leaving a room in which a grand jury was hearing testimony concerning allegations of corruption in the construction industry. The picture illustrated a story with the headline: "CORRUPTION CALLED A WAY OF LIFE IN NEW YORK BUILDING INDUSTRY."

Clarissa tossed the paper on the table and went to the phone and dialed the number of the Howard's stable. The phone rang and rang and rang.

"Listen. This is really something," Diana said, and she read from the newspaper. " 'The multi-billion-dollar New York City building industry, which is flourishing as it rarely has in its history, is riddled with corruption and collusion that affects nearly every building, tunnel and road built, according to prosecutors, government officials and industry sources. . . . ' "

And rang and rang.

" 'Many of the illegal activities directly drive up the cost of construction. Others may cut costs for one builder at the expense of others, including workers whose pension funds are cheated and minority groups whose efforts to get jobs in the industry are undermined. . . . ' "

And rang and rang.

" 'Corruption comes in many forms, ranging from petty payoffs to price-fixing and bid-rigging on a grand scale. And it affects projects ranging from the repaving of roads on Staten Island to the refurbishing of the Charleton Hotel to the erection of such buildings as the McDonell Building and La Tour, the latest project of multimillionaire entrepreneur Sean Howard.' "

Finally the groom answered the phone and told Clarissa that the vet had had to go on another call and would not be available until late that afternoon, or possibly the next morning.

"Mr. Howard's in New York," Clarissa said. "I'm going to try and reach him. Please don't let

154

the vet do anything until you've heard from one of us."

"Well, ma'am, Mrs. Howard said . . ."

"I know what she said. Please. I'll call you as soon as I can. If you don't hear from me, obviously you should follow your orders."

"Yes, ma'am."

Clarissa hung up and turned to Diana. "I have to go out for a while, honey," she said.

"And I know where," Diana replied.

"Tell Sarah and Abraham what's happened, will you, Pat? Tell them I took the Jeep to the station. I'll call as soon as I know what's going on. But don't expect me home for dinner."

"Yes," Diana said.

"Yes, I won't be home for dinner?"

"Yes, you're going to see him."

"If I can find him. I'm not sure I know where to look."

She found him on the steps of the New York County Courthouse in Foley Square, eating a hot dog and talking to a wiry man in a rumpled blue suit whom Clarissa recognized from the newspaper photograph as Sean's lawyer. Sean looked like a fashion model in a light green double-breasted suit, a madras cotton shirt, and a dark green tie. He was very tan and his blond hair was even blonder.

Sean didn't recognize Clarissa at first, for she had dressed in something of a disguise, wearing a simple navy French cut T-shirt, lightweight trousers and low-heeled sandals. She had her hair up under a white tennis hat and wore dark aviator glasses. Clarissa's disguise was any other woman's strutting outfit, however, and

Sean couldn't help notice how attractive was the woman approaching him across the plaza, no matter how many things he had on his mind.

"Hi," Clarissa said once she was within earshot, by which time, of course, he knew who she was.

"Clarissa!" Sean said, delight written all over his face.

"I have to talk to you," Clarissa said. "It's urgent."

"You can talk in front of Dan," Sean said. "Oh, excuse me. Clarissa . . . Leeds, this is Daniel Freedman, my lawyer."

"How do you do?" Clarissa said. "I saw your picture in the paper."

"Speaking of which"—Freedman looked nervously this way and that—"there're photogs around."

Sean gave Freedman a look of annoyance, then realized that his caution was not unwarranted. "My car's right over there. Let's go sit down and talk . . . Dan, come along with us."

Freedman thought for a moment, then shook his head. "I think I'll have another hot dog."

"You've had two."

"I think I'll have another one."

Sean waved to Eddie, his driver, to stay where he was, leaning against a concrete planter, getting some sun. Sean had his hand on the car door handle when he heard his name called.

"Sean, old buddy. You're not running out on me, are you?"

It was Bill Middlebrooks, looking tanned and fit and expensively tailored.

Sean introduced Clarissa and Middlebrooks.

Middlebrooks looked her over with a practiced eye. "My pleasure. I met your husband a number of times. I'm terribly sorry about your loss."

Clarissa looked at him without expression, barely acknowledging his commiseration. How odd, she thought, that he looks so much like Sean, yet nothing like him. Beneath his tan, he was sallow. Beneath his fitness, he was flaccid. Beneath his handsomeness, he was ugly.

"I just wanted to say, Sean, that I think everything's going very well," Middlebrooks said.

"For me?" Sean said. "Or for you?"

Middlebrooks laughed. "Well, our interests are really the same in the long run, aren't they? We're both trying to make this a better city to live in."

Sean inclined his head slightly. "Now if you'll excuse me, Bill, Miss Tyler and I have some important business to discuss."

Almost imperceptibly, Middlebrooks made a face of extreme doubt. Then he smiled broadly and made a production of looking at his Cartier watch. "See you very soon, Sean. I hope you had a big lunch. Mrs. Leeds, very pleased to meet you."

Clarissa sucked in her cheeks at the use of her married name, and nodded, once.

Middlebrooks strode off, walking up behind a colleague and slapping him loudly on the back, laughing at his surprise. "Brian, you old son of a bitch. You nailed that slum lord yet?"

"Cocky," Clarissa said.

"Very," Sean said.

In the backseat of the car they sat at either

end of the wide seat, sitting sideways to face each other. Clarissa told Sean about the accident, about Diana, about the vet, about the call to Susannah, about the groom, about everything. "I had a horse that foundered. I nursed it back to health. I was sixteen, and things like that matter a lot to a sixteen-year-old girl, but it matters to me now, too. And it matters to Diana. It's work. It takes time. Hot water. Epsom salts. A lean diet. Walking. Aspirin. Bute. She'll never be ridden again, but she'll be able to walk, to run on her own, to live. Please Sean. I'll look after her myself. It's partly my fault, anyway. I let her eat too much new grass, and it's the protein in new grass that causes laminitis."

Sean only half heard what she said, so happy was he to be in her presence again. And he heard not the anguish in her tale, but the enthusiasm, the desire to do everything possible to keep the poor animal alive. It quickened him, as well. He reached for the phone in the panel behind the front seat and dialed a long-distance number and waited, the phone tucked into his shoulder.

"It took the groom a while to answer when I called," Clarissa said.

"It's nice to see you," Sean said.

"I'm sorry about the call to your wife," Clarissa said. "I didn't know you were in town. I hope it doesn't . . ."

"It will," Sean said. "Things haven't been going very well between us. She flipped out over that crap in the *Post*. And there've been a lot of accusations made about me in connection with this investigation. Susannah almost acts as if she believes them. Susannah—" Sean turned with abrupt annoyance at a tap on the window. Middlebrooks had his hands pressed against the glass like a spectator at an aquarium. "Damn," Sean whispered, and pressed the button that lowered the window. "What is it, Bill?"

"I just remembered, Sean—excuse me, Mrs. Leeds—"

"Miss Tyler," Clarissa corrected him with a smile. "My husband's dead."

Middlebrooks faltered. "Y-yes . . . of course . . . Sean, I just remembered that I forgot to tell you to give my regards to Susannah. I assume you call her every day when you're in town. How's she enjoying Bermuda?"

"Fine. She's working hard. On a play."

"I heard about that," Middlebrooks said. "Say, give her my congratulations, will you? I'm just as pleased as can be at her good fortune. Tell her I—"

"I'll give you the number if you like, Bill. You can tell her yourself."

"I have the number, actually," Middlebrooks said. "Maybe I will call her. You wouldn't mind, would you, Sean?"

"Not at all. Now excuse us again, Bill, but we're running out of time"—he held up a finger to indicate that the phone had finally been answered. "Evan? This is Sean Howard. Hold on just a moment, will you? . . . It's almost time to get back inside, Bill, and I have to get this matter straightened out. It's about one of my horses."

"About your horse?" Middlebrooks said dubiously.

"Yes."

Middlebrooks stood straight and brushed off the palms of his hands, which he'd rested on the doorsill. "See you inside, Sean. Good-bye, again . . . Miss Tyler."

Clarissa stared straight ahead. She simply couldn't bring herself to be civil.

Into the phone, Sean said, "Evan? Thanks for waiting. I understand Maggie's foundered. Well, I don't see the need to put her down. Not just yet. This is the first time. It might only be a mild case. Let's give her a few weeks. See what the vet prescribes and start doing whatever he suggests. . . . Yes, I'll speak to Mrs. Howard. . . . Good-bye, Evan. I'll keep in touch."

"Thank you," Clarissa said when he had hung up.

"I wouldn't have had her put down myself," Sean said, "if anyone had consulted me. It's I who should thank you, and I do."

"You're welcome . . . " Clarissa saw once again the pain in his eyes, a pain greater than the pain she had seen before. "This is a very difficult time for you."

Sean heard that it wasn't a question. "What's happened is that someone—I don't know who—has told the grand jury that I've been party to a scheme to defraud investors in my project. It's complicated. I won't bore you with the details, but . . ."

"I won't be bored," Clarissa said.

Sean smiled. "No. I guess you won't. Another time, perhaps, I'll tell you all about it. Suffice it to say that the allegation is of very great interest to Bill Middlebrooks."

"And to your wife," Clarissa said. "You started to say that she thought the allegation must be true. Is that because Middlebrooks thinks it is?"

Sean frowned. "I don't know what you mean."

Clarissa looked out the window for a moment, at nothing. Then she looked at Sean. "Call it woman's intuition. I've never met the man before, and I've never met your wife. But I'd say he's in love with her."

Sean laughed a startled laugh. "Bill Middlebrooks?"

Clarissa put up a finger of warning. "I didn't say she was in love with him. It's just that there was something about the way he asked about her—I know he did it partly to get at me—but there was . . . something." She smiled. "Woman's intution. Don't question it."

Sean held up his hands. "I wouldn't think of it."

"Sean," she asked hesitantly, "do you think it would be like thumbing our noses at the furies if we met back at River House tonight for a quiet little supper? I know we shouldn't be seen in public, but I could fix something simple for us at home."

He reached out and briefly, tenderly, stroked her cheek. "I know how you feel. I can't bear the thought of your getting out of this car and disappearing from my life again. I think we deserve one more last time, too."

They looked at each other wordlessly.

"Here's the key to the apartment," he said finally, handing it to her. "I'll phone the doorman and let him know you're coming. Believe me, the old retainers who staff that place are as close-mouthed as the Sphinx."

She took the key, clasped his hand so tightly he almost winced, and said quickly, "Whenever you get there, I'll be waiting for you." Then she was gone, leaving behind only the special lingering aura of her perfume.

"My God," Sean said. He stood in the foyer of his apartment, blinking in disbelief, for Clarissa had transformed the living room into a flower garden. Bouquets of flowers were on every table and on the windowsills and the mantlepiece. Reds and blues and yellows exploded everywhere, reminding him of fireworks. Through the doors to the dining room he could see that the table had been laid with linen and set with china and silver. In a slim glass vase in the center of the table was a stalk of orchids.

"I got some flowers," Clarissa said.

"I can see that." Still he didn't move. He couldn't, for he was stricken once again by her beauty, and by how she had transformed herself, as well. She had changed from her sensible clothes into a white French lace dress—a long-sleeved overblouse, belted loosely with a silver cord, and a cocktail-length skirt, and beneath it all a simple silk slip with straps so slender they were nearly invisible. On her feet were silver high-heeled sandals. Her hair fell around her shoulders and down her back.

"I stopped at Bendel's," Clarissa said.

"I can see that, too."

She came to him carrying two glasses of champagne. "Dinner's in half an hour. I hope you're hungry."

"Starved." Sean ducked his head in embarrassment and brought from behind his back, where he had been concealing it, a lily, wrapped in paper from the florist's. "This seems redundant."

"It's beautiful. You can never have too many flowers unless . . . unless you don't have enough vases!" She took the lily from him and handed him the glass of champagne and went into the kitchen, where she found another slim glass vase. It was not quite tall enough, but it would have to do. When she returned to the living room, Sean was not there, and for just a moment she had a flash of fear that she had frightened him away with her enthusiasm. Then she heard the sound of the shower running in the bathroom. She set the vase with the lily in it on the coffee table and sat on one of the silk covered banquettes and read the article on the construction business in a newspaper she'd bought on the way uptown. She wanted to know everything about the allegations of corruption.

She was just finishing the long article when Sean appeared at the door. He had dressed in a black dinner jacket, a formal shirt and a white silk bow tie, black tuxedo pants and black patent leather shoes.

"I thought I'd dress for dinner," he said.

Clarissa patted the place beside her on the banquette.

He came to her and sat down.

"Cheers," she said, holding out her glass of champagne.

He touched his glass to hers. "Cheers."

She asked him how the rest of the day had gone and he told her about his testimony before the grand jury and told her more about the anonymous allegations that had been made about him.

"The grand jury only returns indictments, of course," Sean said. "It doesn't convict. Another trial would be necessary for that. But the danger is that an indictment alone would be enough to discourage investors in the project. Without continued financing, the project can't go on."

"Do you think there'll be an indictment?"

"It's hard to know. It's just my word against his—whoever 'he' is. The burden of proof isn't as great as in a regular trial. Hearsay and circumstantial evidence are admissible." Sean set his glass on a table and pinched the bridge of his nose between his fingers. Lately, he had frequent headaches.

Clarissa nudged his hand away with hers and put her fingertips on his forehead.

Her fingertips were cool. "That feels good," Sean said.

"I want you to know that you can count on me to stick by you through this whole thing," Clarissa said.

Sean let her go on soothing him for a while, then took her hand in his and held it to his lips. He looked at her for a long time before setting her hand down in her lap. "You mean, unlike Susannah?"

Clarissa gestured around the living room. "I mean unlike everyone. I don't see anyone else here offering to listen to your troubles, making your dinner, helping you get rid of your headache."

His headache, he realized, was gone. "Did you stick by your husband when he was having his troubles?"

"I tried, but he wouldn't be stuck by. He insisted on going it alone—which was what he finally did—went alone. . . . It takes as much effort to be helped as it does to help. I hope you're up to it."

"I do, too," Sean said, "—because, frankly, my instinct is to go it alone, too."

"That's not an instinct," Clarissa said. "That's just a habit. That's how you've always done things, isn't it?"

Sean smiled. "Pretty much."

"So try doing things another way. You might like it."

"So far, I like it a lot."

Dinner was delicious—artichoke bottoms with oysters and spinach, baked cod with feta cheese, potatoes with dill. Sean got a bottle of 1979 Chateau Laville Haut Brion Blanc from the wine pantry. It went down like water and he got another and they drank it, too. They had Granny Smith apples and brie for dessert. They had coffee in the living room, kicking off their shoes and sitting on the carpet.

Breaking into their companionable silence,

Clarissa gently said, "You started telling me in the car about Susannah. Do you want to talk about it?" she asked.

Sean sighed. "We don't love each other. It's as simple as that. Oh, we feel something—some tie. But it's not an affectionate one. Since she finished the play, and especially since she sold it to a producer, Susannah's developed a lot more confidence in herself, she's become more independent. That's good, of course, but along with that she's become . . . well, I guess resentful is the word. More resentful of the dependence that remains."

"Does she want a divorce?"

"She hasn't said it to me in so many words," Sean said, "but I heard her talking about it with her producer. I wasn't eavesdropping, it's that kind of house. It has big, open rooms and . . . good acoustics. Her producer suggested that she wait until the play was launched. She said divorce was too time-consuming to get wrapped up in until then. She said it might generate negative publicity."

"Lovely woman, that."

Sean smiled.

"Do you want a divorce?" Clarissa asked.

Sean tipped his head back against the banquette and shut his eyes and stayed very still for a long time. "I don't see how I can keep living with someone who doesn't trust me. We've had difficulties in the past, Susannah and I, but her brains are so scrambled with Stelazine by now that she's become utterly unreachable. Every time I suggest she get some help, she flies at my

throat. And now, to top everything, she thinks I'm a crook."

"As Middlebrooks thinks you are," Clarissa said. "Does Middlebrooks really think you are, or does he just hope you are so that he—remember now, woman's intuition—can have Susannah for himself?"

Sean shook his head in perplexity. "I trust your intuition, but I've never thought of Bill as being interested in Susannah—or she in him."

"You said she resented being in need. Resentment, mistrust. It sounds to me as though she wants to punish you. I got the feeling she wanted Maggie put down to punish me—to punish both of us."

Sean nodded. "She wanted me to get Maggie back from the Newmans before we left for Bermuda. I wouldn't."

They sat in silence for a while. Out on the East River a tugboat belched long and low. Sean got up and went to the window. "There's a fog. How odd for this time of year."

"Let's make love," Clarissa said.

Sean turned to face her and sat on the windowsill, his arms folded across his chest. "To punish Susannah?"

"No. Because we want to."

" . . . What about Diana? What about your father's campaign?"

"I'm not proposing that we make love on the street," Clarissa said.

Sean smiled. "What are you proposing?"

"You mean, for the long run?"

He nodded.

167

Clarissa traced the pattern of the carpet for a while. "I'm proposing that we make a commitment—a commitment to the future."

Suddenly, he was beside her, bending to lift her to her feet, raising her in his strong arms as if she weighed nothing, holding her close to him, bending her back in his arms, kissing her long neck, running his hand down her long back, pressing her hips and thighs against his, finding her lips with his and thrusting his tongue deep inside her mouth. Then his hand was on her breasts, then between her thighs.

Clarissa stepped away from Sean and bent her head like a child so that he could unbutton her dress. He pulled it down over her shoulders and she stepped out of it and with one motion pulled her slip over her head and dropped it alongside the dress, then stepped close to him and pulled at an end of his tie to open it and concentrated on the buttons of his shirt.

His smooth, broad chest was horribly scarred, and she touched them tentatively, as if the wounds were still fresh. "Vietnam?"

"Yes."

"How awful. How awful that someone could do this to this beautiful body." And she bent to kiss his wounds, moving her hands down lower and feeling his hardness straining to be free of his clothing.

Sean helped Clarissa finish undressing him and they stood face to face, a little apart, admiring each other's bodies, lightly touching shoulders and arms with their fingertips, sighing with pleasure at the sights and scents and sensations.

Sean lifted Clarissa in his arms and carried her into the bedroom. With one hand, he pulled back the coverlet of the bed and laid her on the cool sheets and made love to her, ferociously, yet gently.

And she made love to him urgently yet slowly, appeasing her long hunger, her long thirst, her long need.

Like flowers, she thought as the passionate force of him surged through her body.

Like fireworks, he thought.

Again and again they made love, finding that the well of their passion was deep and plentiful. Finally they slept, their long bodies graceful on the bed like works of art, dreaming of the future.

Chapter Thirteen

"Sean, this is Diana Leeds. Diana, Sean Howard."

Clarissa stood back as the two people she loved most in the world looked each other up and down in the center of the guest house living room, hoping they would love each other as much as she loved each of them, knowing, somehow, that they surely would.

Diana took the first step to lessen the formal distance between them, offering Sean her good hand. "Excuse the left hand, Mr. Howard. I'm very glad to meet you."

Sean took her left hand in both of his and held it tightly. "I'm very, very glad to meet you, Diana. And please call me Sean."

He looked at both Diana and Clarissa, and smiled. They made such a pretty picture in their white summer dresses and matching white, low-heeled sandals. Diana's long, blond hair was swept up in back and held by an antique comb. Clarissa's hair fell about her shoulders, which had been turned an olive brown by the sun. She looked Mediterranean, sensual, exotic. Diana looked all-American, down to her sling made from a big, blue bandana.

Sean had testified before the grand jury for three more days, and at the end of each day had returned to River House, where Clarissa waited. She had spent the days in Connecticut, taking walks and drives with Diana, practicing her violin, taking a lesson from Sarah, then taking a train into the city in time to be at the apartment when Sean returned, stopping on the way to buy fresh flowers and something for dinner. They would have a cocktail, then dinner, and luxuriate for the rest of the evening in soul-satisfying conversation and lovemaking.

It was Saturday now. Sean had returned to Connecticut on Friday evening, and gone almost immediately to Clarissa. She'd had a drink ready and dinner in preparation.

That night, Diana had stayed in the main house, having dinner with Sarah and Abraham, playing Scrabble with Abraham, trouncing him by dint of getting *xenon* in a triple-word corner, watching *Sullivan's Travels* on television with Sarah, sleeping in a spare bedroom upstairs. "I want you to have some time to yourself in your own house. The guest house is your house at the moment. I don't want to be the pesky kid everybody has to humor."

"You're not," Clarissa had said. "But I appreciate your consideration, nonetheless."

Sean had spent the day on Saturday catching up on office work that had accumulated because of his grand jury appearance. Clarissa and Diana had gone to the Dells and spent the afternoon exploring its glades and open spaces. They had showered and put on their white dresses and sat in the guest house living room with only one light on, to keep it cool, and listened to a recording of Casals playing Bach's Suite no. 1 in G for unaccompanied cello.

"You can hear the *wood* when he plays," Diana had said. "It's extraordinary."

"It's as if you can hear the soul of the instrument," Clarissa had said.

"That's it," Diana said. "That's it exactly."

Then they had listened in silence. Sean had knocked just as the music ended.

"Perfect timing," Clarissa had said, opening the door and standing aside to let him pass. *Perfect looking*, too, she had thought. Sean was wearing a white silk shirt, tan linen pleated trousers and leather sandals.

"I've been on the porch for a few minutes, listening," Sean had said. "I didn't want to interrupt the music."

This night Sean cooked the dinner, from makings he had had sent over during the afternoon—fettuccine with salsa ai funghi prataioli —sauce with wild field mushrooms!

"Wow," Diana said. "Did you pick them yourself?"

"In a manner of speaking," Sean said. "I picked them out of a bin at the greengrocer's."

Diana laughed.

Clarissa felt warm inside, felt calm and contented.

They ate avidly—the fettuccine and a green salad and freshly baked French bread. Sean and

Clarissa had Mouton Cadet; Diana stuck to Pepsi. For dessert there was spumoni and espresso coffee.

"I'm stuffed," Diana said. "It was delicious, Sean."

"Thanks, Pat," Sean said easily using the special nickname he'd been introduced to earlier.

"Delicious," Clarissa said.

"Thanks, Tyler."

Clarissa laughed—the clear tones of a bell. Hearing its clarity herself, she realized that even the laughs she had laughed with Sarah and Abraham hadn't truly been her laughs, that they had retained some discordance. This laugh was her laugh.

"Sean?" Diana asked.

"Yes?"

"Would you mind if . . .? You see . . . Well, I'm interested in this grand jury business. I've been reading all about it in the paper—about the corruption in the construction business, and so on, and well, I'm interested."

Clarissa put up a cautionary hand. "Sean had a difficult week, Diana. He might not want to talk about it just now."

"It's okay," Sean said. "I want you to know what's been going on. I want both of you to know." And he told them about the long days in the grand jury room, about the aggressive questioning of the government attorneys, about a pattern that had emerged in the questioning that led him to believe he knew the source of allegations against him. "A few years ago, I had a bad experience with a man—I won't say his

174

name because I don't want to malign him until I'm absolutely certain he's the one—with a man who runs a company that makes reinforced concrete. He submitted the low bid for a job, but as I often do I gave the job to a company that bid higher because I thought I'd get better work. The man was furious, livid. He came to my office and ranted and raved and nearly attacked me physically. When the concrete was finally delivered, someone went to the construction site after midnight one night and broke up several large slabs with a jackhammer. He'd apparently bribed a security guard to let him into the site, but a policeman—a cop on the beat—happened by and heard the hammer and took a look and didn't like what he saw. He arrested the man for trespassing. He turned out to be an employee of the man I suspect of making the allegations, but the D.A. was never able to get him to say that his boss put him up to the sabotage. . . .

"Anyway, the questions I've been asked all revolve around that bid on that particular job. They've asked me about other bids on other jobs, too, but they keep coming back to that one. What I infer—I have to infer it since no one ever actually confronts you in a grand jury proceeding—is that this man has been putting pressure on the head of the other concrete company —the one that got the job—to say that I accepted a payoff in exchange for choosing the higher bidder. I don't know the nature of the pressure. I do know that the other company's fallen on hard times lately. The man may be in trouble with loan sharks. He may owe money to his competitor. I don't know. But it seems fairly clear that he's vulnerable to some kind of coercion."

"Wow," Diana said. "It sure is complicated."

"It's been costly," Sean said. "Partly in terms of time, but mostly in terms of what this could do to my reputation if things don't get resolved fairly soon. Grand juries can take as long as they want before returning indictments—or not returning them, which, needless to say, I hope is what happens in my case. Until they take some action . . . Well, despite the concept that you're innocent until proven guilty, being called before a grand jury isn't the best thing that can happen to a businessman."

All the talk of his troubles seemed to Sean to have diminished somewhat the light and warmth that had so far filled the room. With determined hardiness, he smoothly steered the conversation into less troubled waters. Soon they were all chatting pleasantly again of happier matters—Maggie's progress, Diana's upcoming trip to Italy, a new hit movie, Clarissa's music. Sean questioned her with obviously sincere interest and intelligence about the Strad, and felt the joy she took in it communicated to him almost physically.

"Could you be persuaded to play?" he asked her, carried away by the intensity of her devotion to her art.

And why not? she asked herself. If not for these two beloved friends, then for whom?

"Well, there is something I've been working on . . ." she said slowly.

"Don't fiddle-faddle around, Tyler," Diana said. "Just *play*."

Clarissa sat back in her chair, put her hands in her lap and considered them for a moment, then looked up and smiled at the anticipation in their faces. "All right. I will."

She played the Bach Chaconne. She made mistakes—played some wrong notes and missed some others. She got the phrasing wrong at one point and made it sound singsong instead of flowing. But she played magnificently, for she was playing for two people she loved.

When she was done, they didn't applaud. They sat very still, listening to their memories of the music, hoping for echoes from the corners of the room.

Finally, Diana said, "You're incredible."

And Sean said, "I've never sat so close to a violin being played before. You hear more than just the strings when you sit so close. You hear the bow and the fingering. You hear the wood. It's as though—"

"You hear the soul of the instrument," Diana said.

Sean smiled. "That's what I was going to say."

Diana nodded. "I know. It's what Tyler said about Casals's cello. But it was the same with her violin."

Sean smiled at Clarissa. "Can you play it again?"

She shook her head. "I don't think I will. Theoretically, I'm not supposed to play it until

I'm sixty. It's considered that difficult. Not difficult, exactly, but, well, it requires a certain maturity."

"I'd say you were a pretty mature musician," Sean said, and he applauded lightly. "It was wonderful."

"Yea," Diana said, slapping her good hand on her thigh vigorously. "Yea, yea, yea."

Clarissa stood up, bowed to each of them, then put the violin in her case and turned to face them, rubbing her hands together with satisfaction.

"I know that gesture," Diana said, imitating it as best she could with only one hand. "That means you're about to say it's bedtime."

"It's *your* bedtime," Clarissa said.

Sean stood up. "I'd best be getting home."

Diana was to leave for Italy the next day, so there had been no question of her spending a second night with Abraham and Sarah. As much as she cherished the last bit of time with Diana, though, Clarissa felt a wrenching sense of loss that Sean had to go back to his own house. Oh, why can't we all just be together she cried to herself, trying with little success to keep her face from falling apart.

Sean came over to Diana and held out his hands. "Thank you for a wonderful dinner, Pat—"

"You made the dinner. Thank *you*."

"And you made it a wonderful time. Thank *you*."

Diana ducked her head. "I'm sorry about your horse."

"She's going to be all right. And so are you. I was much more worried about you than about

178

the horse. But you're both going to be fine, so there's nothing to be sorry about."

Diana got up suddenly and hugged Sean around the neck with her good hand, pressing her nose and lips into his cheek, laughing and crying at the same time.

Sean hugged her back, lifting her a little off the ground as he squeezed her.

Clarissa nearly wept and nearly laughed, seeing them in each other's arms.

As if reading Clarissa's mind, Diana cried out, "I want you two to be together. I want it so much." Then she let Sean go and turned and ran into the bedroom.

They heard the bed creak as Diana flopped down on it and heard her crying.

"What a mess," Clarissa sighed. "Could we at least go riding tomorrow? I'm so tired of always seeing you indoors." She stopped herself. "No, of course we can't go out together. I'm sorry I mentioned it."

"I'm sorry, too, Clarissa, but we have to be discreet."

"That makes me so sad. I know I said I was making a commitment to the future, but having tasted a little of the present, I wish the future was now."

"So do I," Sean said.

"But it's not."

"No."

Clarissa folded her arms under her breasts and poked angrily at the rug with the toe of her sandal. "Damn."

Sean put his arms around her and kissed her forehead. "I love you, Clarissa."

She kissed his mouth. "I love you, too."

They stood for a long time in each other's arms, feeling the length of each other's bodies, sighing long sighs.

At last Clarissa said, "After your testimony on Monday you're leaving, aren't you? You're going back to Bermuda?"

". . . Yes."

"Monday night?"

"Yes."

"And tomorrow night, you said, you're having dinner with your lawyer."

"Yes, but I'd like to see you afterward. Can you come to River House and spend the night?"

Clarissa shut her eyes and leaned her cheek against his chest, that chest that made her weak with its strong modeling, that made her weep at the scars of his war wounds. "Yes. Oh, yes."

They walked out onto the porch. The night was clear and cool, and there were uncountable stars in the sky. Down by the pond, bullfrogs burped antiphonally. Clarissa leaned out over the porch railing, her head back, searching the sky, looking like the figurehead of a ship. She tried to make some order out of the multitude of stars, but she couldn't find any stars she knew, couldn't assemble them into familiar constellations. She felt in an unfamiliar latitude, in a place she'd never been before. "Maybe when we're sixty. When *I'm* sixty. When I'm sixty, you'll be . . . what? . . . sixty-eight? I'll play the Bach Chaconne and we'll be together."

Sean stood close behind her and put his arms around her waist. "You played the Bach Chaconne tonight. We were together tonight."

Clarissa put her head back against his

180

shoulder. "Yes, with Diana. What a treat to be with the two of you." Clarissa calculated, "When I'm sixty, Diana will be . . . forty-two. My goodness. That's hard to imagine."

Sean smiled, but he shivered suddenly and clasped his arms with his hands.

"Cold?" Clarissa said.

"Scared," Sean said.

She put her arms around him, feeling the tension in his body. "Scared of what?"

"Scared you'll find somebody else. Scared somebody else will find you. I can't reasonably expect you to wait for me until . . . until whenever."

Clarissa leaned back in his arms, tipping her head back and looking past the roof of the porch to the sky. "Orion . . . Cassiopeia's Chair . . . Scorpio . . . the Dippers." Things suddenly made sense again. It was the sky she had known since she was a girl. She knew where she was. She knew where she was going. She lowered her head and kissed Sean on the mouth, running her fingers through his blond hair. "Oh, but you can. And I won't be waiting. I'll be . . . getting ready. Getting better."

Sean laughed. "Better? My Lord. I don't know if I can cope with better. What you are now is overwhelming enough."

"You'll be getting better, too," Clarissa said. "It's been wonderful, these few days. Thank you."

"Thank *you*," Sean said. "Thank you for being the joy that you are."

"Go now," Clarissa said. "Go quickly."

And he went, leaping off the porch with a

magnificent leap, running across the grass with an easy, elegant stride, his white shirt reflecting the starlight and remaining visible long after the rest of him had been obscured by night, so that it looked as if a piece of clothing had become incarnate and was speeding across the lawn, magically.

Clarissa sat on the porch steps and wept.

Chapter Fourteen

Clarissa knew from the furrows in Sean's brow and from the darkness in his eyes that something was wrong.

His brow had been so clear, his eyes so bright, but now, as he hung up the house phone on the wall of the kitchen and stood with his hands in the pockets of his seersucker robe, looking down at the terra cotta floor, there was concern on his face, perhaps even despair.

The house phone had buzzed—someone calling from the reception desk in the River House lobby—just as they sat down to a late snack of cold barbecued chicken, tomatoes garnished with parsley, dill and olive oil, and champagne. Clarissa had come to River House late Sunday afternoon after seeing Diana off at Kennedy Airport on her flight to Rome. Sean had come home at 10:30 after his dinner meeting with Danial Freedman. Clarissa had been lying on the couch in her mauve silk pajamas, reading, and Sean had come to her and lifted her in his arms, as though she were merely a feather, and had carried her into the bedroom, where they made love with an abandon informed by their awareness that this might be the last time for a long time. Then they had gone into the kitchen, Sean in his robe, Clarissa in one of Sean's blue oxford cloth shirts, and had set out the cold food that Clarissa had picked up that afternoon. Then the house phone had buzzed.

"Yes?" Sean had said. And, "Yes . . . Yes, it's all right. . . . Yes, tell him to come up. . . . Yes, thank you." Then he had hung up the phone and stood with his hands in the pockets of his robe, looking down at the floor, his brow furrowed, his eyes dark.

"What is it?" Clarissa said at last.

Sean looked up with a small startle, as if he had forgotten she were there. "Oh, it's . . . It's someone to see me. On business."

Clarissa looked at the clock on the kitchen wall. "At midnight? On Sunday? What kind of business?"

" . . . Personal business."

"Sean," Clarissa said sharply.

"Yes?"

"Who *is* it?"

" . . . It's your father," Sean said.

"My father?"

"Senator Tyler is your father, isn't he?"

"Oh, Christ," Clarissa said, and marched out of the room. She was back in a moment, dressed in a lime silk blouse, white linen pants and white espadrilles, running a comb through her thick dark hair, clutching her watch by its strap in her teeth. She finished with her hair and took the watch from her mouth and strapped it on her wrist. "You'd better get dressed, darling. It'll improve our position. I'll answer the door when he comes up. You stay in the bedroom until I call you."

"Clarissa, I won't let you—"

"Please, Sean." Clarissa gave him a gentle push on the chest to get him moving out of the kitchen. "Please."

Each line of apartments in River House is serviced by its own elevator, which opens directly into a small foyer outside each apartment's front door. Clarissa opened the front door and stood against the wall of the foyer, on which hung framed architect's renderings of some of Sean's projects, her arms folded under her breasts, tapping the rug with one espadrilled foot, listening to the hum of the elevator as it bore her father upward.

Dwight Tyler looked startled to see his daughter standing there waiting. "Why, Clarissa."

"Why, Clarissa, indeed. You knew I was here."

"Now, Clarissa, I—"

Clarissa help up a cautionary hand. "No. Before you say anything, I'm going to tell you what's going on here. You think you know what's going on here, but you don't. So let me tell you. I don't want to have to deal with your preconceptions—with your misconceptions. After you've heard me out, you can talk—but only then."

Dwight Tyler put his hands in his pockets and scuffed at the rug with a black wing-tipped shoe, looking a little rueful. "Won't you invite me in, at least?"

Clarissa raked her hand through her hair, her eyes wide with astonishment. "No, I will not. You're not welcome in here. You invited yourself this far, but you're not going to invite yourself any farther. Now listen . . . Listen well . . . Sean Howard and I are friends. You must know that he's married. You must know, too, that his wife is a paraplegic and that before she had the accident that made her a paraplegic their marriage wasn't going well. After the accident, they stayed married, so he could care for her, but they're not in love. You must know, too, that Sean is the subject of an investigation by the New York County District Attorney's office—an investigation into allegations that are without foundation—"

"That remains to be—"

"Don't interrupt."

Dwight Tyler craned his neck and touched the knot of his blue polka-dot necktie.

"When Sean was called to appear before the grand jury, his wife declined to come along with him, to be by his side during the ordeal. She as much as told him that she believed the charges against him, believed that he'd be indicted and convicted. I don't believe the charges, but even if I had, because he's my friend, I'd have stood beside him. I did stand beside him—"

" 'Stand'?" Dwight Tyler said, rolling his eyes a little.

"Don't be lewd, Father," Clarissa said. "It doesn't become you." Clarissa shifted her position, standing with her hands on her hips, no longer on the defensive, looking like an athlete ready to dart or drive wherever an opening presented itself. "Yes, we've made love. But we don't want to see that knowledge splashed across the front pages any more than you do. We are being very, very adult about this—very, very discreet. And, yes, we're lovers, but we're not plotting a life together. We are making sure that no one will be hurt."

She paused for breath.

"Tomorrow night, Sean's going back to Bermuda, back to his wife, for whom he has a responsibility that, I assure you, he does not take lightly. I don't know when we'll see each other again. I don't know *if* we'll see each other again. I do know that we won't be trying, in the meantime, to see each other in a way that might precipitate a scandal."

"Clarissa." Dwight Tyler took a step toward his daughter, out of impatience with her declarations. He was not a man accustomed to holding his peace. "I'm afraid I can't let you go on without remarking on a number of the points you've made. I've been very forbearing, I must say, to have let you go on for as long as I have." He cleared his throat, touched the knot of his necktie, and held his hands lightly clasped together in front of him—a series of gestures, Clarissa noted, that he made whenever he rose on the Senate floor to make a speech.

"You've got to understand what you're up against. He's had a detective keeping an eye on your friend."

187

"Who has?"

Dwight Tyler sighed. "Middlebrooks. The D.A."

"Ah," Clarissa said.

"I should've realized that. I'm sorry." It was Sean, standing in the doorway behind Clarissa. "Won't you come in, Senator Tyler? I'm Sean Howard."

As the two men shook hands, Clarissa stood back from them and wondered what she would have felt if she were introducing them under more conventional circumstances, if she had brought them together so that Sean could meet her father and so that her father could meet the man that she would very much like to marry. She thought she saw, even in these unconventional circumstances, a flash of respect in their eyes, based, she imagined, on the intuition that enables men to know something about other men from the strength of a handshake.

Clarissa's watch told her it was four o'clock in the morning. Outside the windows the sky was getting pale, the color of . . . She couldn't think the color of what. She was too tired.

Her father was tired, too. He sat in an easy chair, his legs stretched out before him, crossed at the ankles, his hands lightly clasped in front of him, resting on his stomach. He had taken off his jacket hours ago, and had hung it over the wing of the chair. He had loosened his tie and opened the collar of his white shirt. He looked,

Clarissa noted, as he looked on election nights, in his office on Capitol Hill, or at their house in McLean, Virginia, or at home in Louisville— wherever he had chosen to wait out the returns. He looked, as he looked on those nights, confident of the outcome, yet ready to accept the vicissitudes of the career he had chosen. "The difficulty with being a public official," her father liked to say, "is the highly unofficial behavior of the public."

Sean was tired, too. He sat on the edge of one of the silk banquettes, his elbows on his knees, studying the pattern of the carpet. He had taken off his blazer, too, hours before, and tossed it on one of the other banquettes. His sleeves were rolled midway up his forearms. His blond hair fell over his forehead. He looked, Clarissa thought, like an athlete who had just completed one of the most important contests of his career and now just needed to be alone, alone with his thoughts, alone with his aching body, alone with his own private sense of just who had won and who had lost.

At last, Sean looked up and smiled at Clarissa, who was leaning against the arched entryway to the dining room. She had been standing there for hours, it seemed—or had it only been minutes? He wasn't sure.

Clarissa smiled back.

"So you see, Mr. Howard," Dwight Tyler said, shifting a little in the easy chair, "while the matter has all shades of gray for you and Clarissa, for me it's a question of black and white. The way I look at it, the two of you have been having an adulterous affair. It if becomes public knowledge—and it will, I'm almost certain, if it continues—it will do irreparable damage not only to your own interests but to mine as well. My reputation, my candidacy, my party, a lifetime of work are on the line. I know the political game as well as any man in this country, and I'm telling you that the kind of scandal you're brewing—the heyday the media would make of it if it broke—would kill me."

Clarissa shivered. She looked at the weary, careworn face, usually so confident and glowing. She really looked at it, for the first time that night. Suddenly the full force of everything that was at stake—her father's career, Sean's already embattled reputation, Diana's future—hit her like a physical blow. Could she risk so much for love? Hadn't she and Sean already resigned themselves to indefinite separation? Why was she digging in her heels all of a sudden?

She just didn't know what was right anymore, didn't know how to sort out all her conflicting loyalties and desires. She heard her father's resonant voice going in the background—"grand jury . . . Middlebrooks . . . Rachel Owen . . ."—but it was no more than a droning blur. Besides, the real sense of what he was saying had already hit home—she and Sean were playing with fire, and it had to stop.

Suddenly, Sean had his hands on her shoulders. "He's right, Clarissa. You should leave now, with your father—as a bond, if you will, of our promise."

Clarissa tried to clear her thoughts. She shook her head and bit her lip and fought to keep from crying. So Sean had made the decision for both of them, and they were to be denied even their last night together. Finally, she took a deep breath and turned to face her father. "I'm going to get my things. But you please go downstairs now and wait for me in the lobby. I'll be down in ten minutes."

Dwight Tyler sighed, then looked deep into his daughter's eyes and saw how unhappy she was. "Take as long as you like."

"Just ten minutes," Clarissa said.

As she went into the bedroom, Dwight Tyler tightened the knot of his necktie and slipped on his suit coat. He stood ill at ease for a moment, then went to Sean, his hand out. "You're a decent man, Howard. I hope you don't think I believe otherwise. And God knows I sympathize with you. And I wish . . . Well, you're a man any man would be proud to have for a son-in-law. Maybe, if you believe in such things, it'll happen in another lifetime."

"I'm glad to have met you, Senator. I wish it had been under more congenial circumstances."

"And so do I," Tyler said feelingly. "You will never know how much I owe you." And clapping Sean awkwardly on the shoulder, he let himself out of the apartment.

Clarissa had come out of the bedroom and was standing in front of the gold framed mirror on the living room wall, pulling at her cheeks and the corners of her mouth with her fingers.

Sean laughed. "What're you doing?"

"Trying to see what I'll look like when I'm sixty," Clarissa said.

Sean laughed again and went to her and stood beside her, looking at their reflections in the mirror. "You'll look beautiful."

"And so will you—at sixty-eight," Clarissa said. "My brother—I told you about my brother, didn't I? We call him Frère—my brother's a very good amateur photographer. He told me something interesting about mirrors once. When you take a photograph in a mirror, you don't focus on the plane of the mirror, you focus on a point that's twice your distance from the mirror. We're—what?—four feet from the mirror, right? So if we were taking a photograph of ourselves in the mirror, we'd set the focus on eight feet. Do you see what that means?"

"It means we're *in* the mirror, somehow," Sean said.

"Yes. Isn't that amazing? And wouldn't it be wonderful if we were? Wouldn't it be wonderful if we—the 'we' in the mirror—could just turn away, now, turn away from us—the us here in the living room—could just turn away and join hands and walk off into . . . into whatever the rest of the world inside that mirror is like?"

"Yes. It would be wonderful."

They stood for a long while, looking into the mirror, wishing silently but simultaneously that it would happen; that the two people they saw in the mirror would stop looking back at them, finally, and would look at each other, and would turn their backs on them, and would join hands and walk out of sight, to go into the bedroom, to sleep for a while, to wake and make love, to have breakfast together, to plan their day, their life together.

Clarissa shut her eyes and held out a hand to Sean in a way that asked him to do the same.

Sean shut his eyes and took Clarissa's hand.

They stood very still for a moment, then turned toward each other, their eyes still shut, and embraced and kissed, a long, deep kiss that took their breath away. Then they opened their eyes and looked into each other's. They didn't have to tell each other not to look into the mirror.

"They're going," Clarissa said. "I can feel it."

"Yes," Sean said.

"Wish them luck," Clarissa said, as Sean said, "Wish them luck."

They smiled at each other.

"Good luck," Clarissa said.

"Good luck," Sean said.

"Good-bye," Clarissa said.

"Good-bye."

And she was gone, out the door and into the elevator and down to the lobby, where her father waited.

And Sean was alone. Yet he didn't feel alone. He felt accompanied, and he knew it was because what they wished had come true—that the couple in the mirror—the reflections of them—had gone off to have a life together, a life that they were denied. It was, he thought, better than nothing.

Chapter Fifteen

"Frankly," Sarah said, "that wasn't very good. It was"—she shrugged her shoulders—"dull, erratic, frivolous and generally inept."

Clarissa laid her violin on her lap and rubbed the back of her neck. "That bad, huh?"

"Worse, really, given how well you'd been playing it before. . . ."

"You can say it. Before Sean went away."

Sarah ducked her head. "Yes. I never told you this, but the night you played for Sean and Diana, after dinner, Abraham and I eavesdropped. We were in the kitchen, washing dishes, and we heard you through the window. We tiptoed down to the guest house and sat on the grass and listened. It was magnificent, truly magnificent."

Clarissa closed the sheet music of the Bach Chaconne and turned it face down on the music stand. "I'm too young. That's all there is to it. I should be playing Scarlatti. I should be playing Salieri. Something simple and simpleminded."

Sarah put a hand on Clarissa's shoulder. "I didn't mean to be so hard on you. It wasn't all that bad. It's only compared to what you were doing that it doesn't stack up."

"That was in another country," Clarissa said.

It was the middle of August. A month had passed since Clarissa left Sean's apartment in River House. More because she was so tired than because she had any enthusiasm for it, she had acceded to her father's insistence that she accompany him back to Louisville on a plane leaving La Guardia Airport at eight o'clock that morning. She had spent a week at her parents' home, trying to get a grip on herself, trying to keep from being sorry for herself, trying to remind herself that her goal in life was to get custody of Diana.

She succeeded, up to a point, but she was not entirely able to expunge from her mind a feeling —like Sean's feeling—that she was not alone in the world anymore, that she was accompanied. She knew—as Sean knew—that it was because what they wished for had come true—that the couple in the mirror—the reflections of them— had gone off to have a life together, a life that she and Sean were denied. Unlike Sean, however, Clarissa did not think that it was better than nothing. She thought that it was unspeakably sad.

Over her father's protest, Clarissa had returned to stay with Sarah and Abraham, insisting to him that she would be true to her word. Besides, she told him she had made a commitment to Sarah and Abraham and to herself to continue studying music. She would not renege on that commitment, whether the Newmans were neighbors of Sean Howard or not. He acquiesced when there was printed in the local newspaper a photograph of some Louisvillians vacationing in Bermuda and taking part in some social event at which Sean and Susannah Howard were present, he standing behind her wheelchair and smiling down at her.

Clarissa buried herself in music. She was up at dawn listening to recordings, studying books of theory, playing exercises and working on a number of pieces, among them the Bach Chaconne. She stopped only long enough for a light lunch, then took a lesson from Sarah, then practiced until dinner, which she often ate alone, then worked some more. She was in bed and asleep by ten P.M.. Everything she played, she played better and better each day. Except for the Bach Chaconne, which she played worse and worse.

She didn't go riding. She didn't go for walks. She grew pale and her hair lost its luster. She looked, Abraham said to Sarah, "like a ghost of herself, or as if she's seen one."

"She saw a man and loved him and now he's a ghost," Sarah said, "so why shouldn't she look ghastly?"

After dinner one night, chafing against her seclusion and obsessive involvement in her work, Clarissa decided that she just had to get out for a while. Like a driven creature, she set out across the grounds and through the trees separating the Newmans' estate from Sean Howard's, and across the grounds of Sean's estate to the stable. She was surprised at how long it took to make the walk. When Sean had been at his home, she felt as though she could reach out and touch him, that he was close enough to hear her every word, that any time she turned around she might see him standing there just a few feet away. Now that he was gone, his house seemed as far away as if it were in . . . in Bermuda.

Clarissa had seen the groom drive away in his van, and she knew no one would be around. She could visit the brindle mare, Maggie, without interruption, without creating a furor. She had seen Maggie only once since the mare had foundered and had been so depressed that she had been reluctant to go back. The mare had been lying on her side in the stall, for her feet were too painful to stand on. Her eyes had been nearly closed and her breathing was heavy with discomfort. Clarissa had wept.

Now, though, Maggie was better. During their last days together Sean had told her that the groom had been having the mare stand with her front feet in two tubs filled with hot water and Epsom salts. Her ears, which had been lying close to her head, stood upright and twitched attentively as Clarissa entered the stable, using the key Sean had given her. She was munching contentedly on some oats. Her eyes were bright and clear and her breathing was easy and uncongested. Clarissa smiled and patted her sleek coat. "Looking good, Maggie. Looking very good."

Maggie nickered happily. Her eyes said that she recognized Clarissa, and that she was glad to see her. When she had finished with the oats she took the carrot Clarissa offered and wolfed it down.

Clarissa turned over a bucket and sat on it against the wall in front of the stall, watching the horse, watching the horse watch her, wishing that the door to the stable would open and that Sean would come in, come to where she sat, and stand with a hand resting lightly on her head, not saying a word. But he didn't, and after a while she left.

"A penny for your thoughts," Sarah said.

Clarissa shook her head to clear away the memories. She was surprised to find that she was still sitting before the music stand, her violin on her lap, and that Sarah was still beside her in the kitchen. She would have said that hours had passed since she had finished playing. It depressed her that time moved so slowly. At that rate, she would never get to be sixty. "They're not worth a penny. They're not worth a wooden nickel."

Sarah inhaled, ready to say something, then thought better of it and let her breath out. She inhaled again, held her breath for a moment, then said, "Do you know John Keegan?"

"The French horn player?"

"Yup."

"I know of him. I have a recording of his. There's a wonderful piece on it by Dukas. But I don't know him. Why?"

"He's in town," Sarah said.

"Oh?"

"He lives in San Francisco, but he's come east to negotiate a new recording contract. He's also trying to drown the torch he's been carrying for a while. A ballet dancer. She ran off with the premier danseur."

"Sarah?"

"Yes?"

"Why're you telling me this?"

Sarah shrugged. "I just thought . . . I mean . . . Well, it seems that you *are* back in circulation."

Clarissa smiled sadly. "I love you, yenta that you are. And I appreciate your interest in my well-being. Even if I were back in circulation, however, I don't think I'd be interested in a man on the rebound. Men on the rebound aren't choice."

"Well, if you don't want a date with John Keegan, whom would you like a date with? We know lots of interesting men."

"I said, *if* I were back in circulation," Clarissa said.

"When do you think that will be, exactly?" Sarah said. "Or even roughly."

Clarissa shook her head. "I don't know. I wouldn't be surprised if it were a couple of years."

"That long," Sarah said. "I don't think that's a good idea. I know I don't really know what it's like to be in your shoes, but I think that if I were in your shoes I'd get back in it sooner than that. You don't want your vital fluids to dry up."

"Really, Sarah."

"I mean it. The emotions are like anything else. They need to be kept in constant use or they dry up. They get rusty. They get moldy and covered with cobwebs."

Clarissa laughed. "Block that metaphor."

Sarah got up and slid her chair under the

kitchen table. "Just remember, we know lots of interesting men. And whether you like it or not, John Keegan's coming for dinner tomorrow. You don't have to be here, of course. You can have bread and water in the attic, if you like, but—"

"I'd like to meet him," Clarissa said. "He's a wonderful musician. But don't get too pushy. Don't go leaving us alone by the fire or anything."

Sarah spread a hand innocently on her chest. "A fire? In this weather?"

The dinner was pleasant. John Keegan was pleasant—handsome, lithe, smaller than he looked in the photographs on the jackets of his record albums. He was witty and a good story-teller, self-confident without being egotistical, a good and appreciative listener. He was a man whom Clarissa in the past would have liked to get to know. The Clarissa of the present was glad to meet him, felt privileged to be in his presence, appreciated his humor and his wisdom. But that was all. She wondered if her emotions had already become the thing Sarah had suggested—dried up, rusty, moldy, and covered with cobwebs. She knew deep down, though, that was not the case. Her emotions were ripe and ready, but they were engaged already.

One reason John Keegan had come to New York was to explore the possibility of mounting a Broadway show. He had written a play—not quite a musical, but not quite a straight play, either—about a chamber orchestra rehearsing for the opening night of a Broadway show about a chamber orchestra rehearsing for the opening night of a Broadway show, and so on. He had a meeting scheduled the next day with a potential producer.

"Stephanie Chonin. Do any of you know her?" Keegan asked.

"I've heard of her," Abraham said. "I think I may have met her at a party somewhere. In the Hamptons, maybe. Do you remember, Sarah?"

"Does she have red hair?" Sarah said.

"Reddish."

"Then I don't remember."

Keegan laughed. "I thought I was going to have to hang around until next week to see her. She's been in Bermuda working with a playwright on a production she was planning for the spring. But her office phoned and said she was going to be in town tomorrow and had some time free to see me. Seems the deal she was working on fell through."

The significant glances his three companions had exchanged had not escaped him. "Did I say something wrong?"

"Not wrong," Abraham said. "It's just that we know the playwright in question. Susannah Howard. She's our next-door neighbor. It's a bit of a bombshell to hear that her deal has been queered."

"It just happened today," Keegan said. "It wasn't my place to ask for details. I just assumed it was one of those things that happens all the time in show business. Creative differences, it'll probably say in *Variety*."

Sarah deftly changed the subject and it stayed changed through dessert. While Clarissa did the dishes, Sarah came up behind her and put her hands on Clarissa's shoulders. "Are you all right?"

"I guess so. I'm sorry for her—for Susannah Howard. What a disappointment that must be—to have a dream just fall apart like that."

"There are other producers," Sarah said.

Clarissa dried her hands and leaned against the sink. "You remember, though, how hard it was for you when you were starting out. When you couldn't get a management company to represent you. There were other management companies, sure, but the fact that you'd been rejected by the first ones you tried was held against you. It was as though you'd been blackballed."

"I stuck it out, though," Sarah said. "And I finally got signed up. And it's been all sideways ever since."

Clarissa smiled. "Not quite sideways. You're the cream of the crop. I just finished the article about you in the Sunday *Times*."

"That was a nice article, wasn't it? I think the writer liked my breasts. I wore something low cut, over Abraham's protest. He thinks we don't need sex appeal, but I think he's wrong."

Sarah went to join the men in the living room and Clarissa finished doing the dishes. Tears rolled down her cheeks and fell into the dishwater. She was genuinely sorry for Susannah Howard and genuinely glad for her that Sean was with her during this time of tribulation. Feeling sorry and glad at the same time made her cry.

Sean went up the stairs three at a time. Approaching the house after finishing his morning swim, he had felt that something was wrong. He couldn't have said what. He couldn't have said why he felt it. But feel it he did, and he acted on his feeling, breaking into a run, leaping up onto the porch without using the steps, bursting through the front door and going up the stairs three at a time. The elevator—it was one like the elevator in the house in Connecticut—was on the second floor, so he knew that that was where Susannah was. But she wasn't in her room. Nor was she in the sun-filled room that she used as a workroom, the room in which she and Stephanie Chonin had worked for such long hours during the past weeks, trying to shape Susannah's play into what Stephanie Chonin called "box office."

Sean glanced in his bedroom, though he knew for a certainty that Susannah would not be in there. And she wasn't. The only other room on the second floor was the bathroom.

Susannah was slumped on the floor before her wheelchair, unconscious. Around her were the shards of a broken glass tumbler and some small pools of water. In the sink were two empty pill bottles.

Sean cut his foot on a shard of glass as he stepped around the wheelchair and bent to pick Susannah up. He didn't feel a thing. He sat Susannah in the wheelchair and put his fingers in her mouth and tried to make her vomit. She gagged reflexively, but her eyelids stirred. She shifted in his arms, moaning, then came back farther toward consciousness from the place she had been. The vomit, when it came, was watery and gushed onto Sean's chest and onto the white duck pants Susannah wore on her helpless legs. Sean put his fingers in her mouth again, and again she vomited. And again. The third time, there was bile in the vomit, which meant that her stomach was cleaned out. But who knew what had already been absorbed in her system? Sean lifted Susannah from the chair and carried her out of the bathroom, stopping, as an afterthought, and returning to pick up the pill bottles from the sink, pocketing them in his bathing suit. Retracing his steps, he saw blood on the floor and realized that it was from the cut on his foot.

Sean carried Susannah downstairs and out the side door to where his Mercedes—a twin of the one he drove in Connecticut—was parked. He laid Susannah on the backseat, making a pillow of a towel he had left in the car the day before, after a round of tennis at the Racquet Club. He drove at top speed to the hospital, covering the ten miles in eight minutes, terrifying some tourists on motor bikes and nearly forcing a battered blue truck full of farm workers off the road. A policeman on a motorcycle gave chase over the last half mile, but when he saw that Sean was turning into the hospital, he put two and two together and rode on, giving Sean a wave of good luck.

Two attendants had a stretcher ready almost before Sean had opened the rear door of the Mercedes. He stood aside as they got Susannah on the stretcher and quickly wheeled her into the hospital. A young doctor bent over

Susannah, conducting a preliminary exam in motion.

Sean held out the pill bottles. "She took these."

The doctor glanced at the bottles, but didn't read the labels. "Stelazine?"

"Yes. I guess." Sean read the labels. "Yes."

"How many pills?" the doctor asked. He had an accent of some British Commonwealth country—South Africa or Australia or New Zealand. Sean had played rugby with South Africans and Australians and New Zealanders and recognized the harsh nasals.

"I don't know."

"You her husband?"

"Yes."

"Wait in there," the doctor said, pointing to a room off the corridor down which they moved.

"But . . ."

"Please wait in there, mate," the doctor said. "There's nothing you can do right now. Don't worry. She's in good hands."

As they kept moving down the hall, Sean called after them. "I made her vomit. Three times. There was bile in the third vomit."

"Well done, mate," the doctor called back.

New Zealand, Sean thought. Like . . . What was the name of that New Zealand scrim half? Nigel something. Nigel . . . Hewitt.

"You've cut your foot," a pretty blonde nurse said as Sean came through the door.

"It's nothing."

"I'll be the judge of that," the nurse said and pointed at a plastic chair against the wall. "Just sit yourself down there and I'll have a look."

She was an American, or perhaps a Canadian. Her name tag said MAUREEN WRIGHT. She had cool, gentle hands. "My, my."

"It's nothing, really," Sean said.

"We won't have to amputate, if that's what you mean," the nurse said. "But we'll need something more than a Band-Aid."

The cut needed three stitches, by which time word had come back from the Emergency Room that Susannah was conscious and out of danger.

"Dr. Sharrock's our best doctor," the nurse said. "Your wife is very lucky he was on duty."

Sean could tell that the nurse was in love with Dr. Sharrock. He could understand it. The doctor was handsome, athletic, competent. He hoped the doctor loved the nurse. She was pretty and efficient. He hoped everybody in the world was loved in return by those whom they loved.

Sean began to shiver from the cool of the air conditioning, and the nurse brought him a green scrub suit to put on. "Don't go performing any operations, now. Just sit quietly."

Sean smiled and sat in a plastic chair with his foot propped up on another, leaning his head back against the wall. For the first time, his mind formed the concept that Susannah had attempted suicide, had tried to kill herself.

Things between Susannah and Stephanie Chonin had gone badly from the start. Stephanie Chonin had her fingers in any number of pies, and she had spent a great deal of time on the telephone dealing with other matters. Susannah could only wait for her to finish with her business, and Susannah was not good at waiting. Though she was young, Stephanie Chonin had been in show business for a long time, and she was full of anecdotes, of which she seemed to feel a need to unburden herself before she could get down to matters at hand. They were amusing anecdotes, by and large, but Susannah had not been in a mood to listen to quite so many of them, quite so often. And Stephanie Chonin had a commercial instinct that made her uneasy about, if not downright unsympathetic to certain aspects of Susannah's play—aspects that she called "writerish."

"This is fine. This is great. But it's writerish," Sean had once heard Stephanie Chonin tell Susannah about a scene in the play. "Trust me when I tell you that audiences don't respond to things that're writerish. They want spectacle, drama—things that come from your gut, not from your mind."

Susannah had protested: "But spectacle and drama are *written*, aren't they?"

"Sure they are. Susannah, honey, I'm not saying we could have plays if there were no writers. No such luck. I'm just saying that you have to write with guts. Critics don't like writerish plays, either, you should know. They tend to doze off. Gutsy plays keep them wide-eyed and bushy-tailed."

And finally, there had been problems with the play's key investors, who when they had finally read the play to which they had made a commitment based on Stephanie Chonin's description, had found it to be deficient in the ingredients they regarded as essential to commercial success. A play about a young couple whose idealism ran aground on the rocks of reality was fine, but not if that was all it was about. It needed—to be commercially successful—more sexual tension. For example, one investor wondered if the man, instead of throwing himself into his work after the tragic death of the couple's child, might have a torrid affair with a woman beneath his station—an exotic dancer, say, or even a prostitute. Stephanie Chonin thought that was a great idea.

"Sean would never have done anything like that," Susannah had said.

"Forget about Sean," Stephanie Chonin had said. "This is fiction. Make things up. Forget about the truth. The truth may be very interesting to the people involved, but it's not box office."

Susannah had remained steadfast. The key investors had thrown up their hands and torn up their pledges. Stephanie Chonin had tried to interest other investors, but there had been no takers. She had finally said that she was dropping out of the project. That had been the day before. Sean had driven her to the airport.

"Your wife is very talented," Stephanie Chonin had said. "For a first play—the first draft of a first play, really, it was very sophisticated. But it needs a great deal of work, and she's not willing to make the necessary compromises. In many ways, she's like the protagonist —idealistic, stubborn, and finally, self-destructive. Don't you agree?"

"I haven't read the play," Sean said.

Stephanie Chonin made her eyes wide, then

nodded with understanding. "I don't suppose you have. You don't come off badly, though— that is, the character who could be said to be you isn't an unsympathetic character. In fact, he's much more sympathetic than the guy the heroine has an affair with. He's . . . Well, maybe I shouldn't say anything more."

Sean fought off a desire to know more about the man. Had he really existed? Had he truly been a rival? "No. I don't think you should."

Stephanie Chonin offered her hand. She wore rings on every finger and three bracelets on each wrist. "You're an interesting man. Your dedication to caring for your wife is quite remarkable. I suppose it's vulgar of me to say this, but . . . well . . . if you ever find yourself back in circulation, give me a call."

In his car, driving back to the house, Sean had smiled sadly at his reflection in the rearview mirror. That he was attractive to women was something that rarely occurred to him. That he might ever be back in circulation—he had never really been in circulation at all, given that he had married so young—was not something he ever thought about. He was committed—to the care of Susannah and to the company of the woman whose reflection abided with his in the mirror on the wall of the River House apartment.

"You can see your wife now. But only for about five minutes." It was the pretty blonde nurse. She was on her way off duty and had changed into street clothes.

Sean realized that he had been in a half-sleep

—not dreaming, just remembering the events of the past few weeks. He stood tentatively on his wounded foot. "This feels better already."

The pretty nurse handed him a wooden cane. "Use this for a few days to keep your weight off it. And don't do anything rash. No marathons, or anything like that."

"I wouldn't even consider it," Sean said.

Susannah seemed to have shrunken. She looked like a child, curled up on the big white bed.

"Do you think I'm a fool?" she said when she saw Sean standing beside her.

"No."

"Do you think I'm crazy?"

"No."

"What do you think?"

Sean put a hand on her shoulder. It felt hard and cold, even through the sheets. "I think you overreacted to a disappointment. A big disappointment, I'll admit, but not the end of the world. There're other producers."

"They'll want the same kind of changes," Susannah said. "I'm not prepared to make them. I wrote the play to say something about me. In that sense, I wrote it for myself. I'm its best audience. I don't require changes. Maybe I'm the only audience it's intended to have."

"On some level, the play is successful," Sean said. "Stephanie is the first to admit that. That's why she got involved in the first place. Write another play, using the talent that made this one successful to the degree that it is, but also making it the kind of play that people are likely to put up money to produce, and pay money to see. You can't simply ignore the commercial requirements. They're a fact of the art form you've chosen to work in. Put this play in a drawer. All writers I've ever read about or talked to have a play or a novel or short stories or poems in a drawer. It seems to be necessary —required, even. Maybe some day you'll come back to it, and change it, make it better. It can only benefit from your maturity, from your experience with other plays."

Susannah's eyes were dull. She didn't seem to be hearing what he was saying. "While you were driving Stephanie to the airport yesterday, Bill Middlebrooks called."

Sean's neck hairs bristled. "For me?"

"For me. He said you'd been seeing that woman while you were in New York."

Sean wanted to shout, *And what about you? Was there a time when you saw him? Fucked him? Is that true, Susannah? Did you have an affair with him? Are you still?* "Goddamn him! I'm not trying to undercut your anger. I'm not trying to make it seem that it's his fault that you found out. I know it's my fault. But it pisses me off that he'd call you. Not only that, I don't think it's ethical. I'm under investigation by his goddamn grand jury."

Susannah shook her head slowly, as if to say none of that mattered. "I wanted you to see her."

" . . . Wanted?"

"I know you'd be annoyed at me for not coming with you while you testified. I know you'd turn to her—and that she'd be there for you. I wanted that."

Sean shook his head. "I don't understand."

212

"I've been nothing but a burden to you, Sean. I've exploited your kindness, and I'm ashamed of that."

"I haven't done anything I haven't wanted to do."

"I know you believe that, but it's not true. You knew very early in our marriage that we weren't right for each other, but you hung in there. You gave me a child in the hope it would make things better—and it might have, but it didn't. When I tried to go back to work, you helped me. After the accident, you took care of me. You've been taking care of me. But it isn't what you've wanted to do. You haven't wanted any of it. And I think it's time you got free of me, lived your own life, found a woman you really love, made more babies."

Sean brushed the hair away from her forehead. "Don't worry, Susannah. I'll never leave you."

Susannah wept. "How can you be so good?"

A dour nurse put her head in the door and said that Sean would have to go.

"I'll be back this evening," he said, bending to kiss Susannah's cheek. "Is there anything you want from home?"

"Where did you get that outfit?" Susannah said.

"I was getting cold in my bathing suit. A nurse gave me this."

"Why do you have a cane?"

"I cut my foot on a piece of glass."

"God, I'm clumsy," Susannah said, and draped an arm over her eyes.

Chapter Sixteen

The grand jury indicted fifteen men on a variety of charges. Sean was not among them. After reading the story in the *Times* about the indictments, Clarissa did a dance of joy around the kitchen. She decided to go visit Maggie. If she could not share the good news with Sean, she could at least share it with his horse.

The groom was not around. Clarissa knew that he worked elsewhere in the mornings, and that he would not be at Sean's stable until the afternoon. She let herself into the stable and sat on an overturned water bucket in front of the mare's stall.

"We did it. We did it, we did it, we did it." Clarissa clapped her hands gleefully. "Take that, Mr. District Attorney. You jerk."

A car came up the driveway. Clarissa's heart pounded. The groom was friendly enough, but she didn't want him to find her there. Maybe it wasn't the groom. Maybe it was Sean. Her heart nearly stopped. No. It couldn't be Sean. Could it?

She got up and peeked through the window of the stable. It was a blue compact car. She didn't know the make. A man got out. A small middle-aged man in a rumpled gray suit. He was balding, but combed his hair to conceal it, thereby calling attention to it. He went to the back door and opened it and went inside. He hadn't used a key. He'd used something from a small leather case he'd taken from the pocket of his suit coat.

"A pick? A burglar?" Clarissa went to the phone that hung on a wall of the stable and put her hand on it. The staff was on vacation. The house was ripe for picking. Then she took her head away. Something—she didn't know what—told her the man wasn't a burglar. Something else—she didn't know what—made her think she knew what the man was up to. She went to the brindle mare and rubbed her nose. "Sorry I can't stay, Maggie, but something's up. I'll tell you all about it the next time I see you." Then she slipped out the door of the stable and locked it. She went around the rear of the stable into some trees and made her way along a rise of ground that hid her from the house. When she reached the Newmans' estate, she ran.

Sarah was in the kitchen, making a cup of tea. "Been walking? It's a beautiful morn—"

"I'm taking the Toyota. Where's the key?"

"In the car. But I need it. I have to go to—"

"Take the Jeep."

"Abraham took the Jeep. Where're—"

"I'll phone you." And Clarissa was gone.

Sarah stared after her open-mouthed.

"Jesus," she finally breathed, shaking her head in wonder.

Clarissa parked the Toyota in a grove of trees by the side of the road below Sean's driveway. She waited twenty minutes before the blue compact came down the driveway and drove past her. She counted to ten, got as far as six, then started after it.

She followed the blue compact to New York. It was a beautiful morning and traffic was light. Clarissa enjoyed the driving. She had driven only a little—to the store and back, or to the station to pick up Sarah or Abraham if either of them had gone into the city. She hadn't driven on a parkway since she had lived in Washington with Peter, a hundred years ago. As she drove, she hummed the Bach Chaconne.

Traffic in Manhattan was heavier, and it took almost as long to get downtown as it had to reach the city limits. The blue compact parked in a garage near City Hall and Clarissa parked the Toyota there, too. She followed the balding man into an office building and into an elevator and rode with him to the twenty-second floor. He went into the office of District Attorney William Middlebrooks.

"Bingo," Clarissa said to herself, and took the elevator back down to the lobby. She found a pay phone and called the *New York Post*.

"Penelope Hammill," she said when the switchboard answered.

The voice was brusque. "Penny Hammill," it said.

"Clarissa Leeds," Clarissa said just as brusquely.

"Who? Oh. Yeah. Hey, what can I do for you?"

"You want a story?"

"Sure. Hey, what happened? You and Sean Howard getting married?"

"You know where the D.A.'s office is? Middle-brooks's office?"

"Sure. What's up?"

"Meet me in the lobby. Make it fast. Oh, and can you track down a license number for me?"

Penelope Hammill laughed. "What's this, anyway? A 'Kojak' rerun?"

"There's nothing amusing about this, I assure you," Clarissa said urgently. She recited the blue compact's license number, which she'd memorized. "That's a New York license. Have somebody check it out for you while you get over here. You can call in once you're here."

Penelope Hammill laughed again. "Yes, ma'am."

The *Post* was nearby, on South Street, and Penelope Hammill made the trip in ten minutes. "Hey, I'm glad there are no hard feelings about that item I ran. But news is news, you know!"

"There'll always be hard feelings," Clarissa said. "But maybe this is a chance to atone for that."

"Atone?" she said. "No one's suggested I atone for anything since I graduated from Our Lady Queen of Martyrs."

"It's never too late," Clarissa said, and she told Penelope Hammill about the balding man.

"You tailed him all the way from Connecti-cut?" the reporter asked incredulously.

Clarissa shrugged. "Beginner's luck."

"I'll say. The times I've tried to tail someone I've either lost them inside of ten blocks or I've run into them and sort of advertised my presence."

"Call your office," Clarissa said. "See if they've got anything on that license plate."

"Aye, aye," Penelope responded, but there was an appraising look in her eye as she surveyed Clarissa that hadn't been there before. She called her office and found that the car was licensed to a Richard Singleton.

"Well, what do you know?" Penelope Hammill said. "I thought it might be old Dick from your description."

"You know him, then?"

"He's an investigator in Middlebrooks's office. Licensed to snoop. He's a decent guy, I guess. He does his job well. So what do you think?"

"I think," Clarissa said, "that having failed to get an indictment against Sean Howard out of the grand jury, Middlebrooks is trying to get something on him some other way. I think your friend Singleton either took something from Sean's house or left something that, if found, would make Sean look very bad."

"Why would he do that?" Penelope Hammill said. "Not Singleton—who's hardly a friend, by the way. Why would Middlebrooks do that?"

"He's ambitious," Clarissa said.

"He is that."

"He's also . . . Well, I can't prove this, but it's something I feel—"

"A woman's intuition?" Penelope Hammill said.

Clarissa smiled. "Yes . . . I think Middlebrooks is having, or once had, an affair with Sean's wife."

Penelope Hammill waggled her eyebrows. "So he'd like Sean Howard, so to speak, out of the picture?"

"So to speak," Clarissa said.

"And what do you think Singleton left at Howard's house? Or took?"

"Let's ask him," Clarissa said.

Penelope Hammill laughed. "Us? We?"

Clarissa shrugged. "You ask him. You're the reporter. I can pretend to be, if you want, but why resort to that when I've got you?"

"You really do have me, don't you?"

"I thought you'd be interested in a story, that's all."

Penelope noticed what Clarissa had learned long ago to pay no mind to, namely, that Clarissa was a magnet for the eye of every man who was passing through the lobby of the office building. Penelope Hammill was beautiful in her own way—she had a pert and perky Irish face and a small, wiry body—and the two of them were causing a great deal of commotion. "Before we rush into the fray, what do you say we have a Coke or an iced tea and talk things over? I feel sort of on display around here."

"Fine," Clarissa said.

They went into a coffee shop off the building's lobby and sat in a booth. Penelope ordered a black iced coffee, Clarissa an iced tea.

"You know, my friend Jim Morgan still has a thing for you," Penelope said. "He told me about your violin contest. You really set him on his ear—musically and otherwise. I'm surprised he hasn't pitched a tent on your doorstep or something. Jim's usually very intense when someone catches his eye."

"He may have pitched a tent," Clarissa said. "I haven't been around much."

"So I heard." Penelope leaned her forearms on the table and spoke conspiratorially. "It's true, then?"

"What's true?" Clarissa said.

"That you and Sean Howard are—" she waggled one hand in the air, "you know . . . friendly."

"We're friends, yes."

Penelope Hammill laughed. "Come on, Clarissa. May I call you Clarissa? If we're going to work together, you're going to have to be a little bit forthcoming. I heard that you and Sean Howard had quite a thing going, back when he was testifying before Middlebrooks's grand jury."

"From whom did you hear that?" Clarissa asked.

Penelope Hammill laughed. "My lips, unfortunately, are sealed."

"Come on, Penelope," Clarissa said. "May I call you Penelope?"

"Penny, please."

"Well, Penny, if we're going to work together, *you're* going to have to be a little bit forthcoming."

"Touché," Penny responded. She sat back for a moment and looked around, then leaned forward again. "Middlebrooks was peddling that rumor. Not in person, but through one of his flunkies."

221

" 'Peddling'?"

"The 'flunky' called me and asked me if I'd be interested in a bit of gossip about one of the grand jury witnesses—namely, Sean Howard. I said sure and he said before he'd tell me he wanted my assurance that I'd print it."

"Do you do things like that?" Clarissa said.

Penelope Hammill made a sour face. "Never. Which is what I told him. He said in that case he'd peddle it elsewhere. I said good luck. A couple of hours later he called back and said he'd decided he'd give me the gossip without a promise that I'd use it."

"Meaning he hadn't been able to peddle it elsewhere," Clarissa said.

"Precisely. He said the gossip was that Sean Howard was having a fling with the widow of a United States senator. I said you mean Clarissa Leeds and he said yes. I said that's it? He said don't you like it? I said I didn't see what it had to do with anything—anything connected with the grand jury, that is."

"Good for you," Clarissa said.

Penelope Hammill shrugged. "I don't know about that."

"You didn't print it, did you?" Clarissa asked.

Penelope Hammill held up her hands innocently. "What do I look like—a rumor monger?"

"I'm just surprised, that's all."

"That I have ethics? Lots of people have. It's a valuable tool. People tell me things they think I'll want to hear and then I get to decide whether I want to use them or not. If people thought I was scrupulous, I'd miss out on a lot of good info! So, Clarissa, is it true? You were

222

tête-à-tête the night of the blackout, you know."

Clarissa sipped iced tea through a straw and thought for a moment. She needed an ally—there was no question about that—and Penelope Hammill was a formidable one, indeed. But could she be trusted? Face to face, there was a straightforwardness and decency to her that Clarissa would never have imagined possible based on her columns alone. Besides, wasn't this a gamble she just had to take?

So, Clarissa told her everything—about Acapulco; about the night of the blackout; about the times in Connecticut and the times in town; and finally about Sean's irrevocable commitment to Susannah, her own devotion to Diana, and the solemn promise they both had made to Dwight Tyler.

When she had finished, Penny said, "God! What a story. You should write a book about it. It'd be a best-seller. You'd make a fortune."

Clarissa, who had been tearing her napkin into strips while she talked, arranged the strips into a neat pile in front of her on the formica tabletop.

"I understand," Penny said. "You'd rather the story had a happy ending. To hell with the fortune, right?"

"Right," Clarissa said.

Penny rubbed her hands together briskly. "So. What do we do next? I mean, if what you think is true—that Middlebrooks is trying to pin something on Sean Howard, trying to get something on him the grand jury couldn't, well, that's not just a story; that's a front-page story with a very large headline."

"I thought you might think so," Clarissa said. She slumped a little in the booth and looked at Penny sadly. "I don't know what we do next. Now that the adrenaline's worn off a little, it doesn't seem possible to do anything. I mean, we can't just walk into Middelbrooks's office—or even into Singleton's."

"True. But they don't spend all their time in the office. Particularly, Singleton doesn't spend all his time in his office. In fact, he spends a great deal of time in the Lion's Head. You know it?"

"I know it's a bar in the Village. A writers' hangout."

"Yeah, it has a reputation as a writers' hangout, but it's really a hangout for people who like to think they're writers, and like to think that other people who think they're writers think they're writers, if you follow me. Singleton thinks he's a writer. He's actually written a book, unlike most of the Lion's Head regulars . . . a book about his days as an FBI agent. I think it was remaindered the day it was published. I haven't read it. I wouldn't subsidize the worm."

"Penny?" Clarissa said.

"Yeah?"

"Get to the point."

"The point, Clarissa, is that Singleton likes to drink and he likes to talk. He particularly likes to drink with and talk to pretty women, of which, if I do say so myself, we are two. So what we do next, I propose, is wait until he's off work and get over to the Lion's Head and buy Singleton a drink or two and listen to him talk.

He knows me, of course, so he won't spill everything, but he might spill a little more to you, if I were to spot a friend at the bar and go off to chat with him for a while, leaving you two to get better acquainted."

She leaned back to get a better look at Clarissa. "He may know you from photographs, of course, but you look to me like the sort who can transform yourself with a hat and a pair of dark glasses, without doing damage to the basic allure, of course. What I propose is that you go to my apartment for the rest of the afternoon. It's at Eighty-third and East End. Rest up. Send out for a bite to eat. If there's anything in my refrigerator, it's probably something that can talk and do simple mathematical calculations. You'll find some hats in the bedroom closet and several pairs of sunglasses in the dresser. I'll go back to work and meet you at the Lion's Head around seven o'clock. Take a cab, I think. A car'll just be a bother. Leave yours in my garage. We'll see what we shall see. How does that sound to you, partner?"

Clarissa smiled. "It sounds terrific."

Penny shrugged. "Yeah, well, sometimes things like this look great on paper, but smell in the flesh. For all we know, Singleton might bring some chippy along with him. For all we know, it might be his bowling night. But it's worth a shot."

"It's worth a shot," Clarissa agreed, "partner."

It *was* Singleton's bowling night . . . or his poker night . . . or his night to visit his mother. At any rate, he wasn't at the Lion's Head. Not that night. He was there the next night, however, and he nibbled enthusiastically at the bait they dangled.

"Middlebrooks has gone off the deep end," Singleton said. "You know what I mean?"

"Not exactly," Penny said. "Do you know what he means, Diana?"

Clarissa nearly forgot that Diana was the name she had chosen to go by—Diana Tyler, a friend of Penelope Hammill's from Washington. She shook her head. "Nope."

Singleton peered under the brim of the big straw hat Clarissa had taken from Penny's closet and tried to see through the dark glasses she had borrowed from her.

"You never told me you had such pretty friends, Penny."

"Likes attract," Penny shrugged. "Off the deep end, how, Dick?"

Singleton smoothed the strands of hair that covered his bald spot and gave Clarissa what was meant to be a suggestive look. "Maybe we could, uh, go someplace a little quieter later? Just the two of us. No offense, Penny, but I assume you have got something cooking."

"You know me, Dick, I'm booked up till the end of the decade. But before you run off, I'd like to hear a little more about Mr. Middlebrooks. Off the record, of course."

Singleton looked around the room, then made circles in the air with a finger next to his ear. "You know what I mean?"

"He's insane?" Clarissa said.

Singleton laughed indulgently and tried to see between the buttons of Clarissa's pale blue silk blouse. "Not certifiably. But it's the only explanation. Unless . . ."

"Unless what, Dick?" Penny said. She toyed with the top button of her cherry red silk blouse and ended up leaving it open.

Singleton tried to arrange his face and look her straight in the eye. Then he shrugged. "He's under a lot of pressure to bring this construction industry thing off. If he doesn't, he's up shit's creek without a paddle." He started, and touched Clarissa's hand solicitously. "Forgive the language, Diana, darling. It's just, well, around the office people tend to talk like it was an army barracks."

Clarissa retrieved her hand and put it in her lap. "Pressure from whom?"

Singleton looked at Penelope Hammill. " 'Whom'? Your friends say 'whom'? This I didn't know about you, Penny."

"As I explained, Dick," she said, "Diana here writes for the *Washingtonian*. It's a D.C. version of *New York Magazine*. She covers the art and classical music beat. She's very cultured."

Singleton smoothed his strands of hair. "I like a woman with culture."

Penny sat up straight. "Well, I'll be. Isn't that Tom Schactman?" She waved at someone at the bar and explained to Clarissa, "Tom's an old friend. I haven't seen him in years. He just published a book about Woodrow Wilson. I really should go congratulate him. I wish I'd read it.

227

It's on my coffee table, at least. Either of you know anything about Woodrow Wilson so I can sound knowledgeable?"

"Not me," Singleton said.

Clarissa shook her head.

Penelope pushed her chair back and stood up. "Oh, well. I've winged it before, I can wing it again. Please excuse me. I'll only be a minute." And she went off, her arms open. "Tom, Tom, Tom."

Singleton leaned close to Clarissa. "So, Diana. Tell me about yourself."

Clarissa indulged him in vapid and flirtatious pleasantries for a while, all the time adroitly leading the conversation back to the real matter at hand.

"Middlebrooks isn't married, is he?" she finally said once she'd gotten him on to the subject of his work and his clearly less-than-beloved boss.

Singleton sat back heavily. "Oh, no. Don't tell me you got a thing for him, too!"

" 'Too'?"

Singleton sighed. "He's one of those guys who looks at a girl and she flops for him. Pardon the expression, Di."

"What kind of girls?" Clarissa said.

"All kinds; tall, short, stacked, not-so-stacked; blondes, brunettes, redheads."

"Married women?" Clarissa said.

Singleton shrugged. "I guess."

"You don't guess, Dick. You know."

Singleton played with the ashtray.

"I'll tell you what," Clarissa said. "I don't want you to tell me anything you don't want to, but if I'm right about one of the women who . . . flopped for Middlebrooks, will you at least tell me if I'm right?''

"Hey, what is all this? What are you after?" Singleton asked suddenly.

Desperately determined not to overplay her hand, Clarissa forced her voice to become languorous, nonchalant. "Let's just say," she purred, "that I have my very good reasons, and I could be *very* nice to anyone who helped me satisfy my girlish curiosity."

Singleton watched, mesmerized, as she slowly began to stroke the side of her neck.

He was completely undone. At that point, he would have sold his mother down the river to "satisfy" this female. Clearing his throat, he said, "Well, let's have it. Which particular name do you have in mind?"

"Susannah Howard," Clarissa said in a totally uninflected voice.

Singleton shot looks over both shoulders at once, it seemed to Clarissa, so quickly did he do it. "You don't mean Susannah Howard, Sean Howard's wife? The real estate guy? The guy who's putting up that building at Times Square? Le Tower?"

"La Tour," Clarissa corrected him.

Singleton cocked his head. "The way you said that, I'd say you speak French. Is that so, Di?"

"A little," Clarissa said.

"I like a woman who speaks some foreign languages!"

"About Middlebrooks and Susannah Howard, Dick . . ."

Singleton smoothed his strands of hair. "A

couple of years ago—I don't remember how many . . . must've been five or six—I went up to Middlebrooks's apartment one weekend to do some work. He lived in River House, over by the FDR. You know the place?"

"Yes, I know the place," Clarissa said.

"What a place! The views had views! You could see all the way to fucking Montauk, just about. Pardon the expression, Di. Anyway, there we were, working away, and the doorbell rings. I mean, it's not the kind of place where people come around selling magazine subscriptions, if you know what I mean. I figured it must be a neighbor. Middlebrooks didn't answer it. I said, 'You want me to?' And he said, 'No thanks,' or words to that effect. 'They'll go away.' I noticed how he said 'they.' A lot of times, people don't want you to know if it's a man or a woman they're talking about, they'll say 'they' when what you'd expect is that they'd say him or her. You ever notice that, Di?"

Clarissa nodded. "So it was a woman."

"Well, the doorbell kept ringing and ringing, like whoever it was knew he was home and wasn't going to take no for an answer, and finally Middlebrooks got up and went out to see who it was—or, I guess you could say, to see what the fuck she wanted. We were working in the dining room. My coat was in the front hall. I was dying for a smoke. I thought it was a good time to have one, only my coat was in the hall. So I went out and got my cigarettes and there was Middlebrooks having this real intense like whispered argument with this woman—"

"Susannah Howard," Clarissa interjected, her pulse quickening.

"Well, I didn't know at the time it was Susannah Howard. I didn't know Susannah Howard from Mata Hari at the time. But a couple of years later, I read the paper about how Sean Howard and his wife got clobbered by a drunk driver out on the Island. Her picture was in the paper, and it clicked with me that she was the woman Middlebrooks had been arguing with, the woman who rang the shit out of the doorbell. She lived in River House, too, her and her husband. I figured she and Middlebrooks were . . . you know."

"But they're not still?"

Singleton shrugged. "I couldn't say, except . . ."

"Except what, Dick?"

" . . . Well, I walked into Middlebrooks's office the other day—that's the kind of place it is; nobody's door is closed to anybody else, not even the boss's—and the boss is on the phone talking long distance. I knew it was long distance 'cause he was talking real loud, like maybe it was overseas or something, and what he was saying was, 'But I still love you, Susannah.' " He shrugged. "I mean, I wasn't eavesdropping or anything, I just wanted to tell him something and it's the kind of place where when you got something to tell somebody you just walk in his office. When I heard that, I walked out, of course. I don't know if he even knew I'd been in there. He was standing by the window, looking out . . . Say, Di, I know a restaurant near here that has terrific

French cooking. What do you say we go there? You could try your French out on the waiter. I'd get a big kick out of hearing that."

Clarissa slowly moistened her lips with her tongue. "Didn't I read something about Sean Howard recently? Something about his being indicted by a grand jury?"

"God, you're hot on this whole business," he groused impatiently. "All right, all right," he relented, as the beginnings of a serious pout began to form on her mouth. "You read about his *not* being indicted. Middlebrooks tried his damnedest, but he couldn't get anything on him. Not even . . ." He swallowed what he had been going to say.

Clarissa leaned forward, her elbows on the table. "Not even what?"

Singleton looked toward Penelope Hammill again. "Not a word of this to Penny."

Clarissa held up a hand, fingers together, thumb extended. "Not a word."

"Promise?"

Clarissa laughed. "Dick, really."

Singleton smoothed his strands of hair. "It's complicated. I'll skip the details and just give you the bare bones. The bare bones is that Middlebrooks tried to get a guy to tell the grand jury a story that Sean Howard took a payoff from a contractor to accept his bid for a job even though it wasn't the low bid. I know that for a woman this is all very mysterious stuff. Women don't really understand this kind of thing. But I think you follow me so far, don't you?"

"So far," Clarissa said.

"Anyway, the jury didn't buy the story," Singleton said. "The guy they heard it from is a very sleazy guy. He's got mob connections up the whazoo, if you'll excuse the language, Di."

"Meaning Middlebrooks has them, too?" Clarissa said. How she longed to be rid of this odious little man! "Mob connections, that is," she went on, widening her eyes.

Singleton peered under the brim of her hat. "You wear those glasses all the time?"

"My eyes are very sensitive," Clarissa said.

Singleton smiled. "Anyway, the grand jury didn't buy the guy's story. I don't think his own mother would've bought it. It looked like just what it was—that the guy was singing to save his own skin. Which was just what it was, because Middlebrooks was prepared to make a deal with the guy to let him cop a plea to another rap if he'd help Middlebrooks nail Sean Howard."

"Because he's in love with Sean Howard's wife?" Clarissa said.

Singleton folded his arms on his chest. "You said it, I didn't."

Clarissa looked him straight in the eye. "If you know all this to be true, how can you work for Middlebrooks?"

Singleton met her look, beaming. "I'm quitting. End of the month. Moving to Texas. Going to be chief of security for Alamo Oil. The thing with Sean Howard isn't the half of it. It's the tip of the old iceberg."

"Oh? And what's the rest of the iceberg?"

Singleton looked again toward Penelope Hammill.

"I won't say a word to Penny," Clarissa said.

Singleton smoothed his strands of hair. "Middlebrooks is hurting for money. He's a gambler, and not a very good one. He's lost a bundle lately on the ponies, on pro sports, on just about anything they take bets on. Middlebrooks would be against the sun rising—that's the kind of gambler he is. The mob has its hooks in him. They loaned him money, then loaned him more, then told him they'd lighten up on the vig if he'd do them a few favors."

"The vig is interest, right?" Clarissa said.

Singleton sat back in his chair. "How's a girl like you know a thing like that, Di?"

Clarissa shrugged. "The movies, I guess. What kind of favors?"

Singleton shrugged. "You know, like maybe not pursuing investigations into certain areas, and trumping them up in others. Like maybe bargaining pleas here and there were certain mob types who'd had the misfortune of already being indicted or arrested. Like that."

Clarissa studied her hands for a moment. "It's wonderful about your new job, Dick. But even so, how can you just walk away from such a unscrupulous situation? Wouldn't you like to see something done about it?"

Singleton hugged himself, as if suddenly cold. "I don't like to rock the boat. I got the Texas job 'cause Middlebrooks gave me a recommendation."

"Did it ever occur to you, Dick, that maybe he just wants you out of his hair? I mean, knowing as much as you do."

Singleton's voice was weak. "Maybe so."

"I think you should nail him, Dick. Or help, anyway. Tell Penny what you told me. She'll write a story about it and somebody will look into it—some official investigation. Your job's not in jeopardy. You've already quit. And as for your new job, well, I would think that Alamo Oil would be proud to have such an honest man as its chief of security."

Singleton hugged himself tighter. "I don't know."

Clarissa reached out and touched his arm. "Why don't we talk about it some more—over some French cooking?"

Chapter Seventeen

"Excuse me, but aren't you Sean Howard?"

Sean looked up from the day-old *Wall Street Journal* he was reading at a table on the veranda of the racquet club. The word that came into his mind to describe the woman was bawdy. She had a great flowing mane of blonde hair, a heart-shaped face, a pug nose, bee-sting lips. She wore a pink crocheted sweater that invited speculation as to whether the voluptuous breasts beneath it were bare or covered by some form-fitting, flesh-toned garment. There was no speculation necessary as to whether she wore panties beneath her tight white pants. She leaned over Sean's table, precariously balanced on pink strapless shoes with very high heels. "Yes."

She spread a hand on her expansive breast as if to still her fluttering heart. "I was sure it was. How nice to see you again." Her voice was breathy and high.

"Again?" Sean said.

She puffed out a small breath of exasperation. "Oh, don't you remember? It was in New York. At a party. I don't remember whose party. After a while they all run together, if you know what I mean."

"In your case, yes, I do," Sean said. "In mine, I don't go to many parties. I remember each of them pretty well."

She clucked her tongue against her teeth. "I think it was at George Sherston's. You know George, don't you?"

"Yes, but I don't remember a party at George's."

She flung her hair away from her face and put a fingertip to her lips. Her brow furrowed with the effort of concentration. "It was in 1976. The Fourth of July. George had a party on his roof to see Operation Sail. Afterwards, there were fireworks."

Sean remembered the party. He had stopped by long enough for one drink, then left, unable to cope with the crowd. "I'm sorry, but I don't remember meeting you."

"Lourdes," the woman said emphatically, and stood up straight, her hands on her hips, displaying her attributes.

Sean laughed. "I *know* I've never been to Lourdes."

The woman pulled a chair away from the table and sat on its edge. "*I'm* Lourdes. Lourdes Christianson."

Sean put a hand to his mouth and tried to pinch away a smile. "An interesting name. Are your parents . . . religious?"

"They're dead," she said, and made a face of ineffable sadness.

"I'm sorry," Sean said.

She brightened. "Anyway, that's not my real name. It's my stage name. My real name is"— she smiled cutely, as if realizing that he had nearly trapped her into telling her real name—"well, never mind what my real name is. Do you like it?"

"Your stage name?"

"Yeah."

"It's . . . unique. I'll say that for it."

She slumped a little. "Unique means one of a kind, doesn't it?"

"Yes."

She sighed. "Then it's not unique. Not really. I . . . well, I stole it. There was a girl in *Playboy* named Lourdes—Lourdes Ann, really—and I thought it was such a neat name. And well . . . I took it for myself."

"And? Has it worked?"

"Worked?"

"Have you gotten any acting jobs?"

"No. I mean, I go to all the auditions, but, tsk, I can't even get arrested."

Sean laughed. He was enjoying himself. He had never talked to a woman like this and there was something . . . exotic about her. He looked around and noticed the consternation she was causing among other members of the staid old club, who were having a hard time concentrating on a match between two of the club's better players on the court just below the veranda. To them, she was clearly unique. "What brings you to Bermuda, Miss Christianson? It is Miss, isn't it?"

She flung her hair back. "Yeah. I was married once, a long time ago, to a guy from home. It

239

didn't work out. He was into motorcycles." She flicked a shoulder cutely. "Hard to imagine, isn't it? Being more interested in riding motorcycles than in riding me?" She leaned back in her chair and covered her mouth with both hands. "What am I doing talking like that? You don't even know me! What you must be thinking!"

Sean was blushing, in spite of himself. "You were saying how you happen to be in Bermuda."

She lowered her hands slowly and folded them primly in her lap. "I came with Tim Scott. Do you know him? He's a member of this club."

"I know the name," Sean said. "He's a sailor, as I recall."

She raised her hands momentarily in a gesture of helplessness. "Is he ever. Out on the water every day at dawn. Stays out until sunset. I've hardly seen him in the time we've been here."

"You don't sail?" Sean said.

She made a face of revulsion. "You get all *wet.*"

"I don't sail much," Sean said, "but that's my memory of it, too."

She leaned forward, gripping her knees excitedly. "You know what I do like to do?"

"What?"

"Swim nude." She sat back and covered her mouth again. "Listen to me!"

He smiled. "You get wet doing that, too, don't you?"

She flung her hair back. "It's *different.* When you sail, the wind blows and your wet clothes stick to you." She shivered. "It's yucky. But swimming"—she flicked her shoulder again—"it's . . . it's sensual." She said it sensually, working her mouth around it to draw it out as long as possible.

Sean looked at his watch and folded up the newspaper. "It's time I was getting home. It's been nice talking to you, Miss Christianson. I hope you enjoy your stay."

She put an imploring hand on the table. "Would you take me home?" She sat back and covered her mouth again. "God. I didn't mean that. Not that way. I meant . . . Oh, God, what you must think of me."

"Do you need a lift?" Sean said.

She relaxed and looked at him with grateful eyes. "Yes. Tim dropped me off here on his way to the yacht club. He thought I might enjoy playing tennis. But . . ." she sighed, and looked around despairingly, "there are only men here, and tsk, men don't like to play tennis with women."

Sean looked around at the members trying not to look her way too overtly. "I'm sure you'd have no trouble at all finding a game."

She raised her shoulders and let them fall. "Maybe not. But I don't really want to play, anyway. You get so sweaty."

Sean smiled. "True. I'll meet you in the parking lot. I have to go through the men's locker room to get my things."

She hugged herself. "I wish I'd seen you play. I bet you're good."

"Average," Sean said.

She looked at him coyly. "I bet you're good."

She was sitting on the fender of his Mercedes when he came out the locker room entrance, her legs crossed, her face up to the sun. The parking lot attendants had decided to check to see that the doors of the cars in the lot were locked, and were working in her direction.

"All set?" Sean said, unlocking the passenger door and holding it open for her.

She put a hand to her throat and stared. "Is this your car? I didn't know. Really, I didn't. Isn't that amazing? Out of all the cars in this lot, to pick yours?"

Sean just smiled, handed her into the car and shut the door. Getting in the driver's side, he saw in the rearview mirror, the parking lot attendants glaring at him. "Where to?"

She was sitting sideways in the bucket seat, gripping an ankle in her hands. "Are you married?"

"Yes."

"Do you ever . . . you know . . . fool around?"

"No," Sean said, and did not feel that it was a lie. What he had had with Clarissa was not fooling around.

"Ever tempted?"

"No," Sean said, and did not feel that that was a lie, either. His emotions for Clarissa had not been born of temptation, but rather of destiny.

"Because I'd sure like to fuck," Lourdes said. She had her head tipped back a little and her lips parted provocatively.

"Who put you up to this?" Sean said.

The question knocked her off stride and she shook her head swiftly back and forth. "I . . . I don't know what you mean."

242

"I asked at the desk on the way out if you were a guest of Tim Scott's," Sean said. "They told me you'd said you were a guest of mine."

Her jaw trembled. "No. No."

"Yes, yes," Sean said. "And ruling out that you'd been seized with an overwhelming desire to get to know me, it seemed logical to assume that someone had put you up to it. Someone I might know."

She turned to face front and hugged herself, her face petulant.

"You don't have to tell me," Sean said, "but you'll probably have to tell the police, whom I called."

"Noooo." It was a wail of despair. "Why did you do a thing like that?"

"Because I don't like to waste time," Sean said. "You've handled this so badly, you really shouldn't be surprised that you screwed up."

She was crying. "I just did what he told me."

"Who?"

She said a name, but it was waterlogged and incomprehensible.

"Who?"

She turned suddenly and put a desperate hand on his arm. "Let me go. Please let me go. I have a car here. I'll just drive off and you'll never see me again. I won't bother you again. I didn't want to hurt you. I was just doing what he told me."

"Who?" Sean said evenly.

She turned away and fumbled at the lock.

Sean patted the console by his left hand. "It locks from over here, as well, and you can't unlock it unless I do, and I don't plan to until you tell me who put you up to this."

She pummeled at the floorboard with her heels. "No."

"It's getting hot in here," Sean said. "You'll get sweaty."

She was crying again and said the name again, wetly.

"Bill Middlebrooks?" Sean asked.

She stamped a foot. "I *said* Bill Middlebrooks."

"Why?" Sean said.

"Why what?"

"He wanted you to seduce me, yes?"

She gave him a disgusted look. "No shit, Sherlock."

"But why?"

"Ask him."

"I will. But in the meantime, I'm asking you. As will the police."

"Noooo."

Sean leaned his head back against the headrest.

She sighed. "He couldn't get an indictment out of the grand jury, so he wants to get you some other way. I'm a professional photographer. I've done some work for *Playboy*—behind the camera, not in front of it. That's where I got the name. I got in some trouble. Drugs. A guy I was seeing is a big coke dealer. He got wind that the narcs were on to him and skipped town, leaving me with the stash, leaving me to take the rap. Middlebrooks offered me a deal. He said if I'd do a little job for him, he'd knock the charge down to a misdemeanor. Possession for personal use. I said okay. I mean, what the fuck was I supposed to do—go to the slammer for my fucking so-called boyfriend?"

"I assume there were going to be pictures of our . . . assignation," Sean said.

"It's kid stuff," she said. "A timer that'd take a frame every sixty seconds. You wouldn't even have known it was happening. I get pretty noisy when I get going."

"What about cameras? Aren't they pretty noisy?"

She gave him a look. "You know anything about cameras?"

Sean smiled thinly. "No."

"Well, they don't make them noisy anymore."

Sean ran a fingertip around the steering wheel. "I don't quite understand. My going to bed with you, and pictures to prove it, wouldn't get me indicted by a grand jury."

"No, but it'd sure as hell get you divorced."

Sean had to laugh. "Divorced? Why would Bill Middlebrooks want me divorced?"

She gave him another look. "Think about it, sweetheart."

He thought about it, but couldn't think why. Unless . . .

She was sitting forward and looking around. "The cops don't move real fast in this part of the world, do they?"

"I didn't call them," Sean said.

She stared. "You motherfucker."

"But I will call the cops in New York. What did you say your name was?"

"Diane Arbus."

Sean laughed. "I know a *little* about photography." He leaned back against the headrest. "It doesn't matter, really. There can't be that many women photographers for *Playboy* who're in trouble on narcotics charges."

" . . . Janet Broughton."

Sean reached for the console and unlocked the doors. "Have a nice day, Janet. Oh, Tim Scott doesn't have anything to do with this, does he?"

She shook her head. "I met him on the plane on the way down. I needed a name to drop. Lucky, huh, that I should hit on a guy who's a member of your club?"

"Very lucky."

She laughed. "Not really. He was wearing one of those stupid fucking blazers."

Sean laughed. "I hope you get out of this with as little damage as possible."

She opened the door and swung out of the seat. "Your wife's a lucky woman. Men don't usually turn me down. I can't think of one who ever has." She walked across the parking lot toward a white rented Camarro. The parking lot attendants came racing to her aid.

"Bill Middlebrooks?" Carolyn Evans said. "For a handsome, well-built, well-dressed man, Bill Middlebrooks is one of the most boring, dull, colorless men I've ever met."

"Was he really around that much that you've met him?" Sean said. "I know he went to school with me, and lived in River House, and lives near us in Connecticut, but I never had a sense that he was around that much. I guess the husband is always that last to know."

"I suspect that affair is too strong a word to

describe what he and Susannah had, Sean," Carolyn Evans said. "I suspect that it was an infatuation—he is attractive, after all, and you and Susannah were having a hard time of it. With the benefit of hindsight I think I can say that I saw that they were interested in each other. I can only say, with . . . well, call it woman's intuition—What are you smiling at?"

Sean shook his head. "Go on, please."

" . . . Well, I think that he probably showed his true colors when Susannah was crippled. I suspect he got rather quickly as far away from her as he figuratively could."

"But he's still pursuing her now," Sean said. "Or he's pursuing her again. I wonder why."

Carolyn Evans pursed her lips. "Perhaps he needs money."

Something tingled along the length of Sean's spine. What the hell was he dealing with here?

Carolyn Evans had come to be with Susannah after the suicide attempt. She hadn't been welcomed by her daughter, whose depression had gone into remission only temporarily, then had returned with a vengeance. It was a rare day when Susannah even sat up in bed, let alone got out of it.

Sean had welcomed his mother-in-law, however. He didn't know how he could have gotten through the days without her. He saw in her qualities—compassion, wisdom, forcefulness—that he had never noticed before—or perhaps that had never been so manifest, given Carolyn Evan's habit of seeming to be foremost a great wit. She and Sean spent a great deal of time together—playing tennis, staying up late playing backgammon and talking, and taking walks on the beach before dinner—as they were doing now. Sean wondered if Susannah herself had ever possessed the qualities he perceived in her mother. If she had, what had caused them to shrivel so? It wasn't the accident—her smallness of spirit predated that by a long time.

" . . . Needs money," Sean repeated. "And he hoped that by getting me in jail he'd have access to Susannah—and her money? That sounds a little convoluted to me."

Carolyn Evans snapped her fingers. "That's it. He needs money to pay gambling debts. It's just conjecture, but now that I've said it, it sounds absolutely right. He's a very poor gambler. I remember now that he was terrible at backgammon. Do you remember those River House backgammon tournaments?"

Sean nodded. Those were the days when he had worked from dawn till midnight, but he remembered hearing about the cutthroat games played far into the night.

"And he was with us once at the race track, for the Belmont Stakes," Carolyn Evans said. "I seem to remember that you were in Europe. It was the trip when you were smitten by the Eiffel Tower . . . He lost a small fortune playing long shots. Poor gamblers have no faith in the possibility of a sure thing. They think the gamble is in taking risks, not in slowly accruing your assets." She stopped and faced Sean. "But whatever Bill Middlebrooks is up to, his gambit brings up another question—the future of your relationship with Susannah. Do you really think

—to continue with the gambling metaphor—
that it's worth continuing to play the hand
you've been dealt?"

Sean smiled. "It is only a metaphor. What
Susannah and I have is more an investment
than a game of chance. We have stock in each
other."

Carolyn Evans made a face. "Metaphor or
not, I like mine better. Remember, Sean, the
money on the table isn't your money any longer;
it's foolhardy to keep spending your money to
try to reclaim it."

With a bare foot, Sean drew a curve in the
sand. "Susannah needs a reason to live. I'm not
that reason. I may never have been. But I can at
least help her find one. Whether it's in trying
again to write a play—or to rewrite the one
she's written, to make it, in Stephanie Chonin's
words, box office. Or whether it's something
else—something we don't even know about,
something that hasn't occurred to us yet. Whatever it is, perhaps I can inspire her, encourage
her in those ways. I don't mean to disparage
you, God knows, but, well, you're—"

"Her mother," Carolyn Evans said.

Sean smiled. "Yes."

They moved on along the strand. Storm
clouds were massing on the horizon, like sol-
diers awaiting last minute orders before
launching their attack.

Carolyn Evans laughed suddenly. "Tell me
the truth, Sean, were you the least bit tempted
by this . . . this floozy?"

"She was less a floozy than she pretended,"

Sean said. "She seems to have a good mind. She'd just gone off on the wrong track at some point. But no, I wasn't tempted."

"Not in the least?"

"No."

"It is . . . I suppose it's none of my business . . ."

"You can ask," Sean said. "I trust you to ask a reasonable question."

Carolyn Evans stopped and studied the waves for a while. "We're going to have a bit of a storm, it looks like."

"Yes," Sean said.

She turned to face him. "Is it loyalty to Susannah that keeps you from being tempted by an attractive woman, or is it loyalty to Clarissa Leeds?"

Sean kept his eyes on hers for a moment, then looked away. The storm clouds had sent out scouts, which scudded low over the graying water. "If Susannah and I were no longer married, I would not be interested in getting involved with any other woman. Is that what you're asking?"

"Any woman other than Clarissa Leeds?"

"Yes."

"But you can't involve yourself with her?"

Sean shook his head. "No. For her sake. She's involved in a custody proceeding. And her father is running for the vice-presidency, for God's sake. I made a promise."

They walked on again, to the jetty that was their usual turning point, then headed back toward the house.

"And what about Middlebrooks?" Carolyn

Evans asked. "What do you intend to do to—what is the expression—blow the whistle on him?"

"I called my lawyer," Sean said. "But he was in conference. He'll call me back about seven or seven-thirty. I don't have any idea what he'll recommend, but whatever it is, that's what I'll do."

"Do you think you should've let—what was her name? Not Lourdes—God! What a contrivance—but her *real* name?"

"Janet Broughton."

"Janet Broughton. Do you think you should've let Janet Broughton go off scot-free? She is your only means of implicating Middlebrooks."

"I'm not a policeman," Sean said. "I have no authority to hold her in custody. And I didn't want to have to explain this whole thing to the local police. It's too complex for them—or anyone, for that matter. It may not be a police matter at all. It may be the kind of thing . . . Well, I don't know. I'll have to talk to Dan before I have any idea of how we should proceed."

The first raindrops pocked the water of the bay. The waves ran farther up the shore, claiming new territory for themselves. The clouds covered half the dome of the sky and an eerie light—almost brown—suffused everything, making everything look as if it were dusted with ochre.

They hurried and made it to the house just as the rain began coming down in torrents.

Susannah sat by the living room window,

and it was a moment before they noticed her. She seemed to have shrunken in size, and looked like a child in her chair.

"You're up, Susannah," Sean said. "How wonderful."

"I hope you'll join us for dinner," Carolyn Evans said. "Sean has put up with enough of my chitchat."

Susannah's voice was barely audible. "There was a phone call for you, Sean."

"Dan Freedman? Damn, I told his secretary to tell him to wait until—"

"It was a newspaper reporter," Susannah said, even more softly. "A woman named Penelope Hammill. Isn't she the one . . ."

"She wrote the column, yes," Sean said. "What did she want?"

Carolyn Evans cleared her throat. "I think I'll take a quick bath before dinner." She walked to the stairs and went up them briskly.

Sean switched on a lamp on a table by the window and pulled a white wicker chair close to Susannah's wheelchair. "What did Penelope Hammill want, Susannah?"

"Clarissa Leeds," Susannah murmured.

Sean shook his head. "I'm sorry. I don't understand."

Susannah frowned. "I don't understand, either."

"Did she leave a number?" Sean said.

"No," Susannah said. "She said she didn't know when she'd be able to call again, and didn't know where she could be reached. So she talked to me. We talked for a long time." She laughed suddenly, a deep, full laugh. "Bill Middlebrooks."

Sean took her hand. It was ice-cold. He warmed it in both of his. "What did this reporter say?"

Susannah didn't seem to have heard. She stared unseeing at the rain that drove against the big picture window. She seemed not to hear the racket it made against the glass, either.

"Susannah?"

She turned her head slightly, but kept her eyes on the rain. "Yes?"

"Did Penelope Hammill tell you something about Bill Middlebrooks?"

Susannah brightened slightly. "A man broke into the house. The Connecticut house. She saw him and followed him—"

"Penelope Hammill saw him?"

Susannah looked annoyed. "No. Clarissa Leeds. She saw him and followed him. He went to Bill's office. He works for Bill. His name in Sinclair—Singer—Single—"

"Singleton?"

Susannah nodded.

"I met him during the grand jury testimony," Sean said. "What else did she say?"

"She's quite wonderful," Susannah said wistfully.

"Penelope Hammill?" Sean said.

Again the look of annoyance. "Clarissa Leeds. She seemed to know exactly what to do. I don't know that I'd have known exactly what to do. I'm certain I wouldn't have known exactly what to do." The sound of her own voice seemed to be lulling Susannah to sleep.

"Let me put you in bed, Susannah," Sean said. "You made a big effort getting out of bed and getting downstairs. You're tired."

253

"I haven't finished my story," Susannah said. Sean sat back in his chair.

". . . Clarissa Leeds followed this man and found out he works for Bill and called Penelope Hammill and the two of them went and talked to him—"

"To Bill Middlebrooks?"

"No. To Singer—"

"Singleton."

"Yes. They talked to Singleton and he told them Bill wants to have an affair with you—" Susannah laughed than and shook her head slowly back and forth. "No. No, no. That's not it at all. Singleton told them Bill wants people to think *you* are having an affair with another woman. . . . He hid some letters in the house. Letters I was supposed to find . . . Letters from this woman to you." Susannah turned suddenly and looked directly at him. "Sean?"

"I haven't been having an affair, Susannah," Sean said.

She waved a hand. "Oh, I know that. What I was going to say was that I'm not having an affair with Bill."

"I didn't think you were."

"He wanted me to . . ."

". . . I've figured that out."

"I slept with him a few times, a long time ago. It was after the baby died. Can you understand that?"

". . . Yes . . . Let met take you upstairs, Susannah."

She put her hands between her knees and made herself stiff, as if to resist any attempt to move her. "After the accident, I didn't think I could be with you. Not because I held you responsible, but because I didn't want you feeling responsible. I . . . I called him. I asked him to come see me at the hospital. He wouldn't come. I called him again. I said if he loved me as much as he said he did—he said he loved me, Sean—he would take me, live with me, love me. He laughed. Bill *laughed*, Sean. He said, 'Don't you think things are different, now, Susannah? If we can't fuck, we don't really have much going for us, do we?' "

Sean stood and got behind Susannah's chair and started to turn it. "Come to bed, Susannah. You've completely overextended yourself."

"Wait."

He stood still.

" . . . She loves you, Sean. Clarissa loves you. Look at all she's done for you."

Sean pushed at the chair.

"Wait! I want to look at the rain for a moment longer. Switch off the light, will you, please?"

Sean did, and the blackness outside seemed to burst through the window and surround them. The rain racketed at the window. The palm trees groaned and their leaves hissed and shivered.

"It's no night to be out, is it, Sean?" Susannah said.

" . . . No."

" . . . Take me upstairs now, Sean. There's something I want to show you. A letter from Bill. It's . . . well, it's intimate, I'm afraid, but I think you should see it."

Chapter Eighteen

"What day is it?" Clarissa said.

Penelope Hammill laughed. "Your sense of time gets all screwed up when you're working on something like this, doesn't it? It's Thursday."

"No. I mean the date."

"The tenth, I think. Or maybe it's the eleventh. Why?"

"I have to be in Washington on the fifteenth."

Penelope Hammill laughed. "I think you'll make it. What's in Washington?"

"A custody hearing. I'm trying to get custody of my stepdaughter, Diana. Her mother's contesting it."

"You were going to tell me about Diana," Penelope Hammill said. "Now's a good time."

They were sitting in Sarah and Abraham's Toyota on West Eleventh Street in Greenwich Village, just down the block from a townhouse where William Middlebrooks had an apartment, a pied à terre he used when he had to stay overnight in the city. In just a few minutes, they—or rather, Penelope Hammill—was to meet Sean Howard and his lawyer, Daniel Freedman at a coffee shop on the corner of Sixth Avenue, and go to Middlebrooks's apartment. That afternoon, Penelope Hammill had phoned Middlebrooks at his office and told him that she had some information suggesting he had tried to influence testimony regarding Sean Howard and that he had also tried to entrap Sean Howard and to plant evidence that would make it look at though Sean Howard was having an extramarital affair.

She didn't mention the gambling debts, or the sentence rigging, wanting an ace in the hole. Did he have any comment? Without a word, Middlebrooks hung up the phone. She'd called back immediately, but Middlebrooks wouldn't come to the phone. So she had spoken to Middlebrooks's flunky—the one who had tried to get her to print a rumor about Sean Howard and Clarissa. She had told him to tell his boss that "Sean Howard wasn't interested in going to Lourdes."

" . . . What the hell does that mean?" the flunky asked.

"He'll know," Penny had said.

Five minutes later, Middlebrooks had called back and suggested that she meet him at his apartment at eight o'clock that night. She hadn't told him that she would be accompanied by Sean Howard, who had flown in from Bermuda that morning, and his lawyer.

Clarissa leaned her head against the headrest and looked up at the trees that hung over the parked car. "What can I say? Diana is the top. The best. Outstanding. Diana is . . . well . . . Diana."

"And what're your chances of getting custody?"

Clarissa sighed. "They'd be better if I were married."

"Wouldn't all our chances be better if we were married," Penny quipped.

Clarissa turned to look at her new friend. "You don't strike me as the marrying kind."

"I don't strike men as that, either," Penny said. "Or at least they never ask me . . . Are there any candidates?"

After a beat, Clarissa said, "No."

"Not other than Sean Howard, you mean?"

Clarissa nodded her head. "Yes. But therefore, no. He's not a candidate, so there're no candidates."

"He's bound to be grateful to you for what you've done," Penny said. "If Middlebrooks had gotten away with this, Sean Howard would at best have had to go through a very ugly scandal. The kind of thing that could damage a man's professional reputation forever. He could've been put out of business, even if . . . well, even if he hadn't wound up divorced."

"I would've done it for anyone," Clarissa said.

"Oh, come on," Penny said. "I know you're a good Girl Scout and all that, but let's not pretend you wouldn't do things for Sean Howard that you wouldn't do for anyone else. But it sure would have been understandable if you hadn't done *anything*—hadn't followed Singleton, hadn't called me . . ."

Clarissa shook her head. "I don't understand."

Penny smiled and patted Clarissa's hand. "Of course you don't. That's why you're so special. You don't have an ounce of guile in you."

Clarissa laughed. "I *still* don't understand. Are you going to explain it to me, or aren't you?"

"If you *hadn't* done anything," Penelope Hammill said, "Sean Howard might've ended up a marriageable man."

"Ah."

"Ah, indeed."

"That never occurred to me," Clarissa said.

"Of course not."

A cat jumped out on the hood of the car, startling them. It was a black cat. It lay on its side on the hood.

Clarissa smiled. "The hood's still warm. Cats like warm places. Even in summer they like the warmest place."

"It's a black cat," Penny said. "I don't like it."

"You don't strike me as the superstitious kind."

"At times like this, I get very supersititious. Call it caution." She drummed on the dashboard with her fingertips. The cat turned its ears toward the sound. "I don't know. Middlebrooks has a good chance of talking his way out of this. Singleton's an anonymous source, and this chippy in Bermuda Sean's lawyer told me about doesn't sound like a world-class citizen. I don't think he's desperate."

You know, Penny, I've had some experience

with desperate men. My husband, don't forget, was a suicide. You can't really tell until they snap just how far gone they are." She looked at her watch. "It's time for you to go . . . I wish I were going with you."

"I think you should come. What the hell— this isn't a illicit rendezvous. This is important stuff."

" . . . I promised I wouldn't see him . . . I can't."

"Well, wish me luck," Penny said. "Hey, where'd that cat go?"

"It jumped down, I guess."

"Did you see it?"

"No."

"Neither did I. Damn, that's spooky."

"He was a nice cat," Clarissa said.

"There are no nice cats," Penelope Hammill said. "Wish me luck, goddamn it. I'll need it for sure, now."

"Good luck."

She got out of the car and walked down Eleventh Street toward the coffee shop, to meet Sean Howard and his lawyer.

Clarissa leaned her head back against the headrest. She hadn't slept well the past few nights on Penny's couch—she had been too wired—and she was very tired. The waiting had taken its toll on her, too—the waiting for Penny's progress reports on the phone calling. And now the waiting which seemed the most interminable of all, knowing, as she did, how close she was to Sean.

She dozed.

And dreamed:

She was riding on a beach, bareback—riding Maggie, the brindle mare. It was a lonely beach, reached, on the right, by high cliffs. No, they weren't cliffs; they were buildings—high-rise towers of steel and glass. Up ahead, there was one that looked like La Tour, a model of which he had on a table in his study in the River House apartment. The sun glinted off the topmost floors of the building, and was reflected into her eyes.

No. It wasn't the sun. It was flames. The building was on fire.

Clarissa kicked the brindle mare with her heels and galloped across the sand toward the building. Reaching it, she dismounted before the mare had fully stopped and raced up the long tiled drive to the building's entrance. The doors were not doors at all, just a painted trompe l'oeil.

Clarissa stepped back and tipped her head way back to try to see the top of the building. It was obscured by smoke from the fire. She thought she heard voices, but not crying for help, merely talking animatedly.

She went around a corner, and there, resting on the ground, was a wooden scaffold, attached to ropes that ran all the way to the top of the building. Clarissa climbed onto the scaffold and hauled on a rope. Her end rose off the ground; the other remained where it was.

"Wait," Penelope Hammill called. "I'll help you." She was getting out of a Toyota she had just driven up, and she climbed over the railing of the scaffold and grasped the other rope. "Ready when you are."

"One, two, three, *pull.*"

They rose as if mechanized. Soon the beach was far below them. They were so high that she could see, out over the ocean, the curvature of the earth.

They felt the heat from the flames.

At last, they reached a balcony, and hauled themselves over its railing and peered into the thick smoke.

"This way," Clarissa said, and led the way around a corner of the balcony. A window had been broken and they could see into the room beyond—a restaurant, filled with diners who ate their meals calmly, oblivious to the flames that ate away at the ceiling of the room, and to the smoke that billowed about their heads.

"How'd you know this would be here?" You're like goddamned Wonder Woman." Penny said.

Clarissa stepped through the broken window and walked to a table where a man and woman sat, sipping coffee. The man wore a soft white shirt and loose white pants. He had navy espadrilles on his feet. He smoked a pipe. The woman wore a long white robe, like a hospital gown.

"Sean?"

"Hello, Clarissa." Sean stood and shook her hand.

"I've come to help you. This is Penelope Hammill."

"We've met briefly. How do you do, Miss Hammill?"

"Fine, thanks," Penny said, shaking his hand. "Although it is a little warm up here."

Sean smiled. "Do you know my wife, Susannah? Susannah, this is Clarissa Leeds and Penelope Hammill. Susannah Howard."

Susannah nodded her head slowly, but didn't speak or take the hands they offered.

"Susannah's been ill," Sean said.

Clarissa tugged at his sleeve. "Sean, we have to get out of here. The restaurant's on fire."

Sean looked around in puzzlement. "It's fine here. There's no danger."

"Sean."

He took her hand away from his arm, gently. "I can't go, Clarissa. I have to stay with Susannah."

"We'll take Susannah with us. We have a way down—outside—a scaffold."

Sirens sounded far below. At first, Clarissa thought they were cats wailing.

"Hurry, Sean. Please. We'll take Susannah."

Susannah lifted a hand and waved it languidly. "It's all right, Sean. I'll be all right."

"Let's get the hell out of here," Penelope Hammill said.

"You take Sean," Clarissa said. "I'll take Susannah."

Penny led Sean away.

The sirens were closer. Searchlights probed into the smoky gloom.

Clarissa got behind Susannah's wheelchair and hauled on it. It wouldn't move. "Have you got the brake on?"

"The wheels don't turn. They're only decorative," Susannah said.

Clarissa put an arm behind Susannah's neck and the other under her legs. "I'll carry you out."

But she couldn't lift her.

"The chair and I are one," Susannah said.

From the window, Penny called, "Hurry, Clarissa. Hurry."

"I can't come. I have to help Susannah."

"It's all right, Clarissa," Susannah said. "I'm fine."

Clarissa backed away reluctantly.

Susannah sat stupefied in her chair, oblivious to the chaos around her, and Clarissa's panic rose in her throat to strangle her.

The searchlights shone in Clarissa's eyes, blinding her.

Penny pounded on the window. "Clarissa. Clarissa. Clarissa!"

Someone was pounding on the window of the car. "Clarissa. Wake up."

Clarissa shook her head to clear it. Bright lights shone in her eyes—the lights of an ambulance, parked facing the wrong way in front of Middlebrooks's house. On its front was the word AMBULANCE in mirror image.

Clarissa rolled down the window. "Oh, God. He didn't kill himself did he?"

Penelope Hammill shook her head, but her face was white and there was perspiration on her brow.

"What happened?" Clarissa said.

"Let's go somewhere and have a drink. I'll tell you about it."

"Hello, Bill," Sean Howard had said, moving in front of Penelope Hammill so that Middlebrooks couldn't close the door. "You know Miss Hammill. And I think you know my lawyer, Daniel Freedman."

"Umm," Freedman said.

Middlebrooks looked accusingly at Penelope Hammill. "You didn't say anybody else would be with you."

"I didn't say they wouldn't," she rejoined.

"Let's go inside, Bill," Sean said. "It'll be more comfortable."

Middlebrooks led them to his study. On its wall were framed diplomas and photographs of Middlebrooks with various movers and shakers. Middlebrooks poured himself a glass of Scotch, full to the brim, with no ice or water.

"Nothing for me, thanks," Penny said. She sat on the couch, crossed her legs, and took out a notebook. Sean sat on the arm of an easy chair. Daniel Freedman leaned against the fireplace mantelpiece.

"Anthony Zito," Penny said.

Middlebrooks sipped his drink and smiled. "Yes?" He had lost his suntan and was sweating.

"Of Zito and Sons Construction Company, Inc. He's facing one to three for income tax fraud. A source tells me you promised to get his sentence reduced in exchange for some testimony—testimony that Mr. Howard here . . ."

"Who's this *source*, Miss Hammill?" Middlebrooks said. He took a long pull on his drink.

" . . . that Mr. Howard here took a sum of money from Mr. Zito in exchange for giving Mr. Zito's firm a contract to do some work on La

Tour even though Mr. Zito's firm didn't submit the low bid."

"Who's the source, Miss Hammill?"

" . . . Furthermore, that you ordered one of your operatives to place in Mr. Howard's home some letters—fabricated letters—that would lead the casual reader to conclude that Mr. Howard was having an affair . . . an affair of which further documentation was to have been some photographs taken, as well as participated in, by a young woman named Janet Broughton, who, like Mr. Zito, although for different reasons, faces a jail sentence—unless she does what you ask her to do. Or is it 'tell' her to? I'm not sure. At any rate, do you have any comment?"

Middlebrooks winced down another swallow. "Who's your source?"

Penelope Hammill shot a glance at Sean. She had played her hand rather more quickly than she should have. It seemed rather less imposing on the table than when she held it close to her chest.

Sean saw the look and stood up behind the easy chair, his hand on its back. "Speaking of letters, Bill," Sean said, "Susannah showed me one you wrote her just a week or so ago. . . ."

Middlebrooks held the glass to his forehead, then registered that it had no ice in it and lowered it and looked at it foolishly.

"I had no idea cocaine was so expensive," Sean said. "I guess when you use as much as you said in the letter . . . The gambling was to raise money to support your habit, is that it?"

Middlebrooks craned his neck almost imperceptibly.

"And your efforts on behalf of various indicted mobsters—that was to get them off your back about the money you owed them . . ."

"Mr. Freedman here has been in touch with the U.S. Attorney's office. They have the letter. They've also interviewed Janet Broughton and have arranged interviews with a number of people from your office, as well as a number of people, Mr. Zito among them, you've had . . . business associations with."

Middlebrooks took a step forward, his hand out. "Sean, do you think we could—"

"No," Sean said. "There're no more deals to be made. You son of a bitch. I don't give a fuck that you tried to get me. You couldn't've gotten me. I'm clean, and you know it. But I resent your trying to use Susannah. I resent—"

Middlebrooks stuck out his chin, changing his tactics. "I've *fucked* Susannah."

Sean started to move from out behind the chair, but Freedman hissed a warning.

"Fucked her better than you ever fucked her. Fucked her till she screamed."

Penelope Hammill cleared her throat.

"Fucked her, Sean. Do you hear me? Fucked her. And she loved it. She begged me for more. She couldn't get enough. She wouldn't let me alone. Calls to the office. Ringing my doorbell in the middle of the night. Wanting to fuck. Fuck, fuck, fuck." Middlebrooks laughed hysterically, swigged his drink, and choked on it. He coughed a wracking cough.

Sean gripped the back of the chair until his

268

knuckles were white. "But then you turned your back on her, Bill. When you really might've done something for her, that's when you really fucked her. And now, now that you're desperate, you're trying to fuck her again. You tried to get me out of the way so you could get your hands on her again. To get her money to pay your debts, to pay for your habit. Were you planning to kill her, Bill? It'd be easy enough, with someone in her condition. You could just leave her out in the rain, roll her over a cliff, making it look like an accident. Then you'd have all her money, and no responsibility. Was that the plan, Bill?"

Middlebrooks wiped saliva from his mouth and mucous from his nose with the sleeve of his shirt. "Yes," he spat, then looked startled that he had, and put out a hand, as if to retrieve it. "No! No, I didn't mean that. You can't . . . you can't use that against me. You don't have a god-damn thing on me. You fucking scumbag, Howard. You're just pissed off 'cause I fucked your wife and did it right, which was something you could never do."

Sean hurled the chair aside and went toward Middlebrooks. Middlebrooks put out his hands defensively. Then his eyes went empty and his knees wobbled and he fainted.

"Fainted?" Clarissa said.

"Just keeled over," Penelope Hammill said. "Hit his head on the edge of this steel-and-glass bar cart. Made a nasty cut. Sean's lawyer called the ambulance. They took him to Saint Vincent's. It's just around the corner. The U.S. Attorney ordered the police to baby-sit him. It's just as well he passed out. If Sean had hit him, it might've been trouble. He asked about you, Sean did."

Clarissa sighed.

"And he asked me to thank you for all you've done."

"It was nothing," Clarissa said.

"He's going back to Bermuda in the morning."

Clarissa nodded.

"He didn't *ask* me to give you this, but I think he'd like it if I did."

"Give me what?"

Penelope Hammill leaned over and kissed Clarissa on the cheek.

Clarissa smiled. "*I* liked it."

Chapter Nineteen

It was still raining in Bermuda. It was raining as though it would never stop. The wind howled and the rain pelted at the windows. The waves had occupied the beaches and were threatening the roads that ran along them.

It was hard enough to make oneself heard by someone in the same room, let alone by someone at the other end of a telephone connection. Yet Sean had spent most of the afternoon and evening on the phone, trying to get his life back in order, trying to focus on things that remained to be done rather than on things that were over and done with, trying to understand that people who read in the newspaper that he was a principal in the drama starring just-resigned District Attorney William R. Middlebrooks weren't being nosy when they asked him to tell them a little more than had been in the paper—only naturally curious. After a while, he got tired of shouting into the phone and decided he would deal with some matters by writing letters. If the recipients wanted to know more about his role in the drama starring Bill Middlebrooks, they would just have to wonder.

He removed his typewriter from its case, set it on top of his desk, got a stack of white bond and a stack of carbon sets, found a sheet of Ko-Rec-Type in a drawer and pulled his swivel chair up to the desk. The phone rang. Sean was going to ignore it, but it rang and rang. He finally answered.

"She seems like basically an okay kid," Daniel Freedman said.

Sean laughed. "Who, Dan?"

"Your blonde friend. Janice Broughton."

"Janet. She called you?"

"Knows you're my client, I guess."

"How? I didn't mention it."

Static cracked on the line. "Guess she read about me in the paper. I got profiled on account of winning that case."

"What case?"

"The Frattini case. You're not my only client, you know. Although the profile mentioned your name as being one of my better-known ones. I guess she figured you being such a nice guy and all it wouldn't hurt having your lawyer for hers."

" . . . How do you know she's blonde?" Sean said.

Freedman laughed. "Came up here to see me. Not bad. Not bad at all. Surprised you . . . well, never mind."

"I heard on the radio that some of the gangsters Middlebrooks made deals with have started to talk," Sean said. "Hoping for even better deals, I guess."

272

"I guess," Freedman said. "How're you doing?"

" . . . Okay," Sean said.

"She was right close by the other night," Freedman said.

Sean spoke curtly, "Who, Dan?"

"Your friend, Clarissa. She was waiting for Penny Hammill just down the block."

"I thought she might be."

"She was."

" . . . Is there anything else, Dan?"

" . . . Not that I can think of . . . You'll probably have to give testimony about Middlebrooks."

"Just let me know."

"I'll do that . . . Susannah okay?"

"Yes."

"Well, I'll talk to you, then."

Sean hung up the phone and went out the door and down the hall to the living room. He turned out the lights and stood by the window looking out at the storm. So wet it was that it was like looking into a giant aquarium. He wouldn't have been surprised to see fish swimming by. He shivered and hugged himself. After a moment, he realized that it was not just events that made him cold; a door was open somewhere. Its banging was a new sound among the cacophonous sounds of the storm. He went looking for it. The staff had the night off.

It was the kitchen door, the door Susannah used when she went outside, for it opened onto a gently sloping ramp that led down to the swimming pool and the gazebo, where Susannah liked to sit. Or rather, where she had liked to sit, before the partnership with Stephanie Chonin had fallen through, before she had tried to kill herself. But she had said at lunch that day that she wished the weather would improve. She felt like sitting in the gazebo again.

Sean shut the door and got a mop from the cupboard and mopped up the rain that had poured in onto the floor. He put the mop away and went upstairs. The door to Carolyn Evans's room was half open. The door to Susannah's room was closed. A light shone under it. He could hear Susannah's voice. She was talking to her mother, Sean guessed. He was glad of that. He had been afraid that Susannah was going to turn away from her mother forever. Sean didn't want to interrupt.

He went down the hall to the Small Room—that was what they called it, The Small Room—that looked out over the swimming pool. He wanted to be sure that the pool attendant had stored away all the pool furniture, as he had asked him to earlier that afternoon. As he opened the door, he nearly cried out, for there was a figure standing by the window. At first, he thought the figure was standing outside the window, for she—it was a woman—seemed to be being buffeted by the rain. But it was a trick of the light, which made it look as though the rain falling outside was falling, as well, on one of the walls of the room.

"Carolyn?"

"Hello, Sean. I'm sorry I startled you. I just wanted to see what things were like on this side of the house. About as bad as the other sides, I'd say." She laughed. "Will it ever stop, do you think?"

"I thought . . ."

"Yes?"

"I thought you were in Susannah's room," Sean said. "I heard voices."

Carolyn Evans shook her head. "No. Are you sure?"

"I heard her voice, in any case."

"Perhaps she's on the phone."

"I don't think so. I was on the phone until— Oh, my God!"

"What, Sean?"

But Sean was gone, running down the hall to Susannah's room. It was empty. On the table beside the bed, a small cassette tape recorder played—Susannah's voice.

"Sean?" Carolyn Evans called.

Sean ran to the top of the stairs. "Call the police, Carolyn. Tell them to send an ambulance right away. Susannah's outside somewhere."

"Outside? But . . ."

"Call the police!" Sean leaped down the stairs three at a time and ran into the kitchen. He grabbed a yellow slicker from the closet by the door and put it on as he ran down the sloping ramp toward the pool. She must have gone this way some time before, or her mother would have seen her from The Small Room.

He ran to the gazebo. It was empty.

He stood rooted to the spot. Where to look? Which way to go? Other than the gazebo, Susannah had no favorite place in good weather, and even if she had, would she go to it in weather like this?

The chute.

Years ago, before her accident, Susannah had loved to ride her bicycle. She had especially loved to ride down a stretch of paved rode—it was a driveway, really, for it was on their property and was not used by anyone but them —that led from the main driveway down to the beach. It had originally been a footpath, and had been paved so that they could back trailers down it carrying small sailboats—Sunfishes and Lasers. Susannah had liked to pedal furiously down the drive—they called it the chute—then lift her feet from the pedals as she reached the sand of the beach to see how far she could go before the wheels of her bicycle lost their battle with the grasping sand. She had sometimes done it over and over, like a small child.

Sean ran toward the chute. It was a hundred yards or so, but it seemed like miles. The rain filled his mouth as he ran, nearly choking him. Each time he lifted a foot, the wind slapped at his ankles, trying to knock him sprawling. He ran as low to the ground as he could, as he had in his rugby days. His wet clothes weighed tons; his Topsiders were filled with water.

At the top of the chute was Susannah's afghan, sprawled on the ground like a dead bird.

Sean ran down the chute, fighting to keep from falling headlong, gyrating his arms to keep his balance. The wind filled his slicker like a sail, and he thought that he might fly.

The wheelchair had gone a surprising distance in the wet sand before toppling on its side. Susannah was not beside it.

But her track led away from it. She had dragged herself on her hands and arms—ten, twenty, thirty, forty, fifty yards before collapsing from exhaustion. She lay facedown, her arms straight out over her head, as if in the middle of a swan dive. Her feet were bare and she wore only a thin nightgown.

Her pulse was faint, but it was there.

Sean picked her up. The wind knocked him onto his back. Its gusts seemed to laugh at him, to inquire imperiously just who he thought he was: trying to keep his footing on his own was one thing; but with a helpless burden? Hah. Hah, hah, hah.

Sean got to his knees and made his way like that to the wheelchair. He laid Susannah down for a moment, righted the chair, and put her in it. He had to pull it backward across the sand; pushing it was out of the question.

At the end of the chute, he turned the chair and pushed it slowly up the ramp. Like Sisyphus, some idle part of his mind was able to think; only when he got to the top he wasn't going to let his burden roll back down. He slipped and fell flat and the chair crashed onto his head. Blood poured down his face and filled his mouth. He held the chair with a shoulder as he regained his feet, and pushed on up. He pushed and pushed, his head down, not letting himself look up, lest he see how far away his goal was.

Finally, he looked up and bright lights filled his eyes, suffusing the night with a brilliance that was, some part of his mind was able to comprehend, like Heaven's. Perhaps he was in heaven, he thought. Perhaps the blow to the head had killed him and he was simply bearing Susannah—and himself—to their final resting place. In that case, why did his head hurt so much, and why was his burden so heavy?

Suddenly, his burden was light, taken from him by strong hands. Angels? No, men in white. Ambulance attendants.

Sean stood with his hands on his knees, fighting to get his breath. When at last he stood and wiped the blood from his eyes and spat the blood and rain from his mouth, he saw that the lights were the lights of an ambulance. On its front was the world AMBULANCE, in mirror image.

"Hello, Sean," Susannah said on the tape she had made and left in the cassette tape recorder in her room. "It's no night to be out, but I'm going out for a swim. I expect you'll find this—I don't have the strength to write a note—and understand. Suicides always leave notes, don't they? In the hope that others will understand. . . In my case, I think it's plain enough. I want to be free. And I want you to be free, too, for you must be very, very tired of living with me—" There was the sound of a laugh, which turned into a cough. Then: "That's really all there is to it. I'd imagined I'd go on for much longer, but there's nothing more to be said. I want to be free—of the pain I feel, of the memories of the pain I've felt, of this wheelchair, of this life. Am I a coward? Am I—Oh, hell, you don't want to listen to this. I've debated it plenty in my own mind. There's no need to inflict it on you. Things will be difficult enough for you for a while, as it is. No sense burdening you with thoughts that you'd argue the other side of, when you heard them—trying to encourage me, trying to get me to see the bright side of things. You always encouraged me, Sean. You were always such a tower of strength. You—Oh, hell, you don't want to listen to that either . . . I love you, Sean. I wish you well . . . I love you, too, Mother. I know you're listening, too. . . . Oh, and one favor, Sean. Please burn the play. The original's on my desk, along with the only copy and a notebook I kept while writing it. Please burn everything. I know I don't have to ask you, but please don't read any of it. Ashes to ashes. . . Good-bye.''

Sean burned the play and the copy and the notebook and the cassette in the same coffin in which Susannah's body was consumed by a crematory's fire. She lived for thirty-six hours, suffering from pneumonia and exposure, but never regained consciousness. The doctors held out hope throughout the thirty-six hours; they said she died not because her body had given up, but because she seemed to have lost the will to live.

Sean burned the urn on a small knoll overlooking the sea. The sun shone brightly and the wind was soft and warm. Out on the water, a sloop sailed downwind. The crew broke out a spinnaker and it filled immediately; it had wide vertical stripes—blue and yellow and red.

Chapter Twenty

"I have something to confess," Penny Hammill said. "I didn't come to Washington just to keep you company."

"Are you working on a story?" Clarissa said.

"In a sense. My story. The story of my life."

"You're writing your memoirs? I bet they'll be exciting."

Penny's laugh rang through the corridors of the District of Columbia Court House, where they sat on a bench waiting for the custody hearing to begin. All up and down the corridor, men turned away, wishing at least one of the two beautiful women were theirs. "Not writing them. Just living them. You see, there's this man . . ."

"Yes," Clarissa said, her eyes twinkling. "Tell me more."

"His name's Philip Cleaver," Penny went on. "He's a writer—a novelist."

"I've read one of his books," Clarissa said. "About a man who falls in love with a famous movie actress—and she with him. She's killed in a plane crash and he can't get anybody to believe that they were lovers."

"*Dawn's Husband.*"

"That's it. It was a wonderful book."

"I'll tell him you liked it. He'll be very pleased."

She looked up at the ceiling, as if at a memory. "We had a thing together a few years ago. It didn't work out—for the usual reasons. He moved to Washington to write in a place a little less crazy than New York. I hadn't seen him or talked to him until last week. He called and said he'd been thinking about me a lot and wondered . . . Well, just wondered. I'd been doing some wondering of my own—about him, about my work, about whether it made any sense to go on doing what I've been doing, about whether I wanted to live in New York any longer . . . We made a date."

"That's wonderful," Clarissa said.

Penny smiled. "I also made an appointment to see the managing editor of the *Washington Post.* He said he knew my work and would be interested in having a chat. He said his only concern was whether I wouldn't find Washington a little tame."

"What do you think?" Clarissa said.

"I think I've had enough wild. I could use a little tame."

Clarissa laughed—not as loudly as Penny had, but loudly enough to turn some heads. "It would be wonderful if . . . No, I better not say it."

"I'll say it," said Penelope Hammill, "It would

be wonderful if we were both living in Washington—you with Diana and me with Philip."

Clarissa rapped on the wooden bench with her knuckles. "I wish. Oh, how I wish."

Penny gave her a look. "I thought I was the superstitious one."

Clarissa smiled. "In this case, I'll try anything. I'll try prayer, voodoo, hocus-pocus."

"You won't need it." It was Lester Roth, Clarissa's lawyer, who had materialized as if from nowhere.

"You startled me, Lester," Clarissa said. She looked at her watch. "You're late. I hope the judge doesn't hold it against us."

Lester Roth hooked his thumbs in the pockets of his vest. "The reason I'm late is I've just been having a little talk with the judge in his chambers . . . along with Peter Dix."

"Who?" Clarissa said.

"Rachel Owen's lawyer."

Clarissa held her breath.

Penelope Hammill took Clarissa's hand.

Lester Roth waved his hands. "Don't you want to know what we talked about?"

"I'm not sure," Clarissa said.

"We talked about your daughter."

" . . . And?"

Lester Roth rolled his eyes. "Don't you get it? *Your* daughter."

"Oh, Clarissa," Penny said, squeezing Clarissa's hand hard.

Clarissa held a hand up to check her friend's enthusiasm. "Why don't you tell me the whole thing, Lester? From the top!"

Lester Roth struck a pose of great accomplishment. "There's not much to tell. Rachel Owen has decided to drop her claim for custody of Diana. Diana is your daughter—legally and aboveboard and no questions about it."

Clarissa couldn't let herself believe it yet. "Decided to drop her claim—why?"

Lester Roth shrugged. "No formal reason was given. None was necessary. I heard some gossip, though."

"What kind of gossip, Lester, goddamn it? Don't make me drag this out of you."

Lester Roth spread his hands innocently. "You wanted to know what we talked about. We didn't talk about gossip."

"What . . . gossip . . . Lester?"

He shrugged. "Well, one of my investigators stumbled across the fact that Owen has quite a thing for young boys. It's a taste he gratifies very, very discreetly, but I'm afraid that if I had to, I could rake up a whole lot of dirt and prove it." He spread his hands and smiled a wicked smile. "Of course, I felt honor-bound to mention this to the Owen's lawyer before the custody case came to trial. I told him I could hardly keep that sort of thing to myself when the welfare of a young girl was at stake. He got up on his high horse and started harrumphing about blackmail, how he wouldn't cave in to it, and so forth. Apparently, though"—the smile again—"his clients took a more temperate view. In return for some—ah—documents I was able to deliver to them, they have formally dropped the whole business."

"Why, Lester, you old scoundrel," Penny

breathed. "You don't look like the type who has it in him to play that kind of hardball!"

"If there was ever a case where the ends justified the means, this was it," Lester rejoined mildly. "I did what I had to do."

Clarissa could contain herself no longer. She whooped with delight and caught the totally disconcerted Lester in a joyful hug. "Thank you, Lester," she cried. "Thank you, thank you, thank you."

He blushed. "All in a day's work, my dear, all in a day's work."

Clarissa looked around her as if she didn't know where she was. "Is that it?"

"That's it," Lester Roth said.

"There's nothing to sign? No forms to fill out? No oaths to swear? No affidavits? No nothing?"

Lester Roth patted the pocket of his suit coat. "I've got the judge's order right here. Case closed."

Clarissa looked around her again. "A phone," Clarissa said. "I have to find a phone. I want to call Diana. What time is it in Italy? You're a journalist. You're supposed to know things like that."

"God, I have no idea," Penny grinned. "Something tells me, though, that Diana won't care what time this call comes in."

Clarissa took both their arms and hauled them down the hallway. "Let's find a phone."

"Are you sure you're in Italy?" Clarissa said. "You sound like you're in the next room."

"I wish I was," Diana said. "I wish I was in the same room."

"Aren't you having a good time?"

"I'm having a great time. I just miss you— Mom."

Clarissa laughed. "You'll be home soon. We haven't talked about it—we couldn't really, until things were officially decided—but, well, where would you like to live? My feeling is that I've had enough of Georgetown."

Diana made an unpleasant noise. "Me, too. Not just our house, but the whole phony neighborhood. Frankly, I'm a little tired of Washington. It's as bad as California."

Clarissa laughed. "Where would you like to live?"

"New York," Diana said.

"Just like that?"

"It's where it's at. It's the capital of the world. It's the Big Apple. The top banana. It's also important that you be somewhere where you can play music."

"I can play music anywhere, Pat. Violins are very portable."

"Bobby says when it comes to music of any kind, New York is the place to be," Diana said.

"Oh? And who's Bobby?"

"He's this boy I've met. He's a little young— only fourteen—but he's kind of cute."

Clarissa laughed. "Would you want to live right in the city?"

"Bobby says if you're going to live in New York,

For Love of a Stranger

you should live right in the city. I'd like to live in the Village. I'd like to live on Grove Street."

"Does Bobby live on Grove Street, by any chance?"

"Yeah. How did you know?"

"Woman's intuition," Clarissa said happily.

They prattled on for a few minutes, until Diana asked in a different tone of voice, "By the way, how's your friend Sean?"

Clarissa took a deep breath. "I don't know, babe. He had . . . a tragedy in his life. His wife died."

"Oh, wow! But, well . . . hey, I know I shouldn't say this, but isn't that sort of good in a way?" Diana asked. "Don't get mad, but isn't it for the best?"

"It's okay," Clarissa said. "I know what you mean. But no, it isn't for the best, honey. He's very sad. He's gone off somewhere to be by himself. I don't know where, exactly. He wrote a letter to Sarah and Abraham, saying he'd be away for a while—"

"How's Maggie?" Diana said.

"She's fine. She's walking very well. There's no sign that the laminitis will come back. She's fine."

"I'm so glad. I worry about her a lot."

"How's your wrist?"

"It's great. I'm going to try playing tennis next week."

"Don't get carried away, Pat. Take things easy."

"Oh, Tyler," Diana said. "I'm so happy we're going to be living together."

287

"I'll see you in a few weeks, Pat," Clarissa said. "I love you."

"I love you, too—Mom."

Clarissa hung up the phone and sat staring down at her hands in her lap.

Penny tapped on the door of the booth. "Everything all right?"

Clarissa opened the door and hugged her friend. "I have bad news."

"What?"

"Pat wants to live in New York."

"Well, there's room enough for all of us," Penny replied.

Clarissa leaned back to see her face. "A few minutes ago, you were talking about moving to Washington."

Penny shrugged. "While you were on the phone, I called Philip. Seems he was thinking a little differently. He was thinking about moving back to New York. Washington's too tame."

"What about your interview at the *Washington Post*?"

"The hell with it. I'll tell the managing editor he was right. I'll tell him I like it wild."

Clarissa smiled. "You really like this guy, don't you?"

Penny nodded. "I like him a whole lot."

"Daddy?" Clarissa said.

Dwight Tyler looked up from a speech he was drafting on a yellow legal pad. They were sitting on the veranda of the house in McLean. A purple haze lay on the crests of the green hills. "Yes, dear?"

"If you're the vice-president, does that mean I'll have to have a Secret Service man living in my closet?"

Dwight Tyler smiled. "Not in your closet, Clarissa, but there'll be one nearby."

"I don't know if I like the idea."

Dwight Tyler laid the yellow legal pad on a low stool next to his chair. "None of us likes the idea, Clarissa. Even less do we like to admit the necessity. But necessary it is."

"I suppose," Clarissa said.

Clarissa's mother lowered the magazine she was reading. "They're usually very handsome, Clarissa."

"Mother, really."

Her mother waved a hand in the air, as if to erase what she'd said. "You're right. That was crude. But . . . Well, your father and I can't help wondering . . ."

"Wondering what, Mother?"

"Well, now that you have legal custody of Diana, perhaps it's time to consider the possibility of finding a father for her."

Clarissa took a sip of her gin and tonic. "I'll marry for love, Mother," she said mildly. "Diana doesn't want a functionary for a father any more than I want one for a husband."

Her mother started to say something, then thought better of it, and lifted her magazine. Then she lowered it. "Dwight?"

Dwight Tyler paused with a pen poised over the legal pad, which he had retrieved from the stool. "Yes, dear?"

"When you say the Secret Servicemen would be nearby, just how nearby did you mean?"

"Whoa!" he said. "This kind of talk is putting the cart before the horse. I don't like it. It's bad luck."

"*Newsweek*, dear," Clarissa's mother said, "called it a 'flood time of enthusiasm' for your ticket."

"Tides turn," Dwight Tyler said.

"Which reminds me, Clarissa," her mother said. "In the same issue there was a mention of your friend, Sean Howard. He was spotted in Montana, or some godforsaken place like that—"

Dwight Tyler interrupted. "Let me remind you, Abigail, that when one is running for national office, there are no godforsaken places."

Clarissa laughed. "I saw the item, Mother. Sean has a friend who lives in Montana. A writer named Ken Forrest. He was in Vietnam with Peter, in fact."

"God, it's a small world," Abilgail Tyler said.

Dwight Tyler put the pad on the stool and cleared his throat. "Clarissa, I know how much Sean Howard means to you. I was most distressed when I read about his wife's death. I sent him a card of condolence. I don't know if he mentioned it to you."

"I haven't spoken to him, Father," Clarissa said. "I sent him a card myself, but that's all."

Dwight Tyler fidgeted in his chair. "What I'm trying to say, Clarissa, darling, is that obviously now the situation has changed. If you should feel, once a suitable mourning period has passed—"

"Daddy, please don't. I don't mean to cut you off, but now is just not the time for me to start wondering about what the future holds in store for me and Sean. It's not fair to him, it's not fair to his wife's memory, it's not fair to Diana, it's not fair to me."

Dwight Tyler cleared his throat. "I believe I understand. I'm sorry if I disturbed you by mentioning it."

"Don't worry about it. I know your heart's in the right place."

"Clarissa," her mother said.

"Yes?"

"Your father and I probably don't say this often enough, but . . . we love you."

David Stein placed the tips of his gnarled fingers together under his chin.

Clarissa laid her violin in her lap and placed the bow on the music stand and closed the sheet music of the Bach Chaconne.

David Stein cocked his head, as if he could still hear the music frolicking about his studio across from Carnegie Hall. He smiled. "So. You have been practicing a great deal."

"Not that much," Clarissa said ruefully. "Not nearly as much as I'd've liked. I've had . . . other things on my mind. But I've practiced some."

"And thought a great deal, from the sound of it," David Stein said. "Even if you have not been practicing with your hands, in your heart you have been making music—as it was clear to me the first time I heard you play that you had been making music in your heart during the years you said your hands were idle."

"I guess I have," Clarissa said, smiling sadly. She brightened. "I hope—You said you wouldn't cash my check until I gave a performance I invited you to. I do wish you'd cash it. I hate to think of the interest you're losing, of the good uses you could put the money to. I hope you'll think of this as that performance."

David Stein shook a gnarled finger at her. "Now, now, young lady. I distinctly said that I would cash the check and use some of the money to buy flowers for your dressing room and a bottle of champagne with which to celebrate. I feel very privileged to have heard you play just now, but I'm afraid I intend to hold on to the check until you give a more . . . public performance."

Clarissa slumped in her chair. "But that might be years. Ages."

David Stein gestured cavalierly. "I'm in no hurry. I don't intend to die for a great many more years. And as for the . . . interest on the money, I can live very nicely without it. I appreciate your concern, but"—he laughed—"but I'm afraid I'm not going to let you off the hook."

Softly, Clarissa said, "I was afraid you wouldn't."

David Stein smiled. "And now, would you play it again, please? You were understandably nervous the first time. I have a feeling that if you play it again, some of the nervousness will have dissipated and you will be able to play
292

with a little less reluctance, a little more lightness."

Clarissa laughed. "Let's hope so."

And she played, forging once again a fine chain of golden sound that made a contented captive of its listener.

And even before she had finished, David Stein wept.

Clarissa went to the old man and knelt before his chair and put her arm around his neck. "Thank you so much for your confidence in me."

David Stein patted her glistening black hair. "My confidence in you is merely a response to your confidence in yourself."

Clarissa sat back on her heels and held his bent hands in hers. "I'm going to be moving to New York in a few weeks. My friends, Sarah and Abraham Newman, are going back to tour soon, and I won't be able to study with Sarah any longer—not until next summer, at the earliest. I was wondering . . . Would you be my teacher?"

David Stein looked grave. "I am a very demanding teacher."

"I'm sure you are," Clarissa said. "I hope you would be."

"I would require much more regular practice than you say you have been able to manage."

"I want to practice more."

"These . . . other things you said you've had on your mind . . . Have they been resolved?"

"Yes. I was involved in a custody dispute over my stepdaughter. I won, and that makes me very happy."

But still he looked grave. "But there's something else, isn't there? Or rather, someone else —with whom things remain to be resolved?"

Clarissa bowed her head. "I'm not sure. There is someone else, yes. A man I loved. A man who loved me. But that was in the past. It was only for a moment. I don't know that that moment can be recaptured. Too many things have happened. Too many lives have changed."

David Stein brushed a strand of hair away from Clarissa's cheek. "If you are in love, you will make lovelier music."

Clarissa nodded.

"Perhaps it is of vital importance that you eliminate these doubts that persist in your mind," David Stein said. "Perhaps you need to find out if, as you say, that moment can be recaptured. If it cannot, it will mean unhappiness for you, I am sure. But it may also mean that you can eventually free your heart to love some other man."

Clarissa looked up and smiled. "You're very wise."

David Stein shrugged. "I am old."

"Not in your heart," Clarissa said.

David Stein smiled. "No. I myself have fallen in love recently—with a woman who teaches young ballet students at a studio just across the street there, in Carnegie Hall. We met at a coffee shop on Seventh Avenue that is frequented by the likes of us—elderly artists."

Clarissa squeezed his hands. "I'm so happy for you."

David Stein looked up at the ceiling. "Therefore, to your question—will I be your teacher— the answer is, 'Yes, but.' Yes, I will be your teacher, but first, you must clear your mind of the doubts that remain in it. When your mind is clear, then we will be at a place it will be good to begin from.''

"So, what're you going to do?" Sarah said. She was on her knees on the floor of her bedroom, packing a trunk with clothes she would wear during performances on their concert tour.

"I don't know," Clarissa said. "I don't think it's appropriate for me to go looking for Sean, to find out what he's feeling."

"It may not be appropriate," Sarah said. "But it sure would get results."

Clarissa shook her head. "It's only been a few weeks since Susannah's death. Coming on top of all the trouble he had during the summer, with the grand jury, he must have mountains of work to deal with, if nothing else. He'll be in touch with me when he's ready. If he wants to be."

Sarah sat back on her heels, her hands on her knees. "Tyler, I don't think conventional attitudes about a suitable period of mourning apply in this case. You and Sean had something vital together—something wonderful and fresh and alive. This is a time you can be of help to him—as you've been a help to him in the past."

Clarissa shook her head again. "Sean and I think alike. I can hear him saying—even though he hasn't said it out loud, on the phone or in a letter—I can hear him saying, Please wait. I'll be in touch with you in time. And I'm saying back to him, I understand. I'll be here when you need me. And I know he can hear me."

Sarah sighed and dipped into the trunk, extracting a long black gown with a deep V-neck. "Do you like this?"

"It's beautiful."

"It's yours," Sarah said, and folded it carefully and laid it on the bed.

"Sarah, I can't."

"You must," Sarah said. "For one thing, I can't wear it anymore. I've gained a few pounds this summer. All the heavy lifting I've been doing. For another, it's never been quite right for playing the cello in. It's quite fitted, and, well, if you'll pardon my crudeness, it's a little hard to get between my legs. For yet another, I want you to have it for your first performance. We'll be so busy this fall, I don't know that I'll be able to be at your first performance. It would mean a lot to me if my dress could have my proxy."

Clarissa smiled. "Sarah, I think we should be realistic about this. I've only began playing the violin again—"

"And brilliantly, I might add. You might add it too."

"Nonetheless," Clarissa said evenly, "I don't think it's realistic to expect me to be giving a performance this fall."

Sarah sat back on her heels again. "Tyler, there're performances and there're performances. I don't expect you to be playing in Carnegie Hall tomorrow, but I don't expect you to be playing in a closet, either. There's chamber music all over New York during the fall and winter. You just have to get connected. I've already given your name to my business manager. He'll probably be in touch with you around the middle of September."

"Sarah."

Sarah slapped her thighs with her hands. "Don't you think I know what I'm doing? Don't you think I'm concerned about my reputation—my credibility? Would I give you a reference if I thought you'd be an embarrassment to me?"

Clarissa bowed her head. "No."

"No, is exactly the right answer. So when he calls, you be nice to him. If you don't think you're ready, say so; he'll understand. If you think it's something over your head, say so; he'll respect you for saying it. But if it feels right, take it. You'll know when it feels right."

"Yes, ma'am," Clarissa said meekly.

"And wear the dress," Sarah said. "It's a very sexy dress. I wear it when I'm not sure I'm playing up to snuff. It distracts the audience."

Clarissa grinned. "You didn't learn that at Juilliard."

"No," Sarah said. "I learned it at the College of Hard Knocks, from which I have a Ph.D."

Clarissa laughed. She was sure that, somewhere, Sean heard her laughing, and was pleased by it.

Chapter Twenty-One

"There's something I've been meaning to ask you," Ken Forrest said.

"Yes?" Sean said.

Forrest lifted his booted feet up onto the railing of the porch he had built onto the back of his house. In the distance, mountains rose up spectacularly. He rubbed his bearded face. Neither man had shaved in days. They were dressed alike in flannel shirts, faded blue jeans, hiking boots. Each held a can of Olympia beer in his hand. "Being a writer, there're certain things I have need to explain that in real life sometimes just don't get explained."

Sean laughed. "I know what it is."

Forrest turned his head to look at Sean. "Oh, yeah?"

Sean took a sip of beer. "You're going to ask me how come I heard Susannah's voice on the tape recorder when I was out in the hall—when I thought she was talking to her mother. The message she left was much too short to still be playing if she went out while I was on the phone."

Forrest was only temporarily nonplussed at being second-guessed. He and Sean had enjoyed an uncanny mental sympathy for years, and both of them had long since stopped questioning it. "Okay, whiz kid," he shot back. "So you can read my mind. Now answer the question, if you're so goddamned smart."

"Actually, I'm not really sure how she rigged it," Sean replied musingly. "All I can figure out is that she set the tape recorder running as a deliberate ruse—there was a bunch of stuff on the tape before the message she left for me. She must have figured that if I heard her voice—muffled, mind you, because the doors in that house in Bermuda are made of solid oak—I'd figure she was on the phone, or talking to her mother, working whatever.

"She fooled me all right," he concluded somewhat somberly, the memory of that storm-lashed night in Bermuda by no means was far from his memory. "By the time I realized she wasn't in her room, it was too late—and that's precisely what she had in mind, I guess. This was one suicide where the victim just didn't want to be stopped in the nick of time. I doubt that she really gave a damn whether I actually got around to listening to that machine to hear her message or not."

"Hey, old buddy," Forrest said, holding out a friendly hand. He knew better than to offer any direct words of compassion. "I'm no expert, but rumor has it that when somebody takes it into their head to go out that way, there's not a goddamned thing in the whole world anybody else can do to stop them." He clapped Sean awkwardly on the shoulder, and then drained his beer in one long swallow.

They were both silent for a little while, carefully allowing the moment of threatened emotional intensity to dissipate a little.

With the sun gone, the whole valley was purple. The sky was dotted with stars although it was still pale blue. Sean felt as though he were on the moon.

After a time, Forrest asked simply, "You got any plans?"

"Plans?" Sean asked., "What are you getting at, Forrest? You're about as good a dissembler as a used-car salesman."

"All right, then," Forrest retorted, pulling the snap top off his sixth beer of the evening. "Here it is point-blank. What the hell are you going to do about Clarissa Leeds? You can't fight it forever, you know. You enslaved yourself to Susannah while she was still alive, always blaming yourself for the accident. Are you going to let her go on running you from beyond the grave?"

"You know, Forrest," Sean shot back, "if you weren't such a stupid son of a bitch, I might actually have to hold you responsible for the things that come out of your mouth. Then I'd have to knock you from here to kingdom come."

"Look, Howard, for once, just cool your jets. I've been reading about the lady in the papers, so she's just naturally on my mind, is all. There's no need for you to bust a gut about it."

"Reading about her in the papers?" Sean

301

asked, his pulse quickening. "What about her?"

"Oh, it wasn't anything that earth-shaking," Forrest answered. "There was a profile of Dwight Tyler in *Time* or *Newsweek*, I think, and it mentioned in passing that the Great White Hope's daughter Clarissa had recently been awarded custody of some kid named Diana."

He went on, expostulating about this politician, and that, about how Tyler was every limousine liberal's idea of the Ideal Statesman but how he, Forrest, knew better than to fall for that shit. But Sean had tuned him out completely. The news that Clarissa was liberated from the constraints that had bound her for all those months came to him like an entirely new lease on life.

Suddenly the malaise that had enveloped him since Susannah's death rushed away. The custody battle was over! He could go home! To La Tour! To Clarissa! His days of hiding out from his need for her had miraculously come to an end.

In a voice tense with emotion, he asked, "Can you get me a pen and paper, Forrest? And then just buzz off for a little while?"

Dear Clarissa,

Having written that, I've stared at this page for a long time, trying to think of the simplest way to say what seems so complicated.

I guess the simplest way is this: I love you. I want you. Can we be together?

Today is Thursday. I will be back in New York Friday evening, at River House.

Love,
Sean

"Clarissa Tyler," Forrest said approvingly when he saw the envelope Sean had left by the car keys in the kitchen.

"I'm going to get a plane out in the morning," Sean said. "Can we stop at the post office on the way?"

Forrest lifted the letter and hefted it, as if its weight would make a difference. "Why not just carry it with you? You'll get to New York before it does."

Sean looked out the kitchen window at the star studded sky. "It's meant a lot for me to be here, Ken. Talking to you about everything that's happened has helped a lot. I guess I'd like the letter to come from this place—to carry its postmark, and maybe something of its spirit."

"Shit, the captain of industry is waxing downright poetic," Forrest said. "We don't exactly have a post office. Just Luke's Lodge—which ain't a lodge, by a long shot—out by the lake. It's on the way to the airport, though, so no problem."

Sean woke in the night to the ringing of the telephone. He held his breath waiting for Forrest to come and tell him it was Clarissa. But how could it be?

In the morning, Forrest was floating several inches off the ground. "I'm going to join you on that airplane. Going to connect to Miami, then Key West. Got a phone call last night from the amazing Maisey. All is forgiven."

Sean didn't ask in what way she was amazing, or even who she was. Forrest's sexual gestes had long since ceased to amaze him.

Luke's Lodge had long ago given up the battle to remain vertical, and listed toward eleven

303

o'clock. So did Luke, and his dog, Herodotus, who smelled of tick powder and bourbon.

"Booze's for his teeth,' Luke explained when he saw Sean sniffing at the dog. "They hurt him something fierce. A little Jack Daniels on a rag does wonders for him. Call him Herodotus 'cause he helps me deliver the mail. 'Neither rain nor snow nor sleep—' "

"Herodotus?" Sean said.

Luke held the letter up to the light. "Connecticut."

"Don't worry, Luke," Forrest said. "Sean here doesn't expect you to carry it yourself."

Luke gave Forrest a look that said he could have if he had to. "Ever tell you about the time I was working up in the Yukon?"

Forrest punched Luke's arm lightly. "Not today you haven't, and you're not going to, you old fart. Me and Sean're taking the big skybird back east."

Luke looked at the letter again. "Sure you don't just want to take this along?"

Forrest punched him again. "Sean here wants it postmarked here. And some spirit, too, if you got any. That's spirit, not spirits."

Luke wagged a thumb at Herodotus. "Dog drinks. Not me."

"So long, Luke. See you in the dead of winter. I hope to bring back someone to keep me warm."

Luke threw them a salute. "Give my regards to Broadway."

"Good-bye, Luke," Sean said.

There was no answer to the letter. No note, no phone call, no appearance at Sean's door. He had waited too long, he told himself. Time had passed and its passage had brought Clarissa new things, new enthusiasms, a new love.

October, November, December. Sean hardly left his office except to visit the construction site. His only exercise was the walk from River House to the General Motors Building at seven every morning and the walk back at midnight, or later. Seven days a week. He worked until eight at night on Election Day before he realized that he had one hour to get to the polls to vote for Dwight Tyler's ticket. Back at the office, he turned on the television and heard that the network's computers were already projecting a landslide victory for that ticket. He turned the television on again at midnight and heard Dwight Tyler's running mate's victory speech. He turned it off lest the cameras show Dwight Tyler and his exultant family.

Sean worked halfway through Thanksgiving Day before he realized what day it was—realized it because he paused for a moment to look out the window and saw across Central Park one of the giant balloon figures that are a trademark of Macy's Christmas Parade, held every Thanksgiving. He gave himself a break of sorts by working only until seven o'clock that night, then going home to eat a turkey dinner with all the trimmings, prepared by the River House restaurant and served in his apartment. While he ate, he watched a college football game on television—Texas versus Texas Tech. It was an exciting game, and he felt a momentary peace— as if he were living a contented life.

On December twenty-fourth, Daniel Freedman stood at the window of Sean's office, looking out over the cityscape, at the last-minute shoppers scurrying through the gray cold in search of something for that distant relative about whom they couldn't have cared less, but were nonetheless obligated to buy a gift for. "Got any plans for tomorrow?"

Sean didn't look up from his desk. "I want to meet with the electrician, but he hasn't returned my call."

"I'm not surprised," Freedman said.

"I don't know," Sean said. "He's usually pretty reliable. He must be tied up on a job."

Freedman snorted. "More likely he's tied up with his wife and kids opening Christmas presents and eating turkey."

Freedman looked at him with almost completely undisguised concern. Sean was working himself to death right in front of Freedman's eyes.

"There's a bash at the law office down the hall," Freedman said cautiously. "You want to drop in for a few quick ones? I went to law school with the senior partner."

Sean leaned forward and retrieved his pencil. "You go. I have work to do."

"Sean!" Freedman said.

"Yeah?"

"Give yourself a break. The thing's back on schedule"—he gestured at the skyline—"I

306

schedule"—he gestured at the skyline—"I mean, you can see the goddamn thing. If I do say so myself, it doesn't look too bad, either. You might just pull off that thing people're always saying needs to be pulled off but nobody's ever been able to pull off—the renaissance of Times Square."

"I hope it'll be a start," Sean said. He leaned back in his chair again. "If I can't meet with the electrician tomorrow, maybe we should go over some of these contracts for the decoration of the theaters."

Freedman laughed. "Maybe you'd like to go ten rounds with my wife."

"I didn't know you celebrated Christmas," Sean said.

"It's not so much that we celebrate Christmas, as that I like to take a day off now and then," Freedman said. "You know what I mean?"

Sean leaned forward again. "I'll use the time to review some future prospects. I am going to build other buildings."

"Not if you don't give yourself a break," Freedman said. "You don't give yourself a break, the only building in your future's going to be the little building you're buried in. Why don't you come out to Brooklyn Heights for dinner? It's been a long time since you've seen the wife. Debbie and her kids'll be there. You'll have a nice time."

Sean leaned back.

"Come about four," Freedman said. "You can work till three-thirty, then come on over. We'll eat about six. You can be back at work by nine."

Sean laughed. "Maybe I'll take the whole day off."

Freedman put his hand to his forehead. "I must have that thing that's going around."

Sean didn't take the whole day off. He worked from seven till noon, then walked the streets in search of any shops that were open to buy presents for Freedman and his family. The only shops he found open sold junk or flowers. He decided flowers would have to do and nearly bought out a store. He sent his car and driver around to load up the flowers—the florist wouldn't deliver to Brooklyn—and take them to Freedman's house. The car was back in time to take Sean across the river, depositing him on Freedman's doorstep at a few minutes before four. The flowers were a big hit.

Sean worked New Year's Eve, stopping at a few minutes before midnight to turn on the small television set in his office to watch the crowds at Times Square ring out the old year and ring in the new. The television correspondent gave a nice plug for La Tour, saying that in it resided the hopes of many New Yorkers that their city had more than a dismal present; that it had a shining future.

At ten minutes after midnight, the phone rang. It was Carolyn Evans, calling from Palm Beach.

"I knew you'd be working," she said. "I just wanted to wish you a very happy new year."

"The same to you, Carolyn. It was nice of you to call."

"Do you have a bottle of something there, at least? You really ought to drink a toast."

"I think there's some brandy."

"Well, go get it and pour yourself a glass," Carolyn Evans said. "I'll hang on. A long-distance toast is better than nothing."

Sean got the brandy and a glass, poured himself a drink and carried it to the phone. He clinked the glass against the mouthpiece. "Cheers."

"Cheers," Carolyn Evans said.

They drank.

"How are you, Sean?" Carolyn Evans said. "How are you really?"

"I'm well, and you?"

"As well as can be expected. Last year was not a good year for us, was it? Next year can only be better."

"I don't see having any free time before March or so," Sean said. "But maybe we can get together then."

"I'd like that."

"I'm afraid I sold the Bermuda house," Sean said.

"I can understand that."

"I'd like to sell the Connecticut place, too, but I just haven't been able to put that together."

"Oh, don't, Sean," Carolyn Evans said. "I know what you must feel, but that's a house . . . Well, it would be a wonderful house to have a family in."

"I think someone else will have to be having the family," Sean said.

"I . . . Well, maybe I shouldn't say this, Sean, but . . . Well, I will say it. I met Clarissa Tyler. Her mother's sister has a house here and they were down for a few days at Christmas time— her mother and Clarissa and Clarissa's stepdaughter, Diana, who informs me that she prefers to be called Pat."

Sean smiled in spite of the pain in his heart.

"Sean?"

"Yes?"

"Does that upset you?"

"I wrote her a note when I was out in Montana. She never answered. I guess she has new interests in her life."

"She's a lovely woman," Carolyn Evans said. "And Diana—Pat—is a lovely girl. They're living in New York now. Did you know that?"

" . . . No." He would have to give up walking, now. He couldn't bear to catch a glimpse of her, let alone run into her.

"It would be the easiest thing to call her. Maybe she didn't get the letter."

"I thought about that," Sean said. "But despite what everyone thinks about the post office, letters get delivered. I don't think it would be fair to call her—not when she's, in effect, answered."

" . . . I think you're making a big mistake, Sean," Carolyn Evans said. "I didn't tell Clarissa who I was. There was no point in doing that. But your name came up, by chance. One of the other guests was lauding your vision—La Tour and all that. I watched her face and it was clear to me that she was very interested. And Diana—Pat—well, she was positively beaming. I think you should call her."

" . . . Happy New Year, Carolyn."

"Happy New Year, Sean.

Sean's secretary said that Penelope Hammill was there to see him.

"She doesn't have an appointment," Sean said.

"She said she didn't think you'd give her one," his secretary said, "so she just came up. She's prepared to stay a while. She brought a sandwich and a book."

Sean sighed and got up and slipped on his jacket. "Tell her to come in."

"Would you like part of my sandwich?" Penelope Hammill said.

"No, thanks. But you go ahead." Sean led her to the couch by the window. "What brings you up here?"

The irrepressible Penny opened a brown paper bag and took out a sandwich. "Well, La Tour's going to be finished soon—I don't have to tell you that—and my paper's interested in doing a big special pull-out section on it—"

"Yes. The people who handle publicity for me mentioned that you'd called."

She unwrapped the sandwich. "Oh, hell. I ordered Swiss cheese. This is American cheese." She rewrapped the sandwich and put it back in the bag. "I'm not really hungry, anyway. Did they mention that I want to interview you— a big profile to go along with pieces of the building, on its design, on its various revolutionary aspects, on the neighborhood, and so on? We've got five or six people working exclusively on this assignment."

"I'm flattered," Sean said. "I'm sure the publicist told you that the only interviews I would do would be connected with the building itself. No personal interviews."

"Well, that's what they said, but—"

"But I owe you a favor?" Sean said.

She brushed an imagined crumb from her lap. "Well, I suppose you could say that, although I wasn't going to stoop to it myself."

Sean smiled. "I'm sure you understand."

She shrugged. "I understand I also don't understand. You're a hero to a lot of people in this city. People like to read about their heroes."

"I'm not a fan of the new breed of journalism that considers the private lives of public figures to be fodder for its readers," Sean said.

She pouted. "I don't intend to write gossip. Just facts. Born, raised, educated—like that."

"That's all available from my publicist," Sean said.

"Oh, sure—the dates and places are available. But not the colors, the feelings, the textures."

He turned to face her. "I'm grateful to you for the help you've given me. I know you didn't think of it as that. I know you were just looking for a good story. I do feel, though, that I owe you a favor, and I'll be glad to repay you by making myself completely available to talk about La Tour—for your special section. I'll give you an advance look at things the rest of the press won't see for several months. I'll talk to you about my plans for the future; some very interesting things are in the works. But I won't talk to you about myself. Not one word. Are you interested?"

Penelope Hammill tried to look doubtful, but didn't succeed. She smiled broadly. "Very."

"No personal questions."

"No personal questions . . . Well, just one."
Sean frowned.

"Oh, it's nothing big—don't worry. I just want to know your shirt size."

Sean had to laugh.

"Don't get me wrong," she said. "I'm not making a pass. I'm happily involved with someone, thank you. It's just that . . . Well, a friend of mine happens to know that it's your birthday next week. Isn't that right?"

". . . Yes," Sean said, but he hadn't remembered.

"And my friend wants to send you a present. She has her eye on a shirt she thinks you'd look just smashing in. And, well, I told her I'd ask your size, since I was going to be in the neighborhood."

Sean scraped at the nap of the carpet with a foot. "Miss Hammill . . . Penelope?"

"Yes?"

" . . . You're talking about Diana, aren't you? About Pat?"

"Yes."

"Clarissa . . . ?"

Penelope Hammill uncrossed and recrossed her legs. "Clarissa's . . . Well, she's unhappy . . . She thinks it's rather like a man to just disappear. She didn't expect it of you."

"I wrote her a letter," Sean said.

Penelope Hammill made a face.

"No, I did. I mailed it from Montana. I was staying with a friend. I told her . . . I told her that I loved her, that I wanted to be with her. I asked her if we could be together. She never answered."

Another face. "I can assure you, Sean. She didn't get a letter from you."

Sean went to the window for a moment, then turned to face Penelope Hammill. "I want to make a phone call. Please don't leave. It'll only take a moment and it may be very important."

Penelope Hammill tipped her head in a way that said it was his office, he could do whatever he pleased.

Sean called Forrest's number in Montana. The phone rang and rang. Forrest finally answered, out of breath. "What, goddamn it? Don't you know there's a writer at work?"

"Work, my ass," Sean said impatiently. "Whose brains are you fucking out now?"

"You're a shit, Sean Howard," Forrest shot back. "I wrote my butt off this morning." Then, hearing the urgency in Sean's tone, he snapped to complete attention. "What's up?"

"You remember that letter we dropped off at Luke's Lodge the day I left your place to come east? Well, it was the most important document ever penned—and there's a possibility it never arrived. Any chance you could check with that drunken old fool who runs the post office and see if he has any idea what went wrong?"

"Jesus Christ, I don't believe it! Luke's Lodge is no more. It went down in flames about a—" His voice disappeared in a tinkling of feminine giggles.

"Forrest, for Christ's sake," Sean hissed down the phone wires. "Get your ass in gear and give it to me straight. Lock tonight's delight in a closet and pay attention to me. My life's at stake."

There was a brief pause, then Forrest's voice came again, sounding as sober and correct as a Wall Street banker's.

"Well, old Luke got out all right. Not a scratch. Old Herodotus bought it, though. Luke thinks he started the fire—the dog, that is— kicked over a kerosene heater. Luke's up in Alaska now, running a saloon. I heard about the fire when I was in Key West. It happened the day you and I cleared out for points east and south."

"So my fucking letter went up in smoke," Sean said. "I can hardly believe it."

"Do you think your young lady will believe it?" Forrest asked. "That's more to the point."

"Would you?"

"Not a chance."

"So long, Ken," Sean said. "I'll talk to you soon." He felt sick.

"So long, old buddy. Hey, I can vouch for you if you want. I mean, I don't know what the letter said, but I'll swear it existed."

"*Adios*, Ken. Remember me in your prayers." Sean sighed and turned to Penelope Hammill.

"I think I get the picture," Penelope Hammill said.

"Do you believe me?" Sean said.

She shrugged.

"Will Clarissa?"

She shrugged.

"Christ, a fire," Sean said. "I met her because of a fire and now I've lost her because of a fire."

"Sean?" Penelope Hammill said.

Sean waited.

"Clarissa is . . . very busy at the moment.

Something very important is happening to her in her career—her musical career. I think you should get in touch with her—write her, call her, send her flowers, whatever. But not just now. It would distract her, and I think that might be harmful. I know you're very busy, too, with your building. But if you were to wait until after your grand opening, well, that would be a good time for her, too. Maybe you can work this out."

Sean wanted to work it out now. As much as he cared about La Tour, he cared about Clarissa's career more, and didn't want to do anything that would impede it. "Fifteen, thirty-four," he said.

Penelope Hammill smiled and wrote it down.

The shirt was from Sulka—a blue sea island cotton dress shirt. It was smashing. The note said:

Dear Sean,

Happy Birthday to you. Happy Birthday to you. Happy Birthday, dear Sean. Happy Birthday to you. You know the tune, so just hum along.

I hope you're well. I am. We live on Grove Street in a tiny little apartment that's just right. It has a lot of rooms so we aren't always bumping into each other every time we turn around. Sometimes we bump into furniture when we turn around, but not often.

Tyler doesn't know I'm sending you this present. Penny Hammill helped me pick it out. I hope you like it. Tyler would be mad if she knew

I sent this, because she's mad at you. She thinks you should have gotten in touch with her. She thinks men are bastards. She said so. But I'm not mad at you. I think you're terrific. I think there must be a good reason why you didn't write, or call, or something. Is there? I hope there is. I hope you'll write to Tyler sometime, or call her, or something.

Happy birthday.

Diana Tyler

P.S. That's my name now. Legally.
    But my friends still call me Pat.

Sean's tears fell onto the note and onto the beautiful blue shirt.

Chapter Twenty-Two

It was a rare day for New York—or, for that matter, for anywhere. The sun shone brightly—but not too warmly—in a sky that had been scrubbed of smog by a northerly wind that had blown briskly all night long. By midday, the wind had blown itself out and zephyrs from the south had taken its place. Fifty-one flags—one for each state, with the national flag at the center of the line—flapped sinuously from their poles around the base of La Tour.

La Tour. The Tower. It was truly that—a graceful silver and alabaster shaft rising elegantly into the deep, blue sky in a gesture that seemed nothing so much as supremely confident.

"A true New York building," said the mayor. He winced at the feedback from the microphone on the dignitaries' stand, and said it again. "A true New York building. Standing straight and proud, rising above the mundane problems of the city, manifesting an invincible hope for the future."

A brass band. Baton twirling majorettes. Dancers from the Alvin Ailey company. A pair of jugglers on unicycles. A mime. Clowns from the Big Apple Circus. A drum-and-bugle corps.

Even the prostitutes and pimps and pushers seemed impressed by the shimmering structure. Even the cops who had to cope with the crowds tipped their heads back from time to time and let their eyes follow the building's gentle curves all the way to the top.

"Consider it a gift," Sean Howard said. "A thank-you to a city that bore and nurtured me and encouraged me to strive for excellence."

"You did it," Daniel Freedman said. "I didn't think you'd pull it off, but you did it."

"I'm very happy for you, Sean," Carolyn Evans said. "And very proud."

"It looks even better in the flesh," Penelope Hammill said. "It has . . . character."

"Thank you," Sean said. "Thank you all."

Holding a giant pair of scissors, Sean, the mayor, the governor and the senior senator cut the blue ribbon in which the building's main doors had been wrapped. The band played a fanfare. The crowd cheered. Thousands of balloons were released and soared into the sky, speckling it with yellow and red and blue and green and orange.

The lobby was set with tables for a lavish luncheon at which there were more speeches, more praise, and still more speeches and still more praise. Toasts and more toasts.

"This is New York State champagne," the governor said.

"These are New York City waiters," the mayor said.

"I love New York," the senior senator said. An aide whispered in his ear and he added, "the city *and* upstate."

Photographs and more photographs. Grouping and regrouping and principals. Interviews with television correspondents. One of them interviewed Sean for inclusion in a special on contemporary entrepreneurs.

"Sean, there's someone I'd like you to meet," Penny Hammill said. "Sean Howard, Philip Cleaver."

"The writer?" Sean said. "I've read your stuff. I like it."

"Thanks," Philip Cleaver said. "I like your building. Penny tells me you play squash. I just moved back to the town and I'm looking for a partner. Would you be interested? I play on the varsity at Harvard."

Sean laughed. "Would *you* be interested? I'm only a fair B player."

"Somehow, I doubt that," Philip Cleaver said.

"We're getting married," Penny said.

"Congratulations."

"Would you come to the reception?" Philip Cleaver said. "From what Penny's told me about you, we'd be honored."

"June fourteenth," Penny said. "We'll send you a formal invitation."

Sean didn't want to say yes, but he couldn't say no.

"There won't be anyone there you don't want to see," she said.

Sean smiled. "Thank you for the invitation. I'll try very hard to be there."

"There's somebody here who'd like to talk to you," Daniel Freedman said out of the side of his mouth.

"Who?"

"He's waiting on the second floor—in the room you're using for an office."

"Who?"

"He didn't want to come down because he thought it would look like he was trying to up-stage the senator and the governor and the mayor."

"Dan. Who?"

"Vice-President Tyler."

Dwight Tyler came toward Sean with his hand out. "Thanks for taking a moment to see me, Mr. Howard. I don't want to keep you from your celebration, but I'm passing through town and I wanted to have a word with you."

"I'd be honored if you'd come downstairs and join us, Mr. Vice-President. If you think your fellow politicians would object, I'll take the responsibility for it."

Dwight Tyler waved a hand. "No. It wouldn't be appropriate. I'm here on a personal matter."

"Please sit down," Sean said.

"I'd just as soon stand. I feel more comfortable standing. I feel more comfortable because I'm here to ask your forgiveness."

"Mr. Vice-President?"

Dwight Tyler touched the knot of his tie. "I asked you, last summer, not to see my daughter. I asked you out of concern for my political future. My concern blinded me to other people's personal needs—"

"It was understandable," Sean said.

Dwight Tyler cleared his throat. "Perhaps. But I feel now that I must ask you to forgive me."

Sean smiled. "I do."

Dwight Tyler cleared his throat again. "That's very decent of you . . . Perhaps you've heard . . . Clarissa won custody of her stepdaughter."

"I did hear. I'm very happy for both of them."

Again he cleared his throat. "I was very sorry to hear about your wife."

"Thank you for your note. I was very grateful."

"Okay, Howard. Let's stop waltzing around." Dwight Tyler touched his tie. " . . . Clarissa tells me that you haven't contacted her."

Perhaps a politician would believe the convoluted explanation, but Sean didn't care to find out. "No."

Dwight Tyler adjusted a shirt cuff. "Well, you're free to do so if you care to. I'm not saying you must. I'm just—"

"I understand, sir."

Dwight Tyler came to Sean and put an arm around his shoulder. "You're a fine, fine man, Howard. A hell of a fine man." He cleared his throat, then looked at his watch. "I should be going. I'm on my way to Vermont. Some fences to mend up there."

"Good luck," Sean said. "And thanks for stopping by."

"Good-bye . . . Sean."

"Good-bye, Mr. Vice- President."

That night, there was a black-tie dinner in one of the La Tour's ballrooms. Afterward, in the theater off the main lobby, there was an evening of entertainment.

Sean looked at his watch. "I'm going to slip upstairs for a while," he muttered to Dan Freedman. "There're a couple of things I have to take care of for that meeting in the morning with the bankers."

"I wouldn't leave if I were you," Daniel Freedman said.

"No one'll notice," Sean said. "I'll be back in half an hour."

"Don't say I didn't ask you not to stay."

Sean slipped out of his seat and went out a side door of the theater. Penny Hammill caught up to him at the foot of the escalator to the second floor. "Whoa, there, master builder. You can't walk out on your own parade."

Sean smiled. "Just for a few minutes. I have some documents to go over."

"They can wait."

"They can't really. There's another party after this. And I'll just be too exhausted afterwards. I have an important meeting first thing in the morning."

She stamped a foot. "It can wait!"

Sean laughed, and glanced at the program he'd stuck in the pocket of his dinner jacket. "To be honest with you, I'm not sure I want to listen to chamber music. Surely you can understand why."

"I don't know—a little hair of the dog might not be such a bad thing," she shot back, her voice rising.

Sean put his hands in his pockets and scuffed at the carpet with a patent leather shoe.

She came to him and slipped an arm through his. "Would I ask you to do something that was going to cause you pain? I know you don't know me very well, but I think you know me well enough to know I wouldn't do that."

"I know," Sean said softly.

"The group is supposed to be very good."

Sean nodded.

"You did want chamber music on the program," she said. "With my own ears I heard you say so to your talent coordinator."

Sean nodded.

"And since it's your evening, I really think you're obligated to stay put for all the performances. I mean, you don't want to insult anybody, do you?"

Sean shook his head.

She tugged at his arm. "So? Let's go."

Sean let himself be pulled along. "This isn't the way to our seats."

Penny improved her grip on his arm. "Let's go backstage. It'll be fun to listen from back there."

"I don't want to get in the way," Sean said.

"You won't be in the way."

Clarissa was up at 4:30 that morning, unable to sleep. She sat at the round oak table in the kitchen, drinking a cup of Earl Grey tea and studying the Bach Chaconne. She woke Diana at

6:30 and made a big breakfast for the two of them. She dressed in jeans, a sweatshirt and sneakers and walked with Diana to the Little Red Schoolhouse, on Bleecker Street and Sixth Avenue.

"Know what I don't like about New York?" Diana asked. "When you're in one part of it, it's like the other parts don't exist. People say if you stand on a street corner long enough, you'll see someone you know. But not if that someone doesn't live in your neighborhood. If they live in another part of New York, you could stand on a street corner for a week and not see them."

"Is there someone you've been wanting to see?" Clarissa said.

" . . . Sean," Diana said.

Clarissa put her arm around Diana. "We'll probably see him tonight."

"Are you still mad at him?" Diana said. "Do you believe what he told Penny—about the fire and the letter and everything?"

"We've been through this before, Pat. Yes, I believe him, but I'm still a little hurt that he didn't try again when he didn't hear from me."

"He probably thought it wasn't honorable, or something," Diana said. "He probably thought it would be putting pressure on you, or something."

"He probably did."

Diana pursed her lips. "Tyler?"

"Yes?"

"Don't get mad, okay?"

"Mad about what?"

"Promise you won't get mad?"

"Diana, I don't approve. If you have

something to say, say it. If it's something I'm not going to like, you'll have to take the consequences."

Diana scuffed at the sidewalk some more. "I sent Sean a birthday present. A shirt."

Clarissa smiled. "How did you know it was his birthday?"

"I read it in some stuff Penny Hammill had."

"How did you know what size?"

"Penny Hammill asked him."

Clarissa laughed. "I'm sure he was very pleased."

Diana pouted. "This thing tonight is formal, though, right?"

"What do you mean, 'though'?"

"I mean, if he's going to be wearing a tuxedo and all, he probably won't wear my shirt."

Clarissa smiled. "There'll be other chances for him to wear it."

"Yeah, but if I don't see him . . ."

Clarissa bent to kiss Diana's forehead. "Don't worry, Pat. We'll see him. I can't say for sure when, but we'll see him. Now get inside. You're almost late."

"Almost doesn't count," Diana said.

Clarissa crossed Sixth Avenue and went to a newsstand on Bleecker Street and bought a *Post* with its special pull-out section on La Tour. She walked up to Barrow Street and went to Sandolino's and ordered tea and read every word of the special section. When she finished, it was only quarter to nine. She wasn't sure she could make it through the rest of the day if time was going to plod along like that.

She went back to the apartment on Grove

Street and changed into a skirt and blouse and took a cab to David Stein's studio across from Carnegie Hall for a violin lesson.

"Are you nervous?" David Stein said.

Clarissa yawned, then laughed. "Evidently. When I'm nervous, I yawn a lot."

David Stein smiled. "All my life, I have been a morning person, and for much of my life I have waited until evening to perform music. I have felt my energy draining away until, when the time finally came, I was ready to do nothing but sleep. On the day of the performance, the most important thing is to hold on to some fraction of your energy for that moment when you finally need it."

By the end of her lesson, Clarissa was having second thoughts about performing music. It was only a few minutes after eleven. She killed three-quarters of an hour walking in Central Park, going past the carousel and the skating rink and the zoo, then decided to go down to the Plaza, to see what was playing at the Paris Cinema. As often, it was a French film she hadn't heard of, but she went in to see it anyway. She barely watched it, and when it was over she didn't remember it and still wasn't sure what the title was. All she had been able to think about was that right across Fifth Avenue was the General Motors Building and in it was Sean Howard's office. He wouldn't be there, of course; he would be at La Tour. But it was the closest she had been to him, or to some aspect of him in . . . in centuries, it seemed.

Clarissa took a cab home and tried to take a nap, but she couldn't sleep. She tried reading, but she couldn't concentrate on the words. She turned on the television, and turned it off. She took a shower and washed her hair and dried it. She laid out her dress—Sarah's dress. It was 4:30. She sat by the window in the living room and watched people come and go along Grove Street.

At 5:30, Sarah called. "Nervous?"

"No." Clarissa laughed. "Yes."

"Good. Nervous players are the best players. Players with ice water in their veins play icy music. They've moved our rehearsal time up to 6:15. Can you make it?"

"Yes. Oh, God, yes. Anything to get out of here. Anything to get started. I'll get a cab right away."

"Don't forget to bring the dress."

Clarissa laughed. "I'm not that nervous."

"I'm just speaking from years of experience," Sarah said.

Suddenly there wasn't enough time: calling Diana, who was at a friend's whose parents she could go with later to La Tour; getting her things together—she was nearly out the door when she realized she had forgotten the dress! Getting a cab, getting uptown, finding the stage entrance to the theater, finding her dressing room, the very brief rehearsal—really nothing more than a sound check, changing into her dress, putting on makeup, brushing her hair.

Suddenly they were on stage. Abraham lifted his chin, poised to give the downbeat.

And then they were playing.

Sean felt a thrill at being behind the scenes—the lights, the ropes, the stacked scenery, the stagehands reading newspapers, oblivious to all but their cues, the hushed performers paying tribute to their peers by watching from the sidelines. In taking note of everything around him, it was a while before he focused on the stage.

Sarah Newman played the cello, Abraham Newman the violin.

Penny heard Sean's intake of breath and whispered in his ear. "They just happened to be in town. They thought it would be neighborly to play for you."

The violist was a tall, thin man with only a fringe of hair on his head.

The other violinist was Clarissa.

Penny felt Sean starting to pull away and whispered in his ear. "It's too late. You can't leave."

"I need a word with my driver." He smiled. "I'll be back."

She wore a long black dress with a deep V-neck. Her glistening black hair was held away from her face by silver combs. There was a fringe of perspiration at the top of her forehead. Her full red lips were a straight line of concentration.

When the music was done, there was a long silence that said the audience didn't want it to be over. Then a wave of applause rose up and crashed around the performers on the stage. Sarah leaned over and patted Clarissa on the knee.

Abraham had stood up to face the audience. "This is a very special evening for my wife and for me. Sean Howard is our neighbor in Connecticut. We feel very fortunate that we were able to be here on the occasion of the dedication of this magnificent building. And we are very honored to have been invited to perform. We have another reason to be especially joyful tonight. And we have a sense that you are sharing the joy, for although most of you do not know it, you are witnessing tonight the coming of age of a very talented musician. Let me invite you to share with us the pleasure of hearing Miss Clarissa Tyler play a solo performance of Johann Sebastian Bach's Chaconne for violin.''

As the applause rose up, Abraham escorted Sarah off the stage, followed by the violist.

Sarah kissed Sean on the cheek. Abraham slapped him on the back.

''Thank you for being here,'' Sean said.

''Thanks for this building,'' Sarah said. ''Isn't that some dress?''

Sean smiled. He felt a tug at his coattails and looked down to see Diana standing next to him. She wore a more demure version of Clarissa's dress. Her hair was piled elegantly on her head. She looked like a princess.

Clarissa paused for a long moment with the violin tucked under her chin, the bow poised. Then she played. Her playing sounded like singing. It sonded like the plainsong of angels.

Diana found Sean's hand in the dark and squeezed it in both of hers. He squeezed back.

Clarissa's nervousness was gone by now. She felt in command, in control. The audience helped, for it clearly was anxious to listen; it accorded her the right to be there, for she had won that right herself.

And something told her—she couldn't say what, but something—something told her that Sean was watching from backstage. She liked that that was where he was; she didn't mind that he wasn't sitting in the audience, a mere spectator. He was supporting her by his proximity, giving her strength, performing with her.

When she'd done, the audience was stunned. When they recovered they showered her with a wave of applause that made her heart stop. They called her back again and again, until, finally, they realized that she really meant it— no encore tonight. They resigned themselves, disappointed that she would give them no more, but elated by what she had given them already. Finally they let her go, the applause subsiding at last.

Clarissa's dressing room was filled with flowers—vase after vase of flowers. And on the dressing table was a bottle of champagne . . . and a card, from David Stein. "Thank you," was all it said.

Clarissa found David Stein in the crowd of well-wishers and hugged him tightly. "Thank *you.*"

He took her hand in his bent fingers and held it to his lips. "You played beautifully."

She cocked her head. "But?"

He smiled. "No buts. You played beautifully. It is a piece meant to be played beautifully. There is nothing more to say." Then he shrugged. "As for the Brahms . . ."

Clarissa laughed. "Let's not talk about that

now. We'll start working on it tomorrow."

"And now if you'll excuse me"—David Stein patted the pocket of his suit—"I have some change left after cashing your check and buying you the flowers and the champagne I promised you. I intend to take my friend, the ballet instructor, for a night on the town. Perhaps we'll even go dancing."

Clarissa kissed his cheek. "Thank you, again."

"Tyler, look." Diana stood before Clarissa, Sean in hand.

"Hello, Clarissa," Sean said.

" . . . Hello, Sean."

She had never seen a man more beautiful— tall and lean and strong. There was a little gray in his hair, at the temples, but it suited him, gave him additional authority.

He had never seen a woman more beautiful. Her hair shone even in the muted light of the dressing room. Her stunning figure was wonderfully enhanced by the dress she wore. The trace of sadness that had always been in her eyes before was gone; it had been replaced by confidence.

"Thank you so much for playing tonight," Sean said. "I can't begin to tell you how beautiful it was."

"I'm honored to have been invited," Clarissa said. "Your building's beautiful—everything about it—inside and out. You must be very proud."

They sank deeper and deeper into each other's eyes.

Suddenly Clarissa laughed. "My Lord. Where did everybody go?"

They were alone. The others had slipped out

of the room, shutting the door behind them.

"It's been a while," Sean said. "They must know that we have a lot to say to each other."

"It was kind of them," Clarissa said.

There was a knock at the door.

"We spoke too soon," Clarissa said, and laughed.

At the door was Eddie, Sean's driver. In his hands was a huge rectangular package, wrapped in beautiful blue and gold paper. Sean took the package and thanked Eddie and closed the door. He set the package on the dressing room sofa.

"It's something for you," Sean said. "From me."

Clarissa stood before the sofa, her hands clasped before her. "I know what it is."

Sean smiled. "Of course you do."

Carefully, Clarissa peeled away the beautiful paper. It was the mirror from the wall of Sean's River House apartment.

"I knew it," Clarissa said.

"Of course you did," Sean said.

"They're still there," Clarissa said.

"They always have been," Sean said.

"Just as we said."

"Of course."

"I wrote you a letter," Sean said. "It was destroyed . . ."

She put her fingers to his lips. "Shhh."

" . . . in a fire."

"A fire!" Clarissa said.

"Do you believe me?"

"Oh, yes. I believe anything to do with fires."

They kissed, their bodies striving for each

other through the fabric of their clothing, their hands softly touching—here, there, everywhere.

They stood very still, holding each other gently, feeling their love shaking itself awake from its long sleep, becoming each other, becoming one.

In the mirror, their reflections did the same.

"Will you marry me, Clarissa?" Sean said.

"Oh, yes."

She got loose suddenly and went to the door and locked it. "You probably have to be somewhere, don't you?"

Sean smiled. "There's a reception upstairs. I'll have to make a little speech."

"But not for a while."

"No."

Clarissa went to the sofa, removed the mirror and placed it on the carpet in front of the sofa. "You don't mind roughing it a little, do you?"

Sean smiled. "It won't be roughing it."

Clarissa came to him and stood very close and untied his bow tie. "But we're not going to hurry. Not that I'm not enthusiastic. I just want to draw things out as long as possible."

"I may faint, is all," Sean said.

She kissed his mouth. "I'll revive you. Mouth to mouth."

And they made love on the carpet in front of the mirror, their long, strong bodies joining together to become one, while in the mirror, their long, strong bodies did the same.

Epilogue

Jorge Estrada y Valenzuela was nervous.
Couples were occasionally married in one of the
ballrooms of the Acapulco Regent, but only very
occasionally. More often couples came to the
hotel already married, ready to spend their
honeymoon. Even in the days when easy marriage had been the linchpin of the Mexican tour-
ist industry, couples had arrived at the hotel
already married, often having gotten married
immediately on getting an easy divorce—in
Juarez or Tiajuana. But there had never been a
big, important wedding at the Acapulco Regent
in all the years he had worked there—as a bell-
hop, as a desk clerk, as an assistant to the
assistant manager, as assistant manager, and
now, as manager. Not only was there to be a big,
important wedding, it was to be a double wedding. And it was not to be in one of the hotel's
ballrooms. It was to be in the hotel's famous
rooftop restaurant, the Buena Vista, with its
magnificent view of the harbor, the mountains

around, the sea beyond. To rent the entire restaurant—for the wedding, for cocktails, for a sit-down dinner—not for one wedding party, but for two! This was a sign of bigness and importance, indeed.

But such short notice. He had gotten the first telegram only the week before. Since then there had been dozens more telegrams and hundreds of phone calls. The couples' representatives had insisted that he call them collect, and had pre-paid the cost of answering telegrams. So many details. Food, drink, flowers, an orchestra—not one orchestra, but two, one to play in the roof-top restaurant for the main wedding party, one to play disco music in a lounge on the floor below for the younger guests.

And such important guests. The vice-president of the United States; a famous movie actress; a best-selling novelist. The editor of an important American business magazine. And many, many more whose names sounded to Jorge Estrada y Valenzuela like a register of living legends.

The managers of the other hotels wanted to know what Jorge Estrada y Valenzuela had done to merit such a big, important wedding with such important guests.

"It is actually two weddings," he explained. "Sean Howard and Clarissa Tyler—she is the daughter of the vice-president . . . And the other, Penelope Hammill and Philip Cleaver are get-ting married as well.

They knew that already. They had read about it in the newspaper, which had had a long article about the big, important weddings at the

Acapulco Regent. They had read that Clarissa Tyler was the daughter of Dwight Tyler, the vice-president of the United States; that Sean Howard was an important New York real estate entrepreneur; that Penelope Hammill was an important New York newspaper journalist; and that Philip Cleaver was an important novelist. But who *were* they? Or rather, why had they chosen the Acapulco Regent, which, notwithstanding its spectacular Buena Vista restaurant, was not the finest hotel in Acapulco. It was a fine hotel, but not the finest, not the sort that such important people stayed at, although they might visit its famous rooftop restaurant.

"Have they ever been guests of yours before?" the managers of the other hotels asked Jorge Estrada y Valenzuela.

"Do you think I've had time to go through old registers to find that out?" Jorge Estrada y Valenzuela said. "I have had no time at all! The Secret Service agents have been driving me insane."

"There is no need to check your old registers," the other managers said. "For if such big, important people had been guests before, you would surely remember."

That was true, Jorge Estrada y Valenzuela said. "They have not, so far as I know, been guests of mine before."

Then why, the other managers repeated, had they chosen the Acapulco Regent?

"It is a fine hotel," Jorge Estrada y Valenzuela said.

The other managers shook their heads sadly. "But not the finest. If they had gone to the

Princess, or Las Brisas, we could understand. But we cannot understand their going to the Acapulco Regent."

"I know it's a terrible thing to say," Diana said, "but I sometimes wish Grandpa Tyler had lost the election. I hate Secret Servicemen. They never smile."

"They have a thankless job," Clarissa said. "They have to suspect everybody."

"Well, they could still smile. And it's so crowded with one of them always hanging around the apartment."

"Don't forget, Pat, we're going to be living at River House—and in Connecticut in the summertime. There'll be lots of room."

"I do sometimes forget," Diana said. "I sometimes think this whole thing is a dream."

"It is. A dream come true."

"In that case," Diana said, "it's a first."

Clarissa smiled. "There always has to be a first."

"These fucking Secret Servicemen," Ken Forrest said. "What a grim group. How you going to handle having one under your bed?"

Sean watched Philip Cleaver serve to Dwight Tyler on the hotel's tennis court. "I'll manage."

Forrest watched Dwight Tyler execute a stylish overhead smash, winning the point and the game. "How're you going to handle your father-in-law's overhand?"

Sean laughed. "I won't lob."

"I had a long talk with him last night about you," Forrest said. "He thinks you're hot shit. I tried to disabuse him of that, but he's a tough man to talk off a position he's got a hold on."

"I wish these Secret Servicemen wouldn't call me 'ma'am,'" Penelope Hammill said. "Just because I'm getting married doesn't mean I'm an old maid."

Sarah laughed. "I think that's a contradiction. Old maids don't get married."

"Don't pick on me," Penelope Hammill said. "I'm a nervous wreck."

Clarissa yawned. "I feel fine."

"You've been married before. I've never been married." Penelope Hammill slopped more nail polish on her thumb. "Damn."

"I think I'd like to get married again," Sarah said.

Clarissa gave her a look. "If you say things aren't going well with Abraham, I'll be sick. Sick."

Sarah put up her hands innocently. "I didn't say that. I just said I'd like to be married again. I had a wonderful time at our wedding. I'd have an even better time, now—now that I'm absolutely sure it'll last."

Penelope Hammill looked up from her nails.

"That's an interesting thought. I think I'll tell Philip we should have the wedding in about ten years—when we're sure it'll last."

Clarissa smiled. "If I'm going through with it, you're going through with it."

"What's to 'go through' for you?" Penny said. "You've got it knocked. You're in love."

"So are you, clown."

"Oh, sure we are—but nothing so certifiable as you two. My God, what a story. And with a happy ending to boot."

"The happiest thing of all is that it's not the ending," Clarissa said. "It's the beginning."

Sarah sighed. "I'd like to get married again."

"So do," Clarissa said. "People go through the ceremony again, sometimes—just to reaffirm their vows. We're having a double wedding, already. No reason we can't make it a triple."

"A triple wedding?" Jorge Estrada y Valenzuela said.

"There'll be no change in the size of the party," Dwight Tyler said. "No more food's necessary. No nothing. We just want the minister to know that there'll be three couples exchanging vows instead of two."

But Jorge Estrada y Valenzuela's head ached. He was sure the managers of the other hotels would run him out of town on a rail. It was all so . . . excessive.

But there was no arguing against the wishes of his guests—especially against the wish of the vice-president of the United States. Especially when it was the wish, as well, of his beautiful daughter.

Where had he seen her before—the beautiful daughter of the vice-president of the United States? Something told him that she was the key to the puzzle, for he was sure that he had seen her before. Had she ever been a guest at the Acapulco Regent? He doubted it, for even if she had registered under some other name he would not have forgotten such a beautiful woman. And, sad as it made him to admit it to himself, such beautiful women did not stay at the Acapulco Regent. The women who stayed at the Acapulco Regent were women who were beautiful at first glance but whose beauty could not stand up to scrutiny.

Perhaps she had been a guest at the hotel's famous rooftop restaurant. That was entirely possible, for people came from all over Acapulco to dine at the Buena Vista restaurant, even guests from other hotels—the Princess, even, and Las Brisas. Still, if she had come even once, he was sure he would have remembered, for she was unforgettably beautiful.

And her husband-to-be—didn't Jorge Estrada y Valenzuela know him, too? Hadn't he seen him somewhere before? Had he ever been a guest at the Acapulco Regent? He doubted it, for he had not risen to be manager of the hotel by forgetting such important guests as leading New York real estate entrepreneurs. Perhaps he had come to dine at the famous rooftop restaurant. Still, he should remember. His head ached. A triple wedding.

"I had a dream about this place," Clarissa said. "I'd completely forgotten. It was the night you confronted Bill Middlebrooks. I fell asleep in the car waiting for you."

Penelope Hammill was standing at a mirror in a small room just off the main dining room, waiting, with Clarissa and Sarah, for the wedding to begin. She was trying to get her lipstick to look less garish. "A dream about *this* place? Oh, right—you've been here."

"Speaking of which," Sarah said, "I've never entirely forgiven you for just running off with my car that way. I mean, if you thought you were going to be in danger, you should've asked me to come along. You called Penny up, after all. I missed all the fun."

Clarissa smiled. "It wasn't fun, exactly."

There was a knock at the door and Clarissa's mother put her head in the room. "Time, ladies."

Jorge Estrada y Valenzuela smiled.

When the first couple, Sarah and Abraham Newman—who were already married, he had been told—exchanged vows, he had kept his eyes on Clarissa Tyler and Sean Howard, and had forced his mind to remember who they were. He could not.

When the second couple, Penelope Hammill and Philip Cleaver, exchanged vows, he continued looking at Clarissa Tyler and Sean Howard. He *had* seen them before. He had seen them together. Had they been guests at the hotel? Had they dined together at the Buena Vista restaurant? They had been married to other spouses, he had been told, so it was really none of his business. Still, he should remember. He could not.

Then Clarissa Tyler and Sean Howard stepped before the minister. And he knew! He, Jorge Estrada y Valenzuela *had* seen them before—and together—but from a distance. He had seen them from a great distance. He had been standing at the bottom of the Acapulco Regent and had been craning his neck back to look straight up into the sky and into the ... the smoke! The flames! The fire in the famous roof-top restaurant of the Acapulco Regent! The children! Superman and Wonder Woman!

"Do you, Sean, promise to love Clarissa, in sickness and in health, for richer for poorer, to keep her with you as long as you both shall live?"

"I do."

"Do you, Clarissa, promise to love Sean, in sickness and in health, for richer for poorer, to keep him with you as long as you both shall live?"

"I do."

You may kiss the bride, and you may kiss the groom."

"*Eso es!*" Jorge Estrada y Valenzuela shouted.

Everyone turned to look at him.

Jorge Estrada y Valenzuela didn't care. "*Viva! Buena suerte!*"

Two of the Secret Service agents looked at each other and smiled.